THE FEMALE WARD

The Female Ward

THAMES RIVER PRESS
An imprint of Wimbledon Publishing Company Limited (WPC)
Another imprint of WPC is Anthem Press (www.anthempress.com)
First published in the United Kingdom in 2013 by
THAMES RIVER PRESS
75–76 Blackfriars Road
London SE1 8HA

www.thamesriverpress.com

A CIP record for this book is available from the British Library.

ISBN 978-0-85728-008-4

This title is also available as an eBook.

THE FEMALE WARD
GOD ALMOST EXISTS

Debalina Haldar

THAMES RIVER PRESS

This book is dedicated to Dida, the divine soul who now rests in peace. This is a small token of my love for her.

ACKNOWLEDGEMENTS

I still can feel the excitement I felt when Thames River Press acknowledged my sample manuscript: '*We see a potential and the story falls right in line with the human interest conflicts that we wish to explore. It is for this reason that we are willing to undertake the task.*'

I am deeply grateful to the two friends who were with me throughout the experience that prompted me to write the book. We had a not-so-great, yet a very unique time that we shall always remember.

I thank my editor, Rebecca Lloyd, for working with me and teaching me about the intricacies of fiction writing. I've learnt a lot, and feel highly blessed to have had such a wonderful experience with her. I thank Mr. Kamaljit Sood, my publisher, and his publishing team, for giving me a chance to see my story in the form of a book.

I would like to express my gratitude to all those who gave me the encouragement to complete the story. My college friends, Abhijit, Ananya, Arijit, Baishali, Bibek, Bidesh, Biman, Debranjan, Deepkamal, Durjoy, Manab, Pallab, Prasanta, Prithwiraj, Rupak, Sangkha, Soumesh, Souvik, Suvendu, Suvodip, Tuhin, Vivek have been a great help in the completion of the novel. My sisters and cousin, Bubuli, Tutul and Munia Didi have always wished for the success of this book.

I thank also my colleagues and friends in Thermax Ltd, Ashik, Diwakar, Jeff, Aditya and Rohith, for their love and encouragement and for keeping their promise to me and telling no one about the writing of this book.

Aritro has always been a strong support throughout this project, and I thank him for supporting Mamma and my sisters when I was away from them. And finally to Mamma and Papa whose support was of inestimable value to me while I was in the process of writing the novel ... you don't know what you mean to me.

'We are responsible for what we are, and whatever we wish ourselves to be, we have the power to make ourselves. If what we are now has been the result of our own past actions, it certainly follows that whatever we wish to be in future can be produced by our present actions; so we have to know how to act.'

—Swami Vivekananda

CONTENTS

CONTENTS

AUTHOR'S NOTE

I would like to begin with what this book is not. It is not a sad story of my life which had its turning point on 8th December. I wrote this novel after I was falsely accused, along with two other engineering students, of ragging another student so brutally that she attempted suicide. We three accused were imprisoned for twenty-four days before our case was heard and we were finally given bail. It was touch and go whether we would ever be able to find work because of our arrest and imprisonment. In the end, myself and one of the women were lucky enough to get jobs, but our other friend wasn't placed quickly; most companies refused to take her on after hearing about our experience. Finally, after trying very hard, she did find a job and has moved to her workplace in Madhya Pradesh.

While the experience of being a prisoner was shocking in the extreme, at the same time, the kindness of the other inmates, defenceless, illiterate women, touched me deeply and I'm thankful for that. I shall never forget the deplorable conditions under which these women were living. This was an India I didn't know about before, and now that I have seen it, and for a short while, lived it, I can see that until rich India starts to care enough to tackle illiteracy and poverty it will never be able to call itself a developed nation.

However, another part of the experience that we three girls lived through was degrading and traumatising, and it taught me nothing but cynicism – and I'm not thankful for that. The Indian media hounded us at every opportunity. I saw its awesome strength. Today, whenever I look at the newspapers or watch a news channel I can't make myself believe in the so called facts that they churn out so relentlessly having been one of their victims.

At the heart of this story however is the hideous tradition of 'ragging' that goes on in Indian colleges despite the fact that it is a criminal offence. I had to face it as a student and I know how demeaning the practice can be. I hate the idea that one group of students has power over another group simply because they happen to have arrived at college sooner. Ragging at its most harmless is embarrassing and silly, but at its worst, it attempts to prevent individual students from independent thinking, attempts, in fact, to eradicate freewill.

Some students really believe that being ragged by their seniors will make them mature people, but in colleges where the tradition still goes on unchallenged, since the juniors have no choice in the matter anyway, perhaps it is better to believe this ridiculous idea, than to believe nothing at all. The truth is that if any junior attempts to stand up for him or herself their life in college is made into a living hell through the whole four years of their stay there. Students in the years above them will not help them or socialise with them; they become social pariahs. The juniors get to realise that this will be their fate very quickly and so it is few who dare to stand and fight the system. Some, who cannot tolerate the ragging, leave college, others attempt suicide, and a proportion of them succeed.

While this novel is based on real events, it is nevertheless a work of fiction and all the characters and institutions mentioned in it are entirely fictional.

1. A FUNNY GAME

Asansol Special Correctional Home

Night 11th December 2010 – in the room with yellow walls

I just woke up and remembered quite suddenly that today was my sister Tutul's birthday. I think back to the time when I taught her to walk and how she stumbled and then laughed and often fell over. I was only fourteen myself and I felt proud that she trusted me so utterly that she would put her hands in mine and be lead by me. Happy eighth birthday, Tutul, I just wish I could be with you.

Everybody else is asleep around me and I'm staring up at the ceiling high above – it can't have been painted or cleaned since this terrible place was first built. They keep the lights on all night long here, so they can watch us I suppose, in case we try to rob or kill each other or plan our escape. Or perhaps it's just that darkness would give us privacy and dignity, things that prisoners shouldn't have.

Now I'm awake, I may as well start writing in my diary because I know I won't be able to sleep for ages. Today I discovered what Rekha is in prison for; she came over and talked to me for the first time about what happened to her. Apparently, she was walking along a road in her village when she saw a local electrician running towards her and he told her that the house she and her husband rented had caught fire and that her husband was in a very serious condition and was in the local hospital. She rushed back home and found the house completely burnt. On her way to the hospital she was stopped by three policemen in a van who said her husband was dead and that she, the landlord and his wife were to be taken to the police station as part of the enquiry. In the police station, they were put in the prison lockup and the next day after a court hearing, they were sentenced to ninety days imprisonment. Rekha has no idea why she is here at all, and the landlord's wife, Maya, is here too but never speaks to any of us. She lies on her thin blanket and hides her face with her hands. From time to time she sobs, or mumbles to herself, but for the most part she is silent. I don't know what to say to her, or how to make things better for her. She seems to be in shock, and somebody should be comforting her, but everybody else seems unable to deal with her, and most of the prisoners here are much older than Kalpita, Tanusri and me. I did say something to her today, but she just turned her back on me and moaned, so I left her to herself.

Yesterday, in the afternoon, Papa gave me this diary via the guards and I'm going to write down as much as I can about what goes on in this horrible place, and I really hope it gets published some day. For me it has always been more comforting to write down feelings than to talk about them with someone.

It is two o'clock at night; that is exactly what the bell chimes out, one, two. I have no option but to believe whatever information the bell delivers. I wish I had my own watch with me with the green dial; the one Papa gave me after my ICSE results in class ten. Students from all over India had to stay awake until midnight to receive their results on the official website. I received my two digit percentage and shut my eyes to sleep. It was an odd hour to shout and scream with joy or to celebrate. Early morning the next day, I woke up to the soft strokes of a thumb, an index, a middle, a ring and a little finger on my forehead. I smiled at Papa, hugged him and said good morning.

He was hiding something behind his back. He made me close my eyes and said I wasn't to cheat and then he gave me my beautiful watch that I have always loved. He told me that we enter the world with fists closed and when we leave, our hands are open. He said I should make full use of the time given to me for my life.

And thus began the journey of the green-dialled watch to signify times … times when I was happy, times when I was sad, good times and times that went bad, times of laughter and times that brought heart-breaking tears. The guards took my watch off me when I came here, and I don't know where they've put it. I miss it, sometimes I look down at my wrist expecting it to be there, but it isn't, it's far away from me now. Faaaar away.

I have been in prison for a couple of days. I have my friends, Kalpita and Tanusri, here with me at least. Yesterday at noon we were taken in the black prison van to our college where we sat our exam called Protection and Instrumentation. I think I did okay in it. As soon as the van entered the college premises, the reporters attacked us again asking us awful questions and pushing forward to try to get at us, calling our names all the time like we were dogs. We had to cover our faces with the dupattas of our salwar suits. My next exam, Mechanical Machine Design, is two days away and I am totally blank about the subject. I've tried as hard as I can to revise for it, but nothing goes in; I'm in a daze all the time.

As I look around, I can see that there is a strong bond among the thirteen criminals we are staying within the Female Ward of the Asansol Special Correctional Home. They have to share blankets when it's cold at night, and I've noticed them sharing their food with each other as well, and when one of them is sick the others get worried and stay awake all night. Somehow they found an extra blanket for Maya and wrapped her in it tightly hoping that would make her feel better. They are taking it in turns to watch over her.

There are women of different religions, social backgrounds and age groups here. What inspires me every time is that the prisoners forget about these little diversities created by our society. What silly diversities! Here the Muslims offer prayers to the Hindu Gods and to the Tulsi tree as well. I've even seen them have rice, dal and sabzi on the same plate. I was especially surprised yesterday when we were given five boiled potatoes for lunch along with the bad dal and tasteless sabzi. I've learnt from others that potatoes are offered here as a special treat once a week, which the prisoners wait for. But the five potatoes were so nicely divided amongst all of us. There is no rich or poor. I have never seen or heard of anything like this before. They love … they feel … they understand … and they share each other's pain.

There is a tiny girl in this prison who doesn't talk much, and it is because of her and the sweet little things she does that the other prisoners still have hope for the future.

Everyone is being so quiet that I can hear noises out there on the street. The dogs are barking a lot today. I don't know what can be wrong with them, they've set themselves off across the neighbourhood, one of them started it, then the next one and so on, and now they're all barking out there in the darkness. Maybe there are thieves about. Apparently, there are very few or no cars on the road at this hour. I can't hear any noise of horns.

This room is a big hall, painted in dull yellow with spider webs all around especially at the top where the walls meet the ceiling. There are five huge windows with iron bars across them. The panes of two of the windows are broken and they let in the cold air which makes sleeping at night very uncomfortable. The cement floor becomes cold and it gets difficult to walk on it barefoot. I cannot imagine that Asansol, being a place that is only an hour away from Durgapur, is so much colder and difficult to survive in. At one corner of the hall, they keep idols of gods, so we're not allowed to go into the hall with shoes on, anyone caught doing that is in serious trouble with the guards.

Criminals. Yes, that's exactly what we're called. Cursed, ill-fated criminals, and yet, how did someone like Rekha end up in here, or us three who have done absolutely nothing. This is a funny place all right. Shakila Aunty, the Female Ward In-Charge says, 'Yeh Jail Nahi … Yeh Khail Hai'. (This is not a jail. This is a game). After days and nights spent inside these four walls, I realise that Shakila Aunty is, indeed, very right. This is a game. If your son is a murderer, you are a criminal. If your daughter-in-law has committed suicide, you are a criminal. If your husband is a rapist, you are a criminal. If your father is involved in female trafficking, you are a criminal. If you are found in the vicinity of an accident, you are a criminal. In short, if there is a police complaint against you for no viable reason, you are a criminal. And this is a game … a very funny game, at the end of which everyone, except the victims of the game, return back to their normal lives with a smiling face.

Morning 12th December 2010

I'm sitting in a corner of the hall right now trying to study for my exams. The off-white pages of 'Design of Machine Equipment' are here, lying beside me. I don't feel anything at the moment. I can't understand the sentences. Two exams of the semester are already over and there are two more to go. I am very tense since I can't study in this terrific cold. I am crying but trying to make no noise.

This place has brought me closer to nature – to the sun, the stars, the wind, and to the huge banyan tree on the lawn outside. Being here has taught me how to rely more on my five senses and stay alert to everything that is going on around me. Sound is very crucial inside the four walls. We perceive the most about the outside world by sounds – the whistle of trains, the clinking of the keys, the morning siren, the bark of dogs, the noise made by children in the evening as they play outside in the street.

Every morning when the bell rings six o'clock and the red brick walls are still cold from the night before, all the jailbirds or criminals, or whatever it is they call us, wake up shivering and can hear the coarse voice of the In-Charge, Shakila Aunty, calling, 'Gunti! Gunti!' Then we must get up straight away, fold our blankets, and come together outside the hall on the lawn and stand in a line. After a while, the tall and upright figure of Kanta Singh, the keeper of the keys, makes his morning visit to the Female Ward. He opens the gate of the hall every morning and locks it up at five o'clock. He is the counter of prisoners. He does it carefully every day. He makes us sit in two rows so it's easier for him to do his job. He's got a thick white moustache that looks just like a brush and I think he's about seventy, but someone told me he's only fifty. He wears a dark brown monkey cap and light brown uniform and when he leaves us, he stomps his feet on the ground to show everyone how important he is. When he's gone it's time to clean the Female Ward.

Usually each prisoner cleans the whole ward by herself for one day. Today was to be my day, tomorrow Tanusri's, and the day after that, Kalpita's. But we decided to work together and nobody objected. I took the work of cleaning the hall. Kalpita decided to do the doorways and the toilets attached to the hall. Tanusri agreed to clean the lawn. This was our first lesson in what they call jailhold work and it turned our hands white and numb, and the dust that was everywhere made us cough.

Rekha gave me a huge broom so I could brush the dust off the hall floor before I washed it, but it was nearly too heavy to handle and by the time I'd finished, I was exhausted. To wash the floor I had to get water in a bucket from the outside tap, and bringing it back into the hall was a struggle because it was so heavy and I spilt quite a lot of it on the way. Even as I write this my arm still aches. Shakila Aunty shouted at me for making the steps and doorway wet and I got scared and dropped the bucket so that it fell onto my toe. The water was so cold that I couldn't feel any pain at the time, but, looking at my foot now, I think I'm going to lose my toenail; it's going black.

Shakila Aunty kept shouting at me, saying I was working too slowly while I cleaned the floor with a cloth, but the water in the bucket was freezing and I couldn't feel my fingers, and every time I stopped to try and breath on them or rub them together she roared at me like a mad lion and I thought she was going to hit me once or twice. When I'd finally finished, I washed the cloth and left it to dry outside on the lawn and she came running out after me shouting that the cloth was filthy and that I was to clean it again.

Outside the hall, there are five toilets shared by all the prisoners. The taps inside each of them never work and the white pans are never white. They are always stained with bright red and mustard yellow spots. And the doors – well, there are no doors. The toilets are open. I suppose this is done to make sure that the prisoners are doing what they are supposed to do inside the toilets and not something treacherous.

We get our food in aluminium plates and bowls. The rice looks like short cylindrical capsules, very different from and much below the average good rice which is thin and long of course. The dal in here is basically yellow-coloured water and the sabzi is not lagging behind either … devoid of salt and spice as it is. My teeth actually hurt trying to tear apart thick and burnt chapattis every night, and it makes me think of Mamma's soft and tasty ones that are so good they just melt away in your mouth.

While I eat the food, my heart reaches out for where Mamma waits for me. I might be in prison, but they can't control my thoughts and memories at least. I think about Mamma a lot these days and I try to imagine every detail in every room in our house in Kolkata. Doing this every day has become an exercise for my mind, and I think it is stopping me from going crazy in here. I do this. I walk down my street and pretend to see my neighbours. I say hello to them and tell them that I have just been on an errand for Mamma. Then I walk into our house and call out hello to my two sisters. I remember every detail as I walk to my room and lie down on my bed. I can hear the familiar noises of my street, people talking, birds singing, and they comfort me. I try to remember where everything is in my room, what it looks like and what it feels like. Then Mamma comes into my room and sits on my bed, I can even feel the bed move as she does this. Sometimes my imagining is so life-like that I am very shocked to open my eyes again and find myself in prison.

2. GREAT EXPECTATIONS

Three and a half years ago I was an unexceptional first year student of Royal College of Engineering in Durgapur, three hours away from Kolkata. I was very excited to be coming to this particular engineering college because it was one of the best in India. The seniors kept a close eye on all the new students – freshers we were called. They used to taunt us whenever they could about the slightest thing or without any real reason at all. This nasty custom of ragging has been practiced in engineering colleges for a long time. Apparently, ragging, in any form, physical or mental, has been defined as a crime in India. Yet, even though it's a crime and there are anti-ragging laws, it still goes on.

As a first year student, I was a particularly unfortunate victim. The seniors were like treacherous jackals waiting for their prey, and I was one of the freshers they always seemed to go for, and I do know why – it's because I tried to make friends with them on a social networking site before I came to college. The seniors were mostly one or two years older than us and expected to be treated as if they were important or famous, or royalty even.

But there were three times as many of them as us and besides, after a year we'd be regarded as seniors ourselves, so our logic was to just hang on and get through all the bullying until we were safely into the next year. We thought that if we complained to the college about the cruel things the seniors did to us, those same students wouldn't help us with notes, books, ideas and suggestions in our studies and so on.

Before I arrived, I'd always imagined my college to be like the ones they show in movies. I expected college life would make me free, free to wear anything, to say anything and free to talk to anyone, unlike life at school with its heavy discipline. College would be a place where I could wear fashionable clothes like the Bollywood actress Amrita Rao does. College would be a place where people fell in love with each other.

The ragging that went on in engineering colleges was no secret, everybody knew about it and I thought that if I made friends with some of the seniors before I arrived, I'd get off lightly. So I logged onto Orkut, the social networking site of the Royal College of Engineering Rockers Community and tried to get talking to some of the seniors on it. I wouldn't even look at that site now; it was a big mistake thinking I'd get out of being ragged that way. I wish I'd had more insight that it was a bad idea. On the day I first logged onto the site, I sent almost one hundred and fifty requests for friendship with a single click on the 'add as friends' button. On looking back, I think the seniors knew what I was trying to do and were determined to make my life in college hell because of it.

My first day in college was on the 31st of July 2007 and I went there in my pink sleeveless top and my blue slim fit jeans. I was filled with excitement and enthusiasm. Papa walked to the caretaker's office to book a hostel room for me and I followed him without knowing that the office was attached to the boys' hostel. We went past the huge volley court adjacent to the right wing of a big building. On one of the balconies there was a washing line on which there were washed and unwashed briefs, vests and shorts. Blue, green, yellow – all kinds of colours.

I looked upwards. The dull blue paint on the hostel walls was faded and peeling off in places. It looked as if the college hadn't been painted in decades. The walls of the boys' hostel had begun to crumble slightly and there were large patches where there was no paint at all. Even though I was really excited to be at college, there was something about the way the buildings were neglected that made me anxious.

Three boys appeared near one of the windows in boxer shorts, and noticing me, came out onto the balcony. One was very fat, another was well-built and the third was lean and thin. The fat boy's body was almost bursting out of his red boxers. The second guy was looking good in his blue ones. And the third was constantly pulling up his yellow boxers. He was the funniest. I smiled at them.

'Hello Madamji! What's up?' the fat guy cried out.

I looked around to see if the question really was directed at me. I realised that the fat boy was even fatter than I had thought he was before he came out onto the balcony. The flaps of fat on his hairy stomach were really huge. I remembered reading a magazine which said the longer your belt is, the shorter your life will be. This guy will not live long, I thought.

'What's happening, Madamji?' asked the thin guy, struggling to pull up his yellow boxers. By then I was certain that 'Madamji' was definitely me. The third boy was staring down at me and not smiling. He was good-looking though.

'Nothing,' I replied, 'I was just on my way to the caretaker's room.'

'Oh!' the fat boy said, 'the caretaker's room, huh? Do you really think the caretaker can take care of you?'

'Nicely … the way you totally deserve?' the third boy added.

'Why is he *incapable* of it?' I asked, pretending to be genuinely puzzled.

They burst into uncontrollable laughter and I waited for them to finish.

'What's your name, by the way?' the fat guy asked.

'Dishari,' I said.

'Okay Dishari,' he continued, 'we are your third year seniors. We can provide whatever information you want. We sure know this place well.'

'Please tell me about this caretaker.'

'Hmmm … the caretaker is really bad, you know.'

'Really really bad,' the other two repeated.

'Really bad? Like what?' I asked.

'Oh Dishari! Words fail me, he is so bad. He is incapable of taking care of girls.'

Suddenly, the thin boy shouted out, 'If you agree, we can take care of you … especially you!'

In his excitement, he totally forgot to hold his boxers up and they fell down! As Papa and I walked around the college after that I couldn't help laughing as the image of the thin boy flashed into my mind.

Papa left in the afternoon and I spent time talking to girls from my batch and finding four in particular who I liked a lot. I was in my blue mini skirt and we walked down the long corridor between the various rooms. The shabby light showed the nameplates on the polished teak doors; we went past the PDC classroom, PGDC classroom, Trainee classroom and the Xerox room. The corridor led to the conference hall, a vast auditorium full of chairs and with windows all around.

I had considered myself to be a good judge of character and had always relied on my instincts. I read many faces on that day and studied them thoroughly. I met extroverts with non-stop radio-like speaking tendencies for example, Suvodip, Arijit, Bibek and Ananya. Friendly yet not much like a radio were Rupak, Kaustav, Durjoy and Tanusri. Then there were introverts, the types who think a lot before speaking and when they do speak, don't say much and keep their feelings to themselves, for example Bidesh, Biman, Abhijit and Baishali. There was one girl called Kalpita, she was one of the ones I liked, with a peculiar expressionless face who really kept her feelings to herself, so much so that sometimes looking at her face was like looking at a mask.

That evening, we had a short welcome ceremony. The conference hall was filled with the first year students and the teachers sat at a large C-shaped table. The ceremony began with a short speech by our Director, Mr. A. Viharjee. Viharjee Sir was a dignified looking man who wore fine clothes. I think, like everybody else at the ceremony, I was inspired by the speech he gave, but there was something about his expression that gave me the creeps, because it was so cold and unwelcoming.

The speech was followed by a formal introduction by all the other teaching staff. After this, we had to step forward and walk up onto the stage to introduce ourselves. Gradually, the radios, non-radios and others took the microphone. As each of us stood up to speak we were handed a red rose, a blue pen, a black diary and a red box of sweets by one of the teachers.

When it was just about my turn to speak, someone said, 'Heylo, I'm Suvodip. Suvodip Das. It's nice meeting you.' He was one of the first year boys sitting in the front row, and he'd turned around to look at me.

'Hi, I'm Dishari,' I said.

'Your skirt is really nice!'

'Is it? Thank you so much.'

'Oh! That's a pleasure, Mam. Would you mind taking this rose of mine? I don't really like its smell.'

'That would be my pleasure.'

The smell of the rose has inspired so many writers. Even Shakespeare couldn't hold his feelings back about this manifestation called 'rose'. And there was Mr. Suvodip Das with his spiked hair, black Nirvana T-shirt and blue jeans, saying that he didn't like roses! And although I was completely aware that he was trying to flirt with me, I took the rose … sitting with its petals on the thorny stems.

He stared at the skirt I was wearing and I could see that he was thinking up some remark to make, so before he did, I spoke first. 'Do you mind not staring at me like that? It's embarrassing enough as it is being new here.'

'Really sorry Mam, I didn't mean to be rude.'

'Yeah, well, try meaning it just a little bit harder,' I said under my breath.

I went up on the stage to introduce myself.

On my way back to the hostel after the ceremony, the fat boy I had met walked up to me.

'Only this morning, eh,' he began very seriously, 'did we not meet?' I laughed, remembering his friend with the yellow boxers. 'What's funny?' he asked. 'Am I funny? Do you find me funny?'

'No, sorry, no, not at all.'

'Don't you dare laugh in front of a senior!' he shouted.

I was startled by that. 'Sorry, couldn't help it, your friend in the yellow boxers was so funny!' I answered quickly. 'I wasn't laughing at you, just at the memory of him.'

'Hey, you little fellow. Don't you dare be smart in front of me! Why did you take the rose off that guy?'

'I never took it. He gave it to me.'

'Did I ask about the boy and his stupidity? My question was directed to you!'

I was terrified and really hurt as well, in the morning he'd been nice to me, and now he was the opposite.

After that first day, many aspects of college life changed. The students weren't allowed to wear jeans and t-shirts any longer. The boys were in formal shirts and pants, and they couldn't wear belts or watches. I could no longer be Amrita Rao, the Bollywood actress I admired then for her funky dressing style. I wasn't a happy-go-lucky person anymore. New rules were formulated for the girls. All we were allowed to wear were salwar suits with dupattas, neatly folded and pinned. No more fashionable hair clips ... our hair had to be oiled completely and tied in the form of a ponytail. And most importantly, no talking to a boy called Suvodip Das. This was a special rule for me. I was always asked four questions by the seniors. Are you the girl on the Orkut website? Are you the one who was in the boys' hostel in a sleeveless top? Are you the one who was wearing a mini skirt the other day? Did you take a rose from the first year boy?

If the introductions occurred between the freshers ourselves and not between freshers and seniors, how on earth did the seniors come to know? When I was asked these four questions the first time, I realised that the whole college knew about the rose. Tiny little incidents would be blown up into horrible rumours and no one would ever be able to keep a secret here. When was I inside the boys' hostel? I was in the caretaker's room which was adjacent to the boy's hostel.

The consequences were strange. I was asked silly questions, alone, in the midst of hundreds of seniors, which I was expected to answer with great intellect and equal humility. I remember giving my introduction ... 'intro,' as they called it, almost twenty times a day. Also, we had to wish the seniors good morning, good afternoon and good evening Sir or Mam. If we failed to stick to this ritual with any of them, they'd stare at us with horrible expressionless faces but not say anything, and when this happened, we'd shiver with fear for it was certain that they'd be planning our punishment.

The trauma often kept me from having my lunch and dinner. The canteen was a haunted place almost. Each bite of the roti would be in the name of some god in heaven. As I filled my stomach, I could see seniors outside the window waiting to catch their prey. They would lean or sit on the railings or simply stand beside the stairs in a big group of around twenty. Usually, they laughed and talked amongst themselves, and looked frequently into the canteen, waiting for us to finish our food and walk outside where they could stop us if they felt like it. Back at the hostel, something even worse awaited me in particular. Even after the Freshers' Ceremony was over I would be called every night and harangued, and forced to stand for hours at a time, and the reasons for doing this would be things like the fact that I'd exchanged mobile numbers with boys from my class, or that I was wearing a watch on my right hand. I used to wonder if these students ever slept at all.

There was one senior student who used to call me out of my hostel almost every night and he'd make me stand in front of him on the volley ball field and tell him about my past crushes. I get the goose bumps even now, whenever I think about that.

3. A TRIBUTE

Afternoon 12th December 2010

I studied all night for tomorrow's exam and made notes of all the important questions … then a foul numerical problem came up. I still don't have the solution to it. Kalpita is trying to solve it at the moment, but I've given up on it.

One of the female guards, Heera Aunty, an old lady in her sixties, is unbearable. I always get rebuked by her in some way or other. This is the latest: she cannot stand me studying my books outside the hall, and enjoying the winter sun. She will deliberately mock me and say cruel things like, 'You are a girl. Learn some household work. What will you gain by studying? Your duty is to marry and make a nice home for a man.' When she speaks like that to me, it makes me boil with rage, yet I've got to try not to show it. The next moment I'd tell myself to keep calm and that such an insane fellow doesn't deserve as much as a single thought. Then she'll go on and say, 'You'll never get husbands so what is the use of you in the world? You should learn to cook and sweep and clean instead of behaving like men yourselves.'

I'd just written something about Heera Aunty when someone started calling me. But just as I closed my diary to go and see who it was, Heera Aunty tried to take the book out of my hands. She wanted to read what I'd written. I couldn't believe it, I slapped it shut and tried to move away from her and she said that I was being very mean in doing so.

Naturally, it gave me a shock because there was an unflattering description of her that I'd just put in. I got away from her in the end, and this time when I sat down to write again, I made sure I knew where she was and that she couldn't come over and bother me again.

I've been in this terrible place with Tanusri and Kalpita for a while now, and I realise that I can't let myself get too depressed or angry about the injustice that was done to us. I see that I need to be able to laugh and joke about with the other inmates sometimes just to make it possible to be here at all without going mad. I'm worried about Tanusri though. She seems distant and unconnected and sometimes doesn't even hear people when they talk to her. Heera Aunty told me she'd been studying us three and she thought Tanusri was going to crack up, that she should stop thinking all the time, because what was the use of thinking anyway? When I asked how she thought Kalpita was doing, all she'd say was that she was a proud girl. Apparently, the straightforward way Kalpita talks had given her that impression. And about me she said I was still a kid and needed to grow up and that I knew nothing about household work – same old story. I expect she decided this when she saw me messing up the morning's jailhold work today. She seems genuinely worried that things will go badly for me when I'm married if I don't learn how to do housework.

Still, lately I have started to feel deserted, even though I pretend I'm okay. I feel as if I'm surrounded by a huge void sometimes. Now I either think about unhappy things, or about myself. I believe I've almost forgotten how to laugh. I'm worried my face will become long and ugly if we don't get out of this place soon.

Oh, I nearly forgot to write about it. Yesterday, the other prisoners made arrangements for cooking in the backyard. It isn't really allowed, but Heera Aunty agreed when she was promised a huge portion of the food. We three remained inside the hall since we had nothing to contribute to it. But later they took pity on us and let us come out. The prisoners plucked four brinjals from the plant that grows on the lawn. Heera Aunty provided the salt, pepper and the matchstick. They gathered the leaves from around the banyan tree and made a fire with them. There was no knife to chop the vegetables though, so they used the edge of the aluminium plates for that purpose. They used the bathing buckets as pots to cook the food in. The place was a great mess, and the thing they cooked was brinjal curry, and it was lovely. Everyone got a very small portion of it, except Heera Aunty, of course, she got a huge portion. The way the inmates here are so resourceful is one of the things I really admire about them; the way they can make something out of nothing.

Heera Aunty has a painful knee joint. She complains the whole day long, and expects people to sympathise with her, yet she's never satisfied with anything any of us do and so it's hard to stay interested in her knee problem. Of all the guards here, she is the strictest one by far and she's extremely tidy and so when the little girl, Rinki, goes and messes up the lawn when she's playing with the leaves of the banyan tree, and scribbling on the mud with her tiny fingers and pulling up the grass, Heera Aunty runs after her and scolds her and makes her cry. She expects us all to obey her, hold our tongues, help her, to be good, and God knows what else. I sometimes worry that I might lose my sense of humour around her, and there won't be any left when, and if, I ever get out of this bloody place.

Today I noticed a few cockroach wings in the dal on my plate. When I first noticed them the day before yesterday, I thought them to be fried onions and was getting happy since something different had been given for lunch but Rekha told me what they were exactly and I was really disgusted. Then, just today I heard Tanusri shouting at the top of her voice, and when we all rushed to see what was wrong, she showed us that her dal had the fried body of a big cockroach in it. Somebody said, 'Eat it all up, it's good for you, college girl,' and when I look around to see who it was who'd said that, I couldn't work it out.

Today is Sunday. I should be at a movie, or just hanging out with friends. I feel like a bird who wants to fly and whose wings have been mercilessly cut. Sometimes I hear a voice crying from inside me: 'Go out and enjoy the air in the courtyard if you're feeling so bad.' I've stopped responding to it lately. I don't feel like going out there much. I lie down with my blanket a lot. The holes in it let the cold air in, so I don't have to go out there to enjoy the air, I can just lie down and listen to all the noises I can hear like the sound of cars and buses or the whistle of trains outside in the real world.

I started thinking about possessions today. I was watching Rinki playing with a withered leaf from the banyan tree and realised that the poor little thing has probably never seen a real toy. Her mother, Nazma Bibi, was over in the corner of the room and her sari was badly ripped and worn-looking. I stared at my pencil bag and sensed how different my life really is to theirs: I have a case to put pencils in, they don't even have a pencil between them, yet, we are here together in this disgusting old falling down prison. India is so diverse and so extreme. This is what this place is teaching me day in and day out.

My pencil bag has always been one of my most precious possessions and I *still* have it with me here. It's white with silver sparkles and it's got red Barbie dolls all over it. When I was seventeen and Tutul four, she had a Barbie doll as a gift from someone and my pencil bag came along with it. Bubuli saw it and wanted it very badly, but Mamma managed to pacify her with a different one. Then when I took this bag to school and my friends saw it they came out with comments like, 'Oh how sweet,' 'sexy red bag,' 'where can I get one?' It came with me to college, to my college hostel and then, onwards to this filthy prison. Oh pencil bag, you are so precious to me … I owe you my tribute for being with me for so many years.

I'm not really jealous of the Dishari who enjoyed life once, but I have a great longing to have lots of fun and be able to laugh till my stomach aches now that it's the Christmas holidays with the new year on its way.

Every day when the female guards come from outside, I long to feel the cold of the fresh air from their sweaters. In spite of all the difficulties and injustice, you can never crush your feelings entirely. At least, I can't. Right now, I want to dance, sing, move around, laugh and oh so many other things … but I mustn't show it. All the 'mustn'ts' and 'shouldn'ts' are driving me mad or they will, surely, very soon. I can't talk to anyone about these things or I will burst into tears. I have tried to talk to Kalpita about my feelings and she thinks that I am being a cry baby. She says Tanusri already *is* crying all day long and it would be difficult for her to console both of us if I begin to cry too. But crying would be such a relief! I did talk to Shakila Aunty the other day because she has always seemed like a wise woman. She's been in here for three years and I wanted to know how she can stand it, how she keeps her spirits up and she said that time has taught her how to handle unexpected situations in life.

Right now the sun is shining. The sky is blue. The wind is fresh and I am so longing for everything, sitting under the banyan tree – to talk, to be free, for friends, to be alone. I want to cry and I know crying will make things better. But I can't. I am so restless. I can feel my heart telling me: 'Search for fun here in this place.' Although it seems impossible, Rinki manages it. Behaving normally is a big effort today and I am feeling utterly confused. I don't know what to think about … what to read … what to write … what to do. I only know that I am longing for everything, I am full of a blind longing, and aching to somehow be alive in a way this place would like to crush out of me if it could.

If I think of my life in early 2010, it all seems so unreal. I was a different Dishari then … friends all around, little pranks on everyone, a dashing boyfriend by my side, parties, the darling of nearly all the teachers, lots of pizzas, enough pocket money, the apple of my parents' eyes. Who could ask for anything else?

Now I look back at that Dishari as a superficial girl, who has no connection with this Dishari who thinks seriously about life. I would not be the least surprised if someone said to me: 'If I remember, you used to be surrounded by a group of girls and two or three boys. What happened? You were always laughing and at the centre of everything!'

Now what is left of me? I've totally forgotten how to answer back promptly. I would love to get back to my old life … at least for an evening.

I've just been for a walk around the lawn and sat with Rekha and Shrimati Didi for a while. They said I was looking ill and I found I couldn't help but tell them I was struggling with all my feelings. They said that I should calm down and take things bravely as they come upon me. Rekha said she envied me because of my education and because I can read. She said that she once found a book in a dustbin by the roadside and took it home. She'd often turn the pages over and look at the strange black marks on those pages and she longed to know what they meant. She promised herself that if she ever did get any spare money she'd ask the scholar who lived on the corner of her street if he'd teach her reading.

Since I've come back to write more in this diary, I'm feeling a bit stronger. How lucky I am to be able to read and write at all, I can't imagine the lives of Rekha, Shrimati Didi and others, and what's going to happen to Rinki? I heard that the children of prisoners can only stay with their mothers until they're five. I can write down my feelings whenever I want to, and I'm glad about that, otherwise I would be absolutely stifled. I know that I can write well. A couple of my stories are good and I have won the Illuminati 2010 for 'By-lane Dreamers.' It's my best story yet and I'm proud of it.

I am thankful to God for giving me this gift of expressing myself and my feelings through words. I can bring life to everything if I write … my sorrows, my happiness, my courage. I don't know, though, if I can write well enough so that I might be able to become a writer. Maybe it's just a pipe-dream … just like millions of its kind from inside the correctional home.

I haven't done anything to the novel I began to write. I know how I think it should go and what happens in it, at least I do in my mind, but somehow I can't get on with it. Whenever I sit down to try and write it, the words won't flow. But I'm still glad Papa brought it with him all the way from home, so that when I get tired of studying for the exams, I'll still have something with which I can occupy my mind.

But I want to write and write more. That's what I want to do with my life, become a writer, not an engineer.

4. T FOR TERROR

At college, my two close friends, Ananya and Baishali, were day scholars, and we were always together. Baishali was very shy at first, but the more she was with me, the more confident she became. Gradually, she told me about her family in Durgapur. Ananya couldn't be more different, being a party girl who liked Inox movies, KFC, and hanging out with groups of people. I liked her from the moment I met her. She too had lived in Durgapur all her life and she promised to show me around the place at the weekends with Baishali.

I thought I knew Tanusri almost as well as I knew these two girls because I shared a room with her right from the start. She used to be really mischievous and always looking out for the chance to make a joke or play the fool. Kalpita, on the other hand, is the most serious person I've ever met. She clings to her solitude, and seems to be indifferent to things, but I often wonder if it's just an act and that underneath, she is as emotional as any of us. She has this habit of looking people straight in the eyes, but showing nothing on her face, no smile, or anything.

I looked forward to my life in college and hoped that at the end of my four years I'd get a good job and become a successful engineer. Mamma and Papa were really proud that I'd been accepted into this particular college as it had a very good reputation. On my second day there, I stepped out of the Girls' Hostel in a red salwar with neatly folded dupatta in the form of a V and with my hair properly oiled, combed, and tied in a pony tail. I was on my way to my first lesson.

I took a seat in the second row, third bench of the classroom. The blackboard was cleanly polished. There were four fans and five tube lights above us. One of the lights wasn't working properly, on-off-on-off-on-off it went and it made an irritating buzzing sound as it did so. There were spider webs at the corners of the room and you could imagine the spiders tapping their feet as they watched us all. The fans made a sound that caught your attention as well as they thumped round and round. The benches were light brown with names scribbled all over them, Subhayan, Susmita, Amrita. The walls were shabby blue with hearts of different sizes drawn on them. Before too long, the beautiful Mrs. Das, our engineering mathematics teacher, came in and handed out the semester syllabus.

Apart from Ananya and Baishali, I talked to a few boys on that first day of lessons, Rupak was one of them. I asked him what his hobbies were and when he said giving missed calls to friends, I didn't know what he meant, and thought him a joker. I met Arijit who could mimic anyone, including Mrs. Das and his imitation of her voice had a group of boys laughing loudly. Then there were the three musketeers of our class. They were always together ... Abhijit, Biman and Bidesh. They were the quietest boys in the class and were room partners in their hostel. I met Bibek too. He was cool. We talked for a long time about movies. He always sat with his childhood buddy of school days, Durjoy. Durjoy didn't talk much during those days of college.

The seniors stepped inside our classroom after the classes were over for the day. One amongst the thirty or so of them grabbed everyone's attention. He seemed to be their leader. If I am given to judge different personalities, I would always categorize a person in one of the following three groups: The ones who can be easily distinguished from a crowd, commonly known for their over-expressive nature, generally called extroverts. In my dictionary, they are known as paanipuri ... no matter how many times you've been told about the unhygienic way they are made, they are just not resistible. Similarly, these kinds of people have an unusual ability to get your attention even if you are adamant that you won't look at them. Next there are the ordinaries, the ones who can be identified or recognised but there is nothing special about them to distinguish them from the rest. I call them toothbrushes – we use them every day but when asked about the most important things that we have and can't live without, we come up with mobile phones, credit cards, watches, pens, lip balm, hair spray, i-pods, purses, underwear, Mamma, Papa (I mean, is there anything else?) But we forget the poor little toothbrush thing though we are completely aware of its importance. Last there are the introverts, the doormats; the ones who never get noticed even if there isn't a crowd. They don't talk much and sometimes they don't talk at all.

The guy who got everyone's attention was a paanipuri. He spoke with a loud and clear voice. 'Welcome freshers. My name is Aritro Ghosh. I am your second year senior. We are here to get to know you.'

We were asked to give our intro, one by one, starting from the left corner of the last bench.

'My name is Arko Sen. I am from Ranchi …'

The introductions continued. I waited for my turn, keeping my head as low as possible.

'What's up Aritro? What are you staring at?' a thick voice cried out of the crowd.

'Or *who* are you staring at?' emerged another, a shrill voice this time.

'Red salwar!' said a third, and people began to laugh.

I looked up in fear when he said that and everyone in the room was staring back at me. It was my turn to introduce myself and I found my heart beating faster and faster, on-off-on-off-on-off. I stood up and found that my legs were shaking.

'My name is Dishari Saha,' I began. I lowered my eyes and gazed at a scratch on the table in front of me, but I needed to see him; it was *his* fault my heart was beating like that, and I couldn't help looking upwards at his handsome face. He was also looking at me with an expression that I could not understand. I took my seat and my heart was still beating fast.

After the intro session, I went to the canteen with the girls. I did not speak to anyone in the meantime. Yet, I could understand that the brief looking and staring back moment which had taken place between us had been noticed and talk of it would be already spreading through the college. As I walked with my friends past the Engineering Physics Lab, Workshop Building and Graphics Hall to the canteen, I could hear voices, loud and clear, from different corners.

'Hey Aritro, your wife has come. See if she needs food or water or something else. The college park is waiting for you.'

I remembered one of the points from a mobile SMS that I had once received. It said:

Dis is 4 my dear Bengali frnds ...
U r a true Bengali if u fulfil atleast 5 of da below:
U lyk to hav paanipuri, samosa, mishti doi
U hav pet names lyk papai, bubai, munai, shonai
Ur kitchen is full of jars which come free wid diff items
U go shoppin only b4 d Durga Puja
U cant bear a criticism against Saurav Ganguly
U prefer street chowmein ovr restaurant's
U always check d price b4 orderng inside a restaurant
U plan ur day of love @ Saraswati Puja & not d V-day
U r a Rupam Islam fan evn if u dnt undrstnd his music
U update ur facebuk status in benglish (Bengali + English)
U refer ur gf/bf (or ur crush) as 'my wife' / 'my husband'
BENGAL AND BENGALIS ROCK!!!

We took the steps leading to the canteen. Both sides of the entrance were crowded with seniors waiting to tease me. 'Hey Aritro. She's come! Your wife's here at last!'

When we found a table in the middle of the canteen, Kalpita said, 'Are we animals in a zoo, or something? These people are seriously stupid. Are we public property just because we're new?'

'I guess that's exactly what we are,' I said. 'This afternoon I was called for an intro by a group of seniors and one of them was copying my expressions without speaking.'

'That must have been really humiliating!' Baishali said.

'Of course it was,' I said, 'and I think I was expected not to show any feelings about it. I reckon that's meant to be the stupid custom.'

'Hey,' Ananya whispered, 'those seniors over there at that table are talking about us, they keep glancing over here. Don't look now; don't make it obvious you know.'

The five of us sat in silence for a while. Tanusri kept her eyes closed so she couldn't see anything, she said, and Kalpita drummed her fingers on the table. We were hungry. We were waiting for a man we could see in a brown uniform who was taking orders from the tables to come our way. Ananya and Baishali were trying to spy on the seniors who were interested in us without making it obvious, and I was wondering where in the canteen Aritro was sitting.

Finally the man arrived at our table. 'My name is Nilu,' he said, 'you can call me Nilu Bhaiya. I'll be taking your orders. Fish, chicken, egg curry or vegetables?'

While we waited for Nilu Bhaiya to come back with our food, it seemed that the canteen had become even hotter and noisier than it was before. I just wanted to eat and get out of there. I didn't dare to look around me, I think we all felt like that; I know Tanusri did. She and I were both gazing at the red jug in the middle of the table and keeping very still.

Yet no sooner had Nilu Bhaiya brought the food to our table, when three second year seniors came over and sat with us and one of them was Aritro. He sat directly opposite me, but the red jug was between us and hid me from him. I was grateful for that because my face was burning. Yet the relief of it only lasted a few moments because Nilu Bhaiya shuffled back again and took the jug away for another table and I was looking straight into Aritro's eyes. I couldn't eat another thing; my throat had closed up and I couldn't swallow. Aritro stared at me. Oh, he looked so handsome in his red t-shirt. There was something about him which made my heart beat many times faster than normal. In an instant I was overwhelmed with self consciousness, I was aware of how I sat, how I looked, the expressions on my face. I sighed inwardly with relief when he said, 'Let's leave them guys. They can't even eat properly in front of us,' and went away. I felt that I'd just met someone different from the others, someone who could understand my feelings. We finished our food fast and left the canteen.

There were seniors everywhere on the railings, stairs, and along the passage. We had to give our intros countless number of times; it was the college custom and there was no way out of it, it struck me as utterly ridiculous, and I think maybe that was true for a lot of us, but we didn't dare go against the convention.

The next day I was hurrying towards my classroom as I was already late for my lesson, when I was stopped by Aritro. 'Which year?' he asked. His voice was deep and I liked it. 'Which year?' he asked again in a louder voice.

'First,' I said.

'What?' he asked. '*First year*! Listen. Only after the Freshers' Ceremony will you be thought of as a first year student, before that you've got to say you're in the zeroth year if anyone else asks you.'

'Okay, I didn't know that. Thank you – zeroth – hard to say that word.'

'The other seniors might ask you. Now go to your class.'

He walked away and I wondered why he'd bothered to caution me, I was glad he had though.

At night, the same conditions prevailed in the canteen as they had during lunch. When I went there with Kalpita and Tanusri, the place was full of seniors. First year boys were being randomly selected by seniors to offer love proposals to the girls. If a girl accepted, there was no problem. But in case a proposal was rejected, the boy had to do a strange task in front of everyone. One had to sing while scratching his entire body! I sat quietly at the table, waiting for my turn to be a part of this offering and proposing activity and dreading it as well.

'I ...' Bhim, a very shy boy attempted to speak, 'I am sorry, Dada. But I don't propose to girls.'

The hall fell silent at his remark and some seconds later, a great roar of laughter rose up and I didn't know what it was about.

'Well,' one of the seniors asked after a while, 'then what! You propose to boys, do you?'

'I am interested, brother!' someone exclaimed, 'do you wanna propose to me? I am single!'

'And ready to mingle!' the other seniors shouted in chorus.

'Kalpita,' I said as softly as I could, 'look at that guy! There.'

'That thin guy in the blue t-shirt?'

'Yes. His name is Rupak. I met him yesterday in Mrs. Das's class.'

'What's he doing on his knees with a fountain pen?'

'I've been watching him for a while now. I think they're making him measure the room using his pen.'

'You're joking!'

'No. Watch him.'

'The whole canteen?'

'Yes. That's what these people are like.'

We noticed that a boy from a distant table had started singing while he scratched his entire body. 'Aha ki anondo akashe batashe

...' (Oh! What great fun in the sky, in the air ...) The sight of him was so ridiculous that I began to laugh loudly. I couldn't help it, and it took me a moment to become aware that the canteen had fallen silent. All I could hear was the faulty tube light, on-off-on-off-on-off.

The seniors drifted quietly over to my table. The first years sat motionless, like the inanimate tables and chairs. Nilu Bhaiya came into the canteen from the kitchen and stood wiping his hands down the front of his uniform. Tanusri and Kalpita were asked to leave the table to make space for the seniors.

'Did I hear you laughing?' one of the seniors asked me.

I looked straight at him and tried not to blink. I could feel my cheeks burning and the palms of my hands began to sweat. I wanted to say do I really have to answer your dumb question? But I couldn't bring myself to do it. A tall figure emerged out of the group. He was Saikat Bhaiya, from the third year. He kept his eyes fixed on me for some time as if he was trying to work me out.

'So you're the Orkut girl, eh?' Abhinav Da, another third year student said, breaking the silence and moving his glasses down to the tip of his nose so that he could stare over them at me. 'You are the sinner! *You* are the one who thinks seniors can be offered friendship requests on Orkut!'

'Reply,' a familiar voice called out, 'when asked a question.'

I knew it was Aritro but I couldn't see where he was, and didn't dare turn around to find him. 'I wasn't *asked* a question,' I called out. 'He was simply making a statement.'

'How dare you speak like that to us!' Abhinav Da shouted, banging his fist on the table.

'That's a bit melodramatic isn't it?' Tanusri murmured and when I glanced at her, I thought for a second that she was about to smile and at that moment it would've been a bad mistake.

'I didn't,' I said, 'I mean I did ... that is, I didn't think before doing that Orkut thing.'

'You've made a big mistake. You must pay for it,' Abhinav Da said.

'*Pay?* For wanting to be friends?'

'Friends with seniors, yes.'

'Do you realise your blunder?' Aritro asked, stepping forward. I looked down and didn't answer him. 'Go back to your room and think about it then,' he said, 'and don't sit with boys in your class. All girls should sit together on the first bench.'

✦ ✦ ✦

Back in the hostel, Tanusri and I talked about the seniors until late at night. Kalpita had crept away to bed and left us by ourselves.

'Really those guys must lack something in life to carry on like that, they were quite absurd,' Tanusri said.

I thought about Aritro and hated the fact that he'd been involved in that confrontation. 'Yes, completely un-cool,' I said, 'all of them, even the handsome one.'

'Saw you looking at him.'

'I thought he was different from the others, he's not though.'

'We won't ever be like that will we, when we're seniors?'

'Well, I won't be; I know that.'

'What was the name they gave you?'

'Pepsodent, I think it was. Stupid,' I said.

'Because you were laughing. And they called Kalpita Robot, did you hear that?'

'Yes, because she's so serious and because she doesn't show anything on her face. And Bibek got called Maru as he's the only Marwari boy here.'

'And you know Rupak that thin boy – the one you met the other day. He's called Puchu at home and the seniors called him Puchu Mastan,' Tanusri said.

'You know what? If they can give us names that freely, we can do it back. Those three that got us at the end were terrible. I was really scared.'

'Well you didn't show it,' Tanusri said.

'So how about 'T' meaning 'Terror'. Let's have Saikat Bhaiya as T1, and that vile Abhinav Da as T2. I hate him.'

'And what about Aritro?' Tanusri asked.

'Oh we'll think of something even worse for him later.'

5. FLAVOUR OF LOVE

Morning 13th December 2010

I am sitting under the banyan tree outside the hall with my blanket around my shoulders. Part of my toenail has gone black. It doesn't hurt, but I've got a deep cut between my thumb and finger and I'm worried it'll get infected. But now at least I can manage to grip my pen because I've finished my jailhold works and the numbness in my hand has faded away. But my feelings are numb as well, and that's not going to go away soon. Today, I tried to concentrate on studying belt drives when Rinki started shouting about something and I couldn't think anymore. That's when I closed my book and forgot about the spur gears, springs, shafts, fits and tolerances that I still had to study.

As I write my diary, I try to feel the warmth beside Mamma ... I think about being in her arms. The ten o'clock bell rings in my ears like her anxious phone calls before each of my exams. How I yearn to feel her hands stroking my hair and her voice soothing me ... how I wish I could cry in her arms and sleep with my head on her lap and feel safe once again. I wait impatiently for the black van to take me back to college for today's exam. Exam doesn't mean just an exam any more. When I get there I can meet Papa and my friends, talk to them, touch them, hug them.

My friends, Bidesh and Arijit, from my class, have helped me a lot with Machine Design, a subject I've been nervous about. They came here yesterday and explained the question pattern and the possible numerical problems in the test. I've studied in the way they suggested. I thank God for such wonderful friends. I could not sleep at all last night. Bidesh sent some notes for me to study and the guards checked all the pages for anything suspicious and then stamped them with the prison logo. I think that is really stupid. Did they think words could change into guns or keys or bombs? I hate this hideous place, I sometimes think it must be worse to be someone who works here than someone who is captured here.

The notes were very precise and Bidesh had made it very simple with plenty of examples so that it was easy to understand. Now I feel a lot more confident about today's paper. But one thing that is worrying me constantly is what Bidesh told me yesterday. He said Prateem had tried to stop him visiting us. I wonder if Triparna is involved in that as well or if Prateem hates me all by himself and wants to make my life even harder by trying to stop me having visitors.

Lately I have been watching Tanusri. She's not coping with this situation well. Both Kalpita and I have tried to help her, but she cries all the time and won't listen to us. We can't get her to talk to us either. She sits for long periods of time with her hands covering her face, and she rocks backwards and forwards, she's a bit like Maya. I am really worried about her. Not because she hasn't studied anything and might not do well … in that case, I'll try my level best to help her in the exam hall. I am worried that she might go mad. She doesn't even eat properly. We have to force her to eat sometimes and I just hope she doesn't try to do anything stupid like hurt herself.

Morning 15th December 2010

This morning, Kalpita was saying that she can't get used to the sound of the prison bell ringing every hour. I can. I loved it from the very first day. It has been like a faithful friend to me especially at night when I can't sleep. My exam three days ago went well. I am so grateful to Bidesh and Arijit. Their suggestions turned out to be really helpful. Tomorrow is the date of our hearing in court and I'm just hoping and hoping we get bail, I'm so jumpy and over-excited; we'll be out of this place with its cockroaches and misery, I can't wait. I'm counting every hour that goes by until we are sitting in that court room. Papa is trying really hard for me and I know God is with me – he must be – because I'm innocent.

Night 16ᵗʰ December 2010

Ours is a difficult case to fight, apparently. It has been difficult to find a lawyer as well. No experienced lawyer was showing any interest at all. Finally, a friend of Suvodip's father agreed to take on the case for us. Today, we were to have our hearing and were all ready to go to court. I was very eager to get out of the four walls and meet Papa and friends. I prayed really hard that we would get bail. Throughout the morning, I kept thinking about Mamma and Bubuli and Tutul. I had no spare paper anywhere so I've had to write to Papa on a torn off page in my diary and I had the idea I'd be able to give it to him in court, just slip it across to him:

Papa,
Please tell Mamma not to cry for me. I am doing well in my exams. I couldn't talk to her the other day as we had to leave. And this is keeping me upset. Please see that she takes care of her health. Tell Bubuli and Tutul not to worry about me. I'll be out of this place very soon. Tell them that I will come home and play a lot with them. As for you, Papa, you mean everything to me. God has given me the best Papa. I cannot express what you are to me.
Yours forever,
Disha.

I wrote to Suvodip too in the hope that he would also be in court and that I would get a moment with him.

Suvodip,
We haven't talked in almost three years since the rose incident in the first year. But what you've done for me when I needed you most makes me feel that I am so lucky. I have got a chance to understand your friendship. If I've ever been rude to you, please forgive me.
Dishari

The day dragged on from morning to afternoon and then into evening. The van never came to take us to court. I stayed in the same place all day facing the wall. The diary pages were in my hands throughout the day. At some point in time, I felt two small hands slowly removing them from me. It was Rinki and she wanted some paper, but everything written in my diary had become precious to me and so I took out some pages from my practice papers for the exam and watched her in a daze as she tore them up and threw the pieces in the air as if they were leaves from a tree. Then she wanted me to play with her. She took hold of my hands and tried to pull me to my feet. As many times as I wriggled free of her, she took my hands again, so in the end, I did as she said and stood up. She led me all around the prison. I think we were going on a walk together. She doesn't talk very much, but this time she was chattering away and looking up at me from time to time until in the end, I did forget my own misery for a while and found myself smiling at the funny little things she said.

I knew that bail must have been rejected otherwise Papa would surely have come to get me out of this vile place. I have to stay here for another fourteen days – for another 336 hours – before we are called to court again, and I feel terrible about it. Perhaps, on that day, we might get bail. But I have lost all hope. I feel like crying aloud right now.

I was reflecting back into the past today. The seniors whom I had at first seen as treacherous jackals suddenly became good friends to me when the ragging period was over and they helped me when I asked for it. I remember clearly the night I had a high fever and the fat boy got me some medicine. Thank God he was there, and the other seniors too helped me with my work or anything really.

Aritro, who most terrified me, gradually became the man I love, and after three and a half years, still do.

Everyone was quiet today; there were no silly fights between the women, and I think they were being silent to give us three some comfort. Even Rinki was quiet. She's asleep now beside Nazma, and the night is hanging dark outside. Before I was brought here, I had no idea what prisons were like. So few educated people ever find themselves in prison. For me to be here is so strange that I begin to wonder if I'm here for a purpose – I believe everything has a purpose. So maybe I should be making proper use of my time here, not being sad all day and crying like Tanusri does. Maybe it's that I have to tell the world about places like these and how these women suffer. I know how they suffer; I know what it feels like to have justice denied to you.

Evening 17th December 2010

Tanusri has been crying since afternoon again. She told me that she feels like finishing herself. It's the silence that frightens her so in the evenings and at night. Yes, it is very oppressive here and we can't go outdoors before our next exam, scheduled for the 22nd. Sometimes I get really scared and panicky and can't control the way I'm thinking and then I get the idea that we will have to be in prison forever, because it's definitely going to happen to other women in here. Maybe that's what's going on in Tanusri's head all the time.

I always have to whisper to Kalpita and Tanusri when I speak against the police or the present system of law and order, otherwise, the female guards might hear us and we might get into big trouble.

This afternoon Rupak came to visit us. We were very curious to know what had happened yesterday in court. He said the lawyer had argued that section 306 was valid under no circumstance, it should have been 309. I had no idea what 306 or 309 meant, and he didn't know either. Kalpita asked him if the judge had agreed with our lawyer. He looked at each of us and then looked away. I asked if we should take it to mean bail was being rejected. He said the next court hearing was two weeks from now on the 31st of December.

He tried to console Tanusri, assuring her that things would be all right in the end and he told us to concentrate on the exam and not to worry about anything else. But how can we not worry? It is so difficult to concentrate only on the exams. Then he said the public prosecutor thought the *feelings* of other students would be hurt if we were given bail. 'Student emotions' being hurt was what the prosecutor said, apparently. Tanusri started to get agitated again and Rupak said everyone he knew at college was trying to help. A signature campaign was being carried out in all the engineering colleges and our friends were staying out late at night working on the petition and he said that they'd collected thousands of signatures in just one day.

Afternoon 19th December 2010

I am sitting inside the hall with yellow walls and wondering what sections 306 and 309 mean. I have decided to ask Papa when I speak to him after our exam. The guards who accompany us to college and bring us back are better than most of the guards I've come across. They always give us time to talk to our parents and I get time to talk to Mamma on Papa's phone as well.

I am not studying much at present. A local club here donated a second hand Onida colour television to the Female Ward, this morning. I think they have one for the Male Ward as well. It's a great relief, sometimes sitting here doing nothing has made me feel as if I'm going crazy, sometimes my throat gets so tight that I can't swallow.

I have never watched Bengali serials before, because they're stupid and the regular mother-in-law and daughter-in-law clashes are ridiculous. But these are what amuse everyone here and I watch them without complaining because it's better than doing nothing. I want to watch the news channel. I have no idea about what's going on in the world. The minute the television came onto the ward, the older inmates took charge of it and we had no say in the matter.

Shakila Aunty, and one of the female guards had a terrible quarrel this morning. I've never seen anything quite like it before. Shakila Aunty had plucked a chilly for herself from the chilly plant that grows on the lawn. That made the female guard so angry that she shouted like an insane person with a brain disorder. Shakila Aunty was quiet for some time even though it's her who's in charge of our ward. And then, even she started shouting and she's usually really quiet. I found the whole thing very funny. I tried my best to control my laughter. They're not talking to each other now.

It must be horrible for the female guards to work in a prison. They look pretty old, in their fifties or sixties. They must have worked here for a good number of years. I can't imagine how it must be to carry on like they do. Prisoners come and go. Some get bail and others do not and are sent to a worse prison. But the lives of the guards stay the same. They don't have a television to watch in their tiny one room house that's alongside our hall, and come to think of it, they're locked in just like we are, they can't come and go when they please. They're not even allowed to carry mobile phones in prison. I expect this is to make sure the prisoners don't steal them to plan escapes and so on.

We three are the youngest of all the prisoners. The others sometimes treat us like babies. And I can't bear that. Yesterday Rekha said she thought it was tough for us to have to wash our clothes and do the 'jailhold' work since we are 'so small.' She kept fussing and I had to give her a few of my clothes so she could wash them for me. But they're always very nice to us as well. On the days of our exams, I have seen them praying for us. They wait for our return in the evening anxiously. I love this attachment ... especially when they ask us about our exams, what we had for our lunch in college and if the guards were good to us. Dinner in prison is served at four in the evening, while we are still in college writing our papers. But they always keep our food for us. The bad dal, thick rice and tasteless sabzi, oh, and the cockroaches, get cold by then. But I am touched by the way these women who have so little in their own lives, are caring about us, and I eat the food as if it was exquisite because it is flavoured with their affection.

6. EVOLUTION '07

I'd been in college for two months and I quite often skipped dinners and lunches and stayed in my room to escape from the ragging. The hostel was the place where I could hide my misery. But it couldn't protect me from the horrible nights when I would be ragged right through until daylight.

I had to stand in the Girls' Hostel for hours and alone every night and be scolded by the then second year senior girls. They all thought I was going around with Aritro when it wasn't true, although I wished it was. I would've loved to have been able to tell my friends that I was the girlfriend of such a good-looking man.

Every day it was the same story – I would wake up after a traumatic night, move towards college hardly knowing what I was doing, have food in the canteen, come back to my hostel to meet seniors and follow their orders to bring pakoras and fries, and if I was lucky, I would have to fill only ten bottles of water and endure yet another never ending night of being tortured by these girls.

'So how are things with Aritro?' Ankita Di, a senior, asked me once. She was the girl who most terrified me. 'I tell you,' she continued, 'Aritro can stare very hard at times.'

'Like how?' I asked.

'Very raw. I don't know if he does that to you. But he always stares at me. And you know where? At my breasts! God!'

'I've never noticed that.'

'Oh! I'll tell you. He proposed love to me once. I refused straight away.'

I fell sick about him. I went back to my room. I was stupid to have fallen for such a bad guy. He doesn't deserve me I thought, but he's so handsome ... no ... no more thinking about him. I was filled with gratitude to Ankita Di for having told me about him.

I ran into him quite soon after that as I was walking to the canteen with Ananya. He was with a group of second year senior boys and I was filled with disgust when he looked at me.

'Why is your hair down like that today?' Aritro asked Ananya.

She moved backwards slightly and I realised just how frightened she was. 'She's got a marriage ceremony to go to after college,' I said on her behalf.

'Heard that one before,' Aritro replied, 'today marriage, tomorrow birthday, the day after … do you think we're fools?' He smiled at me. The other boys who were standing with him began to tease us … that is, me and Aritro. I felt angry; I didn't want to be associated with him.

'Why are you silent?' one of the senior boys asked me, 'don't you like my friend Aritro?'

I was furious now. Each night I had to stand and be ridiculed by senior girls because of this one lecherous boy. I felt like punching him in the face.

'No,' I said, 'I hate him. I hate the very sight of him. Ankita Di told me how he stares at her all the time. He even proposed to her once she said.'

I looked up at Aritro and kept my eyes unblinkingly on his. He looked horrified as if he'd heard something unbelievable. The others stood there without a word and said nothing to him. I felt triumphant. I watched him trying to meet my gaze and failing. He lowered his eyes, turned, and walked away. Then, at the end of our last lesson for the day, some second year seniors came into our classroom looking very purposeful and quiet. 'Go ahead Ankita … tell,' one of them said.

I was sitting on the first bench along with Ananya and I realised that the seniors were all looking directly at me. For a moment, I thought I'd done something wrong, and my mouth went dry. Ankita Di came up to me and she seemed humiliated and unhappy. 'I'm sorry,' she said, 'I lied about Aritro. He never proposed to me, and he doesn't stare at me either.' She didn't wait for me to respond, but turned around quickly and left the classroom, pushing her way through the girls she came with.

'Dishari, Ankita is not good company,' one of the seniors said, 'she used to admire Aritro and she proposed to him once, but he didn't want her. It got bad then, she sort of forced herself on him – he's such a handsome man – and he ended up slapping her. That was an awful night. We made her come and tell you because he hasn't done anything wrong, we thought you should know.'

I stayed in the classroom after everyone else had left. The fan was making its usual irritating noise. I went through a lot of thoughts … why did I trust Ankita Di of all people … why didn't I go with what my heart longed for … why didn't I use my brains or trust my feelings and instincts about Aritro? Before I realised it, tears were running down my cheeks. I took my bag and walked out of the classroom into the darkness and within seconds I'd bumped into somebody.

'I've been waiting for you,' he said. I rubbed my eyes and found that it was Aritro. 'And I find you crying.'

'Yes,' I said. 'Because I wronged you and I'm sorry. Your friends came to our class and told me everything.'

'*You* shouldn't be sorry for that. It wasn't your fault. But please stay away from Ankita. She's not a good girl to be around.'

'So what happened between you and her?'

'Did you know she has a boyfriend in the fourth year?'

'No, I didn't.'

'Well she has, and she's powerful because of it. She's a second year student with a fourth year boyfriend who's got a gang of his own.'

'Well, what *did* happen between her and you?' I asked him again.

'She kept flirting with me. There was one day when I was in the library and she came from behind and got her arms around me and hugged me and kept telling me how much she loved me, and she was pressing herself into me. It was in a corner and there was hardly anyone in the library at that time of day. I prised her off me and turned around, and I couldn't help it; I was so angry and shocked that I slapped her face.'

'That's awful, Aritro.'

'I know. We haven't talked since then. I hated her on that day and I hate her now, Disha. Can I call you that, do you mind?'

'No. Call me that, it's all right coming from you.'

'Look, stay as far away from Ankita if you can, she's dangerous. She used to get her boyfriend and his friends to torture us when we were in the first year and they were in the third year.'

'You're joking!'

'I'm serious. She got pleasure from knowing we were beaten up because she'd arranged it with her boyfriend. She wanted everyone in her year to be afraid of her, girls and boys, and we were. She loves power. She wanted to be treated like a senior herself.'

'That's pathetic,' I said.

'When I was in the first year, there would be terrible ragging at night. We wished night time would never come. The seniors did all sorts of things to us. Especially Ankita's boyfriend. They even made us strip. Ankita would get the details of our ragging and our reactions to it on her mobile phone from her boyfriend. The next day she'd come to class and make fun of us with her girl friends. They hit us a lot, those guys.'

'Badly?'

'Very hard. On the night after I slapped Ankita, she must have told her boyfriend because he started hitting me as if I was some kind of animal. I was left on the floor of my room with a bleeding tongue.'

'But today her classmates forced her to apologise to me, so she can't be all that powerful.'

'I expect they told her they wouldn't work with her, or speak to her again unless she put it right with you. That's what the boys in my class decided after I was beaten like that. And we still don't help her or speak to her.'

The more I talked to Aritro about his first year days and the cruelty he suffered, and the more I was ragged myself, the more I began to hate the whole thing. However, despite that, slowly, everything around me – the college park and its benches, the corridor and the stairs, the classroom and its doorway, became magical as I shared glances with Aritro while taking temperature readings for Stefan's Constant, or through the back door of the physics lab, or while struggling my way towards forming a hypocycloid, and then down through the Graphics Hall window, and again, while measuring with a tri-square at the workshop door.

The day arrived when Aritro called me over to him. He seemed tense and I was puzzled by his expression. 'Okay Disha ... I will call you. Go back to your hostel,' he said and left quickly. He called me on my phone that night. I was on the balcony outside my room.

'Hello,' he said. 'What are you doing?'

'Nothing. Just had my dinner.'

'Okay. I wish to tell you something today.'

'Go ahead. I am listening.'

'I love you,' he said, and he really hurried with the words.

'What? I can't hear; my phone's not working properly.'

'Nothing. Just generally.'

'Generally what?'

'I love you.'

'What?'

'Ami Tomake Bhalobashi. I love you.'

I had longed so much for this. The day had finally arrived. We had known each other now for a month. I lived every moment of the conversation that day.

'Me too,' I told him.

The night before Freshers' Ceremony was known as The Black Night. I was called out by the senior girls along with Kalpita and Tanusri as we were to be their amusement that evening. We were all wearing the correct clothes and when we reached the room we'd been summoned to we found four girls waiting for us. I'd become so used to the mockery by now that I didn't bother to see who our tormentors were; I kept my eyes downwards, as if out of respect for them rather than fear.

'Oh! Our lady love has arrived,' one of them exclaimed. I recognised the voice of Chitra Di and could not help but look up at the heavy scorn in her voice. I didn't remember seeing her amongst the seniors who'd brought Ankita Di to our classroom that day. And there, just behind her, was Ankita Di herself lounging on a chair and staring straight at me in a way that gave me the creeps. To her left, and sitting on the edge of a bed was Rohini Di with a heavy wooden stick in her hands, and on the floor, cross-legged, was a small girl with a scar on her face, Smita Di.

'Ahh!' Ankita Di said, widening her eyes as she spoke, 'let us see what Aritro stares at every day in the canteen!'

'No, not just her,' Smita Di said, 'let's get a look at all of them.'

'C'mon,' the other two chorused, 'un-pin your dupattas!'

I reached up and unpinned both pins – the right one first and then the left. I could see out of the corner of my eye that Tanusri and Kalpita were doing the same. Rohini Di moved the stick from one hand to the other and back again and I wondered how hard it would be when she struck us with it. She stood up and arched her back and held the stick above her head. Tanusri let out a noise that was half a shout and half a cry.

'Shut up you,' Smita Di said. 'Stupid little idiot.'

'You can't hit us with that,' Kalpita said, 'we'll report you!'

'Who said anything about hitting?' Ankita Di asked. 'We are about to perform an examination. Go on Rohini, check them out.'

Rohini Di moved forward, and raising the stick, poked each of our breasts with it, one by one. 'Soft and round!' she said, and she may as well have been describing brinjals in a supermarket.

'Let's see what they can do with these,' Chitra Di said, and reaching under the bed, she brought out three similar sticks and gave one to each of us.

'I'm not doing it, what kind of a monster do you think I am!' I shouted. 'Do what you want to me, but you aren't going to make me do that!'

'Nor me,' Kalpita said, 'so back off now!'

Tanusri began to cry and so I put my arm around her and the three of us stared hard at the four girls.

'Don't be so dramatic, it's only a joke, we weren't going to make you do anything bad,' Smita Di said. 'God, how serious can you get!'

'We just wanted you to dance. Don't you like dancing?' Rohini Di asked. 'You look like you'd be good at dancing, Tanusri, are you?' Tanusri nodded. 'Show us then, go on. With the stick, dance like a tribal woman. A wild woman.'

Tanusri was too frightened to disobey them and she began to dance, awkwardly at first and then as they cheered her on, faster and more recklessly. But Kalpita and I could see she hated every second of it, so to help her, we started to dance too. We shook our legs, our hands, our tongues. We held the sticks under our arms, between our legs, with our necks, trying to think of the craziest and wildest way to use them to a rhythm the seniors were beating out:

'*Ooga Hu Ooga Hu*
Ooga Hu Ooga Hu
Ooga Booga Ooga Booga'

This was only the beginning. That evening, they forced us to do the most ridiculous things one after the other ... things like offering love proposals to a Hrithik Roshan poster or pretending to be lesbians to amuse Ankita Di. 'Come to me, undress me ... show your feelings ... I am longing for it,' Ankita Di said, beckoning me with her finger.

I stared at her and wondered if there was some way to divert her when Smita Di stood up suddenly. 'Let's see something sensuous now,' she said, turning up the music on her laptop. 'This is my favourite song. Tanusri and Dishari you're crazy in love with each other and at last you are alone together, so let's see you act it out, get really steamy and intimate with each other.'

'What?' I asked.

'I *said* act out a sex scene for us, come on! You have to do what we say, so get on with it!'

'We better do it,' Tanusri whispered, 'maybe they'll let us go after that.'

Tanusri unpinned my hair slowly, and I did the same to hers, and then she kissed my forehead and left her lips lingering there for a moment, and I quickly kissed her back.

'Enough!' Ankita Di shouted, hitting my back hard with her hand. 'How pathetic! You don't know how to be seductive; you've no idea, have you? What a shame for Aritro, he's going to run a mile when he finds out you don't know anything about making love. That poor man!'

It was five o'clock in the morning before they let us go back to our rooms. The next day we slept through the whole morning; we were lucky because it was the Freshers' Ceremony and therefore a holiday and no one came to disturb us. I woke up in the afternoon while Kalpita and Tanusri were still under their blankets. I went to the canteen alone. My tension and panic were sucked deep into my stomach after the previous night's terror, so I walked immune from fear. It was very hot outside. I had a light green umbrella in my hand.

I could see a person walking towards me. He looked like Aritro but again, didn't look like him. He was holding his ears. It *was* Aritro.

'Hold your ears and walk with me,' he said in a frightened voice.

'But why?'

'Please do as I say. Our seniors want both of us to hold our ears. They're my seniors too. I have to do as they say.'

I was really angry with him; I was tired of being told to do stupid things by stupid people. I walked towards the canteen and ignored him.

'What Aritro, your wife refuses to obey you?'

I looked up to see a group of fourth year seniors, then I looked at Aritro, still holding his ears.

'What to do bhaiya,' he spoke in a desperate voice, 'I told her, but …'

I closed my umbrella and remained still.

'Well then,' Bera Da continued, 'propose to her.'

'On your knees!' Jisnu Da added.

'With her umbrella instead of a rose,' Arnab Da said.

I glanced to my right. Bibek, Soumesh and other students I knew were peeping through their windows from the first year hostel, hoping not to be caught staring by the seniors. I looked to my left, and there the third years were laughing and mocking. In the beginning I'd thought the cruelty and bullying that went on unchallenged in engineering colleges was something only the first years had to endure, and that once through it, students could get on with their real reason for being in college. Now I realised that the horrible custom of ragging was like an out of control infectious disease that involved all the years, and it wasn't an innocent little jokey tradition at all, but a vicious custom that in the wrong hands – and there were many wrong hands – quickly became sadistic and terrifying.

After all that Tanusri, Kalpita and I had been through, the Freshers' Ceremony almost made up for it. From that night onwards the first years no longer had to wear formal dress and so the boys had taken off their long-sleeved shirts and formal trousers and were wearing jeans and coloured t-shirts and the girls no longer had to oil their hair.

The college was decorated with paper flower garlands hanging in elegant swathes high up around the walls, and lower down there were fan-shaped designs and snowflakes made in delicate tissue paper. The ceremony took place in the field behind the college in which a wooden stage had been erected with a banner reading 'Welcome Freshers' hung across the front of it. The field was full of chairs and the evening began with the Tilak Ceremony, marking our entry to the first year. The names were called in order of roll number.

'Tuhin Gayen ... Jonty Rhodes ... known for excellent fielding!'

'Suvodip Das ... the Chak de India guy ... Independence Day! Great speech!'

'Pulak Mandal ... Massala boy.'

'Kalpita Das ... Miss Robot.'

'Ananya De ... Didi Didi.'

'Dishari Saha ...'

As soon as I stepped on the stage, the crowd broke into applause, 'Aritro! Aritro!' The spot light on him showed his smiling face. He looked as charming as usual and I could clearly see him from the stage. There was a huge white board that they called the Evolution canvas up on stage and we had to put our names on it and make a declaration. I gripped the red marker and wrote a small note before I signed: Let's build a powerful nation! So finally, we of the zeroth year had been promoted to first year status and our real life in college had begun.

Life was running good and Aritro and I were seeing each other. Every moment spent with him was magical. A couple of months later, we met at the college gate for a date on Valentine's Day. As we walked through the Dreamplex Shopping Complex we came across a live dance show and the woman host, seeing us, called us over. 'Those two lovely people. I want them here!' she said. There was no escape; everyone was looking at us, so we walked up onto the stage and from there I could see a lot of seniors we knew in the audience.

'Your names?' the lady asked.

'Aritro and Dishari,' he replied.

'So you two are our seventh couple today and what we want you to do is dance to the tune we play for you, okay, are you ready?'

I was up for it; dancing was a passion of mine. I looked at Aritro, perhaps he couldn't dance at all, but he looked so confident that I was sure he could.

The song began. The seniors were already hooting and cheering us. As soon as I stepped onto the floor and gave my starting pose, Aritro held my right hand and before I realised it, we were doing something like a salsa, using intricate footsteps, 'quick-quick slow, quick-quick slow.' I had only done Indian classical dancing before and never imagined anything like salsa would come out of me. Our eyes met. Aritro smiled at me and before I could respond he made a cross body turn with a hand swap, and moved me from one end of the stage to the other. The song stopped and we bowed to finish the dance.

We were the winners for the evening and they called us 'The Made for Each Other Couple' and I really wished I could freeze the moment and live like that for the rest of my life with the spotlight on us, the crowd cheering and Aritro holding my hands. For a long time afterwards the moment when our eyes met on the dance floor kept coming back to my mind, because that was the first time I'd seen how beautiful his eyes really were.

The next year, when he was in the third year and I was in the second, we celebrated our one year of love. I kept thinking how one year ago I'd known almost nothing about him yet I'd fallen in love with him at first sight and come to realise over the months that followed how lucky I was to have him as my guy. I remembered all the moments that filled my last year with happiness and how eventful my love story had been. I thought how amazing it would be when I told Mamma about the way our secret love was growing in that ragging-staring-scolding period and how I hated him one moment and yet loved him the very next. I waited for him in the college park.

'I knew you'd wait for me, you little darling!' Aritro came from behind and startled me.

'You're late as usual,' I replied, 'I nearly didn't bother to wait.'

We decided to go and see a film, but I didn't much care where we went; being with him was all that mattered. As the lights went off and the movie started he said, 'You are looking so beautiful tonight, Disha, I really love you.'

'I love you too,' I said. I could feel his arms around me.

'Move back a bit,' he whispered.

I did as he asked. I couldn't concentrate on the movie, I was aware of it going on in the background, but nothing mattered to me except Aritro's hands on my shoulders, my hair, my neck, and then the tips of his fingers on my cheek. I turned my head towards him and I was trembling.

'Can I kiss you?' he asked, kissing my cheeks. Then he drew back and tilted my head up towards him. I could barely look at him.

'Kiss me too, Disha,' he whispered.

Everything around me was silent; it was as if there was no movie and no people around us. I kissed his left cheek and it felt like heaven.

'My other cheek is feeling cheated,' he murmured into my ear.

As I moved my lips towards his right cheek, he stopped me midway. Oh my God I thought while my lips were still pressed against his – we are lip locked! He had tricked me and I loved him for it.

After dinner that night we walked through the park and came to a place where a pit had been dug by a building company. I felt fantastic, I'd never been happier, we'd kissed lip to lip for the first time and I could still feel it.

'I love you Aritro, you won't go and leave me, will you?' I said.

He looked down at me and frowned, 'So if you were to fall into this pit, you'd expect me to fall in with you?' he asked, and before I could answer he'd pushed me into it.

As I brushed the dirt off my hands and shoulders, he laughed and knelt down on the edge of the pit and looked at me.

'You stupid idiot,' I said, 'is this the way you treat your girlfriend on her anniversary?'

'Why did you ask such an idiotic question, then? What made you think I'd leave you?'

I felt like a fool. 'Please Aritro, get me out of here.'

'Not yet,' he replied.

'Okay, damn you, get lost, see if I care!'

He laughed again then and for a moment I really hated him.

'Is that what you want me to do, get lost, walk away from here? Fine, goodbye then.'

'Okay, okay, okay. I'll never ask you that again, it was stupid of me, help me out please, Aritro.'

'Give me those hands then.'

My last date with Aritro before he left college was in the Wonder Vatica, we'd been there on our first date as well when I was still nervous of him. He'd called me over that first time to the huge Ashoka tree near the canteen and because he was my senior, when he asked me out, I couldn't refuse him, even if I'd wanted to. At the Wonder Vatica he ordered two Gourmet Veggie Delite pizzas. I was so shy at first that I couldn't look up at him.

'Are you scared?' he asked.

'Not at all.'

'So, where do you stay?'

'Kolkata, Salt Lake.'

'Affairs ... any?'

'What? No.'

'I mean ... any ... before?'

'No. Not at all.'

'Ok. Your contact number, but only if there's no problem.'

'No. It's ok,' I remained quiet. I was unsure if I should exchange my number with him.

'So what is your number then?' he asked again, and I gave it to him.

I couldn't eat in front of him. 'Please help me eat mine,' I said

'I give up ... can't eat anymore,' he said.

A strange thing happened to me then. I felt hideous to have eaten so much and to see the wasted food in front of us, some kind of feeling of shame crept over me and I found myself saying to him, 'You finish that food, you've got to, it's not our birthright to waste food is it? Think of people who have none, have you ever been starving?'

He looked at me in shock, picked up the pizza slices and ate them in silence, and I watched him do it. I have no idea where my sudden courage came from, but it was there; all my fear of him had left me.

'You know,' I began, while we were on our way back to college, 'I got mathematics honours in Jadavpur University. I think it would have been better if I was there. I could have been with my friends.'

'Good. But what would've happened to me?'

'Why? You have friends here don't you?'

'No one special though.'

I suspect he meant that as a hint he was falling for me. Now that he was leaving college and we were back in Wonder Vatica, it was as romantic as it had been the first time.

'Aritro, remember our first date here?'

'Hmmm. How could I dare forget it? You forced me to eat like an elephant.'

'C'mon. Is it only that which comes to your mind?'

'Oh yes! And the way you scolded me. I was really surprised at you.'

'Now see. Don't you irritate me like that. Don't you have any sweet memories?'

'I definitely do, Disha. Remember the first time we met? I and my friends had come to take your intro.'

'Yes. And you kept staring at me and that made me forget what to say.'

'Those were the best days you know. You always listened to me obediently then.'

'Yes, maybe. But only out of fear.'

'Whatever, Disha. Not like now.'

'What? You mean to say I don't listen to you?'

'See. It's so easy to make you angry. Your chubby cheeks turn red at once!'

'Oh really? And I hope you know what I do when I get red with anger. I can punch really well.'

'Cool down, I'm only joking. And remember once when I said you were on the verge of getting fat?'

'Yes I do. But no one else has ever said that to me.'

'I was joking then as well, Disha.'

'Do you remember the V-day competition we won?'

'Yes, that was great. We really rocked the dance floor. I think there were seven other competitors. Right?'

'Hmmm Aritro, and the judges really praised us, na? We were the couple of the night.' Tears came to my eyes as I remembered that night and our beautiful perfect dance, and the way Aritro looked at me.

'Disha, please don't cry now.'

'But I'm going to miss you so much.'

'I'll miss you too. But don't worry. I'll come to visit you very soon. Brave girl. C'mon don't cry. Remember how we were walking near the college park and you fell inside that big hole?'

'I never fell, you pushed me deliberately.'

'Wasn't it a great experience?'

'Well, it sure was. Should I make you feel the same by punching you? I will punch you.'

'And I will love you.'

'Always?'

'Always. No matter what.'

We left each other that night and I went back to my room and cried. My whole body ached with sorrow and longing.

Next day, in the early morning, he called me to the college park for our final goodbye. I made up my mind not to cry and went to meet him feeling numb and tired. I just wanted to gaze at his face so I would never forget it, so that it was in my very blood. We sat in our usual place in the park and I thought how much time had been wasted in our fights.

'Goodbye, Aritro.'

'Bye, Disha. I pray to God to keep you safe, since you are the only one I have,' he answered.

7. SWEET MIGHT-HAVE-BEENS

Night 19th December 2010

There are sixteen of us now all squashed together in this hideous and stinking room. Kalpita and I are worried about Tanusri. She's become so depressed that she won't even speak to us anymore. She spends her time facing the wall with her back to everyone else, but she's stopped crying at last. She told Kalpita last week that she was frightened of the women in here, the jailbirds as they call themselves. She's scared they'll try to beat us up or rob us. I thought that as well when we first got here, but I don't anymore; they're sad and pathetic women really. Just because they're in prison doesn't mean to say they've committed a crime any more than we have. I told Tanusri that but she just shrugged her shoulders.

I've been wondering why this place is called the Asanol Special Correctional Home – there's nothing special about it that I can see. But the so called criminal women we are living with are interesting. There are too many souls here to describe. Shrimati Didi is one of them. People call her Aishwarya. She wanted to know if I was writing bad things about her and the others. So I read her bits of what I'd written and now, every time I start to write she expects me to tell her what I've put down. The other women call her Aishwarya after the famous actor Aishwarya Rai, but you only have to look at her swollen hands and her bad skin to see that her life has been the opposite to that of the real Aishwarya who rides about in big cars, lives a sophisticated lifestyle, enjoys her social status and material advantage and has a husband who loves her.

Shrimati was married off to a drunkard – she's told me all about her life and how she got into this horrible place. Her big, dark eyes are always filled with tears as she thinks of her five-year-old son. Her journey in life has become one without meaning and it began to go wrong with the death of her mother when she was twelve. Soon after that her father married again and her stepmother came with all her daughters, and even though Shrimati had been sick with fever for weeks, she still had to do all the household jobs. She told me that her stepsisters never did a thing. It was always she, day in day out, washing their clothes, cooking for them, cleaning the house. I was shocked when I heard that; it was exactly like the story of Cinderella. I told her that I would have tried to run away if I'd been in her position. She said she'd thought of it, but before she knew what was happening, they'd arranged her marriage to the horrible drunkard who lived in the street opposite theirs – a man called Raja, who did nothing for a living. He was known in the locality for gambling and molesting young girls. Shrimati's life with Raja was unbearable from the very first day of their marriage. He used to come home drunk every night and beat her up. He often raped her. She showed me scars on her body that he'd made, and there were a lot of them. One night when he was in a drunken sleep, she took the knife he always had with him, the one he scarred her body with, and killed him with it. She said she felt nothing at all when she did it. But afterwards peacefulness came to her, a great calm feeling that was with her for hours before someone called the police and she was arrested.

She never complains about her life here, she might even be glad to be safe from the brutality of how her life would be otherwise. But she does weep every night for her five-year-old son as she thinks of him sleeping in the cold without any warm clothes in the house of her stepmother. No one has ever come to visit her in prison, there is no one out there thinking about her. She says that if she ever gets out, she will find her son, and maybe he will be a grown up man by then, and he will look after her and together they will go far away from this area to where nobody knows them and start a new life where they can get to know each other again.

Yesterday, after morning attendance, Kanta Singh called Shrimati Didi, and she quickly covered her head with her sari and came forward. Kanta Singh lowered his eyes onto her and said, 'Shrimati Didi, I understand that you murdered your husband in cold blood showing no feeling whatsoever and that now, and it doesn't in the least surprise me, you don't have a lawyer to fight your case. I wonder, do you know what this means? I don't suppose you do. Well, as Chief Guard of Asanol Special Correctional Home I consider it my duty to tell you. The consequences are that you will be remaining here in paradise forever. You will never be released. Do you understand? You will never walk through those gates again, you will die in here.'

Kanta Singh left, stomping his feet as usual. Shrimati Didi stood motionless. The portion of her sari covering her head fell off, letting out her thick, black hair. A tear dropped onto her cheek and then another. She closed her eyes and sat down. After a while, she looked up again, and a great shout came from her that was more shocking because throughout Kanta Singh's speech she'd been so still and silent, and then she howled, and it was as if the walls were shaking, and she cried out for her little son and said how the world had stopped her from reaching him.

She doesn't have a lawyer. While I sit to study at night, I often hear her speak in her dreams. 'Babu, don't run ... you might fall down.' That's the only time she smiles, when she's in her own beautiful dream world with her son.

Her story is so depressing. She did murder her husband that much is true. But shouldn't the world look at the situation she had to endure? If she hadn't murdered him that day, he might've killed her.

Nazma Bibi is a prisoner who is lucky enough to have her child here with her. She's the little girl, Rinki, and she looks to be around four, and all of us have a lot of fun playing with her. She's really funny and sweet and all of us smile when we hear her laughing, even Tanusri.

Whenever I sit to study, Rinki watches me carefully. Then, she comes closer and sits beside me. Slowly, she takes the pen from my hand, holds the writing book in front of me and begins to draw on the paper. She feels like some kind of miracle in this ugly place, and it's worth sacrificing a thousand pens just to see her face shine with pleasure.

Nazma told me her story this morning. Rinki's father, Jalal Sheikh, got married, for the second time, to a woman called Salma Bibi. Nazma accepted Salma into the family hoping that it would make Jalal happy and that Salma might give him a son because she hadn't been able to. At first, she and Salma were awkward with each other, but after some months, Nazma really started to like her, love her even, like a sister. They had fun together and Salma was lovely and kind with Rinki. Then one night, after Jalal got home from work, Salma went straight up to him, got hold of his collar and started kissing him. They were both laughing and acting as if Nazma wasn't even there. She told me it felt as if a knife had gone right into her heart.

Rinki was sitting with her toys. Salma picked her up and made her sit outside the house. Nazma was speechless. Then she too was shown the way outside. Before closing the door, Salma said to her, 'It's pretty obvious Jalal and I need to be alone right now, isn't it?'

As Nazma and Rinki sat on the steps outside their house, it began to rain. Nazma felt as if the whole world had turned against her. She couldn't get back into the house and Rinki had a fever and wouldn't stop crying. All Nazma could do was to hug her baby and wait until morning when Salma and Jalal had finished drinking and making love to each other and they would be allowed in again. If that had been all there was to it, Nazma said, she would've smoothed things over and gone on as normal, but Salma was intent on getting Nazma and the baby thrown out permanently. However Jalal wouldn't co-operate with Salma on this and that made her so furious that she went to the police station and claimed that Jalal had tortured her. That was a big mistake because the police took her name and age and discovered that she came from Bangladesh and that she didn't have a legal passport. So Salma was arrested under the offence of trespassing and Jalal was going to be arrested for female trafficking, but he managed to flee before that happened. In the meanwhile, Nazma and Rinki were taken into police custody, and a court decision brought them here with Nazma as an under-trial prisoner. From then on, Nazma told me, Rinki has been growing used to prison life, getting to know the things she cannot do, the places she is not allowed to go. Some of the prison guards are nice to her and, like us they smile at her funny little ways. I think when they look at her playing and talking to herself and see her beautiful innocence they also imagine there is a better life than the one they live inside these four grim walls. Rinki is an intelligent child; I've seen her watching the guards – she knows very well that they are different from the other women in here. When one of them is in a bad mood, and that's usually Heera Aunty, I've seen Rinki creep away very quietly to play in a corner of the hall, or stay very close to her ammu all day so that nothing she does can cause annoyance.

The bell rang once, a few minutes back in the cold night, its shrill noise is still there in my ears like the intense and pious summons of a conch shell on an early autumn morning when the fresh shiuli flower or the Nyctanthes smells better than anything else in the world. How on a Durga Puja morning, the first faint rhythmic drum beats ... Ta-Tak-Tak-Tana-Tak-Tak – Ta-Tak-Tak-Tana-Tak-Tak ... fades beautifully into the atmosphere. I hope I am back at home by autumn. The idea of the power of the Goddess Durga who slays Asura, the devil to re-establish peace and sanctity on earth again is making me nostalgic right now. I love those outings during Durga Puja. I love reconnecting with my friends and parts of my family I don't see so much. I can almost hear the sound of the drums, see the dance with the Dhaks and smell the scent of the Shiuli flower. Just conjuring it all up in my head takes me away from this horrible place.

Morning 20th December 2010

I am staring at the off-white pages of 'Tribology and Condition Based Maintenance'. I can barely recognise the words on the page as my tears fall onto the title 'Introduction to Tribology'.

How are you, Baba? Why don't you come to see me, Baba? Not even on the days of my hearings? Have you forgotten me, Baba? And Babu? How is Babu? Has he caught cold in this winter? Does he ask about me? Even if you don't wish to come to me, please promise that Babu will always be safe under your protection. Please Baba. He is the only one I have. Don't let him die.

I wrote that letter in the afternoon – the letter which creates a bridge for Shrimati Didi to reach out to her father and enquire about her son, the letter which had to wait for months before it got written by someone literate. As I was writing down her feelings, I found everyone in the hall staring at me, and I did wonder then how many more letters I'd end up writing for people.

Dida, my granny, just came into my mind. The last time I spoke to her was the day before we were arrested … that was on the 7th of December. I spoke to her on the phone. She couldn't talk much because she was suffering from a terrible cold and she hadn't been able to breathe properly for over a week. The winter this year is really very cold and everyone is unhappy about it. I think about Granny a lot, living alone in that big house. Even though she has four daughters, including Mamma, and two sons, she's lonely. I can't imagine living a life like hers. Really she should come to live with us, but I don't think she could bear to leave her house because it's got Dadu's memories attached to it. I was only four when he died. I can faintly remember his impeccable white clothes and wooden stick.

Dida, oh darling Dida, how little we understand of what she suffers and how sweet she is. I told her so many times to come and live with us. But she loves her home. That is where she got married when she was only twenty. That is where Mamma and all her brothers and sisters grew up.

Besides all of this, Dida knows my terrible secret which she has carefully kept to herself all these years. She knows how much I love sweets and chocolates. So, every time I stole sweeties that were there for guests in our house when I was a child, I'd call her up and confess it, and she just laughed. I'm sure Bubuli and Tutul also thinks Dida is wonderful. However naughty I was, Dida always stuck up for me. How lonely she must be living in that house alone in spite of the fact that the whole family loves her dearly. It has never occurred to me before that someone as loved as Dida is could ever be lonely. Yet I know that I am loved, and as I write these words I am aching with loneliness.

8. DANGEROUS WOMEN

When I was a second year student, of all the juniors in the first year, there was one, Triparna, who stood out. She obeyed nobody's rules about how to dress or how to behave. On her second or third day at college, I saw her walk up to Aritro and raise her hand to him in greeting and give him her lopsided smile. I was sitting with Ananya in the canteen, and Aritro was outside waiting for me to come out so we could go to a movie.

It was very unusual for a first year student to take the initiative like that, and so Ananya and I walked quickly out of the canteen and stood a little way away from them. We saw Aritro cross his arms and heard him say, 'Stand up straight first and give me your intro.'

'I am Triparna,' she said. 'I live in Tollygaunge, Kolkata. Oh! I've heard that you are from the same place too. Actually we can go home together this weekend. I don't really know the bus or train routes.'

Within a second I was furious and burning with jealousy, and so I walked to Aritro's side. 'Who is your little friend?' I asked, staring straight at her.

'No idea,' he said. 'Just some kid. Let's go if you've finished lunch.'

'Oh sorry,' Triparna said, 'I didn't know Aritro was your friend. Ok bye-bye for now.'

This left a very bad impression on me. I realized then that she was a predator and no man would be safe around her, that she was the kind of woman who had to have a boyfriend at any cost so she could compete with other women. Then when Tanusri and I were in our third year and Triparna in her second, we were cooped up together in the same room on our summer training program at Farakka, and this time she'd become involved with a good friend of mine, Prateem. I'd always taken him to be a rebel, and I'd liked him for that and so it annoyed me that he was so attentive to her.

'So what is it about her, Prateem?' I asked. 'I've seen boys stare at her, are they thrilled or repulsed?'

He smiled and raised his eyebrows. 'Oh, you know.'

'No, I don't know. She snaps her fingers and says do this, do that, and you run off and do her errands.'

'Well she's fascinating.'

'Are you serious? She's in our room you know, and Tanusri watches her trying to get up every morning; she thinks the bed won't stand the weight much longer.'

'You girls are so obsessed about your weight and how you look.'

'Oh, come on, Prateem! Don't tell me boys aren't on the lookout for pretty girls, so what is this thing with Triparna?'

'I quite like big bossy women, I suppose. But I think of her as if she was a guy, you know?'

'So huge, though. I just don't get it.'

'How big she is doesn't matter to me.'

'She once pushed me aside when I asked for her intro! I was so shocked. She literally got hold of my shoulders and pushed me away.'

'That's why I like her,' Prateem said.

'Because she pushed me?'

'No, don't be silly, Dishari. I like her because she's different. Because she's bold and strong.'

Our training took place in a power plant that was quite a distance from the house we were staying in, so we had a van that dropped us at our site every morning and brought us back in the evening. The house we were living in was an ashram with temples, orphanages, gardens and parks inside its campus. Triparna never appeared until the van was about to leave each morning, and when she stepped into it, she literally blocked out the sunlight. One day, in the mechanical control room at the training centre, Tanusri whispered to me, 'You know something, Dishari?'

'What?'

'I've seen Triparna and Prateem sitting very close to each other. I mean very close.'

'Where was that?' I asked.

'Over on the DM Plant.'

'Yeah?' I didn't like the sounds of that and I was wondering if I should talk to Prateem about it.

'They didn't care if anyone was watching, and other students were taking photos of them,' Tanusri added.

'I think Prateem's in love with her, but he doesn't know it himself.'

'She was wearing her most obscene dress, that blue one, you know? I think we should say something to her about it.'

'We can't do that because she'll tell Prateem, and I don't want to spoil my friendship with him,' I told her.

'But shouldn't you warn him that she keeps flirting with boys?'

'I think we should do nothing, Tanusri, at least not right now.'

'But …'

'Let's just wait and see what happens.'

Things were running smoothly enough. Tanusri, Prateem, Triparna and I had to submit a project together on the reduction of boiler tube leakage and non-destructive testing. I stayed awake till late at night working on my laptop and researching the different causes of tube leakages in a boiler and the prevention techniques, their symptoms and the testing procedures for leakages.

'Oh Dishari Di,' Triparna said to me one day, 'since you've already started working on our project and are doing so very well at it, I think you should just go ahead and finish it and I'll copy and paste from your laptop. That'll be all right, won't it?'

'What, me do the whole thing, you mean?'

'You may as well.'

I was sitting on my bed and as she sat down beside me I felt the bed shift dangerously. 'But that wouldn't be team work, would it?' I said.

'The others can help of course, but I'd just mess things up if I was involved, that's all I mean.'

'You're saying you don't want to be in the team?'

'No, I'm just afraid that if I tried to work on the project with you, it'd take twice as long.'

She sure has her way of getting out of things, I thought, but I didn't want to have to work with her anyway. I'd heard a lot about her from girls in her year. They'd said she was selfish, cunning, and calculating. Watching the way she behaved around Prateem made me think she was vain too. 'Okay then, off you go, let me get on with it,' I said.

The following day after dinner, Prateem came up to me and he seemed very tense. 'Dishari, I've got something to tell you and I need your help with it.'

'What's wrong?'

'It's Triparna. She keeps saying she loves me. I like her, but it's all going too fast.'

'Well it's up to you, you have to decide if you want that woman as a girlfriend or not.'

'You're my friend, Dishari, that's why I've come to you for advice. Is she right for me do you think? Tell me honestly.'

'Prateem, since you say I'm your friend, I'll tell you what I know about her. I won't add my personal feelings to it. Then you judge for yourself.'

'Okay. I'm listening.'

'Triparna goes about as if she's smart and trendy – she doesn't bother to question whether any of the clothes she wears actually suit her. Look, I'll tell you something, and I'm not the only one who thinks it, she flirts with boys all the time, you might not have noticed it, but she does. So you know ... work it out for yourself.'

'I think I see what you're getting at, Dishari. She'd go with anyone, that's what you mean. I was frightened of that as it happens. Thank you. I'm glad I know.'

I went back to my room and fell asleep, but woke again suddenly to some shouting outside. The voice I could hear was Triparna's and the words became clearer. 'I never talk to other boys. And even if I do, I treat them as brothers. *Brothers*, I said. Prateem, trust me, you have to trust me. I love you so much and I'm going to get Dishari Saha for saying that about me! However long it takes I'm going to get her, and I'm going to damage her!'

After that, all I could hear were sounds of moaning and Prateem trying to cheer her up and make her stop crying. Bloody Hell, I thought, I shouldn't have told him anything. Why on earth did he ask me in the first place? I felt slightly sick and I realised that something about Triparna really frightened me, although I'd never let her see that. Just as I thought I'd better go back to sleep, Tanusri woke up.

'What're those weird noises?' she asked. 'There aren't wild animals around this area are there? What kind of thing makes a noise like that? It sounds like something out of a horror movie.'

'Believe it or not, that's Triparna crying out in the corridor. Prateem's with her.'

'Have they had a fight? Has she beaten him up?'

'Not exactly. I sort of advised him not to have her as a girlfriend because she's a horrible flirt, and he like an idiot told her what I said.'

The next day, Tanusri discovered that the diary in which she was keeping the details and records of our training was missing and it would be impossible to finish our project without it. We looked for it everywhere and eventually found it wrapped in newspaper behind an old trunk in the corridor. We were so thankful to find it that we didn't speak again until we were back in our room.

'Who could have done this?' Tanusri asked.

'I don't know. At least I say that, but I do know, as it happens.'

'It's strange.'

'Listen, Tanusri,' I said, 'every day Triparna goes to take a bath after training before any of us. I mean, she is the first to occupy the bathroom, right?'

'Yes, that is right, and it would be, wouldn't it, as she's such a bully?'

'But today she told you to go first.'

'Yes. I wondered why she did that.'

'When you were taking your bath, I was in here with her. She was talking about how precious the diary is for our project.'

'Okay. I'm with you so far.'

'I said that since I was completing the project I really needed all the data values in the diary and that you were is doing a great job in recording the data.'

'Thanks for that, but what do you mean exactly?'

'Well, she stared at me for a minute and gave me that crooked smile she has and then asked if I'd fill the water bottle because she was very tired and couldn't move. So on my way back with the water, I saw her in the corridor and wondered what she was doing there if she was so tired. What's the date on that newspaper, Tanusri?'

'It's today's date. And it's the Times of India. I don't think anyone keeps Times of India other than us.'

'Yes, that's true. The other students read Bengali or Hindi newspapers or the Telegraph. That means someone from our room has done it. If it's not you or me, then it can only be Triparna.'

'But how can we be sure?'

'Let's keep the diary wrapped up the way it is and put it on her bed and see her reaction when she comes into the room.'

When Triparna did come back she was singing something, but stopped immediately when she saw the diary and turned to face us both. 'What's this stuff on my bed?' she asked.

'Well, Triparna, what do you think it is?' Tanusri asked. 'What does it look like?'

'How would I know?'

I looked at her hands. They were shaking a bit and her face had gone pale.

'Look,' I said to her, 'Why do you want to sabotage our group work? What's the point of that?'

She shuffled back a few steps and frowned. 'I don't know what you're talking about.'

'We're talking about the fact that you took the diary and hid it, and don't deny it otherwise I'll report you for it.'

'You stupid little kid!' Triparna shouted. 'You two had better watch it from now on, do you hear? You can't go accusing me of theft and sabotage, those are really serious things!'

'We know you did it. We worked it out,' Tanusri said.

That night, when we were all in bed, and she thought we must be asleep, she called Prateem and cried her heart out, saying we'd been cruel to her, called her stupid, and said she was a kid.

When we got back to college it was a relief because we didn't have to be so close to her, but a whole year later, one afternoon, she pounced on Tanusri and me when we were in our room with the door open. She stood in the corridor outside shaking with rage. 'Both of you have shown the lowest possible strata of your kind,' she began, 'how dare you!'

I looked at her, puzzled. 'What on earth are you talking about Triparna?'

'You know as well as I do!'

'I'm sorry, but I don't. Come in if you want to discuss something with us. Don't stand out there quivering like that. You look utterly pathetic shaking like that. What's wrong with you?'

'You told everyone I stole that diary.'

'What you mean from last year?' Tanusri asked. 'Have you been thinking about it all this time?'

'We told Prateem because he was in our project,' I said. 'I don't remember telling anyone else.'

'And Prateem is hardly everyone,' Tanusri put in. '*He* might have told other people though.'

'He wouldn't do that to me. Anyway, I don't care what other people think about me,' she said. 'I just came to tell you that you're scum.'

'You should care what people think of you, Triparna, do you realise what kind of an example you're setting for your juniors?' Tanusri said.

'What do I care about the juniors? I don't give a shit if some trash fellows in this college speak rubbish about me. How dare you treat me like … dirt!'

'Wait!' Tanusri said, 'don't forget that you're talking to seniors.'

'Seniors, what seniors? I'm in the third year now. I don't regard anyone as senior to me.'

She left the room and we sat in silence. She had been so angry that it wouldn't have surprised me if she'd beaten us both up with one hand.

✦ ✦ ✦

There was another girl who puzzled me more and more as the days went by at college. I felt truly sorry for her, but at the same time she drove me utterly crazy. Tanusri felt the same way about her. We did know Nabarupa had no mother, so she had no one whose aachal she could tie to her finger before she went to sleep at night. She was a first year student, one who we could treat as badly as we'd been treated ourselves when we first arrived at college, but we had no intention of doing that.

'I think she does it deliberately,' I said to Tanusri, 'you know – things like leaving the main door open all night.'

'What on earth for though?'

'So we notice her all the time. Every morning, when I get up and go out onto the balcony she appears from nowhere and tries to start a conversation with me.'

'It's her that leaves all the yellow and red stains on the bathroom floor, I keep telling her about that and she completely ignores me.'

'You know she does things like deliberately knocking into me, or standing on my feet.'

'I think she's seriously weird, Dishari. I explained that leaving the main door open could mean that anybody off the street could walk in, rapists, thieves, and all she did was stare at me, no reaction at all.'

'So shall we call her in about the music? I can't stand it anymore. She's playing it at that volume on purpose, I'm sure of it.'

'Yeah, I've had enough of banging on her door and her coming out like that pretending its normal.'

'Vile Bollywood songs. But let's not be too hard on her, there's something very sad about the girl, perhaps it's not having a mother, I don't know.'

The strangest thing about Nabarupa was that she stared at things with her big wide eyes, as if she was in a trance all the time. When she was called for an intro by a senior, she just stared at them. When she was asked to close the door, she stared unblinkingly. When scolded, she stared. It was as if she was staring at infinity.

Once I went to her room. I noticed that she had her book open in front of her but was looking elsewhere. 'Why are you staring at the mango trees, Nabarupa?' I asked.

'I am not feeling like studying. But I know I have so much left to do.'

'Ok. What were you studying? Let me see.'

'It's engineering chemistry. I just fail to understand the reaction mechanisms in the organic portions.'

'You need to concentrate that's all.'

'I've tried. It is impossible. Could you help me with it?'

'I'd love to. But I've got to get on with my own work, I'm behind all ready, I've got a lot of catching up to do.'

'No. what I mean is, every day for one or two hours if you could help me with studies.'

'I'll see if I can find the time, Nabarupa. I can't promise, though.'

'Do you want some biscuits? I've got many flavours … chocolate, orange, milk cream. Here, take whichever you feel like.' She pointed to three huge packets of biscuits on her desk.

'Thank you, but I'm already full. Just had my dinner. You did too, I saw you down there. I'm surprised you want to eat those on top of a big meal.'

'Please, don't worry, you must have them. These are yours. Take them.'

'You keep them,' I said, 'whenever I feel like eating biscuits, I'll come to you.'

'You are so good, you know. I really like your hair and skin. Your eyebrow line is perfect. How do you get it like that?'

'So what about work, let's talk about that.'

'Please give me some tips on how to improve my hair quality and make it like yours.'

'Well, maybe, but your work's the important thing, isn't it?'

After that, she would come to my room with her books every evening and although I tried to help her, her attention kept wandering. She stared at my face when I solved the numerical problems for her instead of concentrating on what I was teaching.

'Nabarupa, look here … have you understood what I've done in this step?'

'No I didn't really get it.'

'That's because you're not concentrating.'

'Okay I will from now on.'

'Good. See I've taken squares of both sides of the equation here.'

'No no … this is not interesting. Let's talk about something else. Shall we watch a movie instead?'

One day, she came to me about some mathematics confusion she'd got herself into, and asked me to solve an integration problem for her.

'Why? This is so easy,' I said. 'Surely you know how to do this?'

'For you it might be easy; you're very clever, but I don't even know how to start.'

'Okay. Give me the pen.'

'You know what?' she said. 'You are my best friend, Dishari Di.'

'Really? I don't know what to say.'

'Yes really. I feel so important when I'm with you. You make time for me, talk to me, we have nice chats together. I've never felt like this with anyone else before.'

'Is that right?'

'Yes, it is. Please, never break this friendship.'

I thought carefully before I spoke again, but imagined that in time she would find real friends and so I said, 'You're very sweet to say such things.'

'No I want to confess something to you today.'

'What is it? Go ahead.'

'I don't actually *have* friends. People of my age don't talk to me. In class, I always sit alone in the corner. I feel terrible all the time. I want to run away from this horrible place.'

'Well why did you come to a college so far away from your home? You must have friends where you live don't you?'

'My father paid lots of money so that I could come to here because he says it's the very best engineering college. Also my uncle and aunt live here and so I can visit them. So it wasn't up to me where I studied. If you really want to know, I don't have any friends back at home either.'

'But I'm sure you're wrong about your classmates. Maybe you're always on your own and that gives others the idea that you don't talk much and you don't really want to be with them.'

'So what should I do?'

'Go ahead and make friends. All you need is a smile. That's it!'

'I have you as my friend now and that's all I want.'

But this is my fourth year in college and I'll be gone next year. Then what?'

'I don't know. Please don't say that, I don't want to hear it!'

'But you have to hear it because it's true, Nabarupa. Go and make some friends in your class. I'm sure they're good people.'

'I didn't realise that you're leaving that soon. So you've only got one year left?'

'Not even a year. A few months, that's all.'

'But we'll still be friends when you leave. I'll come and stay at your place, and you can come to mine, and in the meanwhile, we can phone each other every day!'

'But wait a minute, Nabarupa, I don't know quite how to say this, but friendship is a complicated business. You can't just look at someone and decide they're your friend, like you might have done when you were six.'

'Why not?'

'Because the other person has to want the friendship too.'

'What're you saying, that you don't want to be friends with me?'

'Don't look alarmed, I'm just trying to help you understand. When you're in the second year, a fresh batch of students will come in. You'll be busy with them ... taking intros ... and everything else. Just imagine it. You'll be a senior. That'll be so much fun!'

'If you say so.'

'So should we go back to your mathematics problem?'

'No, I don't want to, I hate studying.'

'What on earth are you here for then?'

'It's not my fault; I just can't do the complicated mathematics problems, the reactions, the electric circuits. Nothing goes inside my head.'

'What you need to do is to try to study for thirty minutes at a stretch for two days, then go on increasing it. It's like an exercise.'

'Will it help?'

'It surely will. So start from today. Then read story books whenever you don't feel like studying.'

'I don't have story books.'

'I have some in Kolkata. Next time I go home, remind me to bring them for you.'

'So when are you going home again, this weekend?'

'No, no ... the next.'

'I'd love to see your home, what's your family like, how many of them are there?'

'Papa, Mamma, and my sisters, Bubuli and Tutul.'

'One happy family! I feel so jealous of you!'

Her loneliness touched me deeply and I began to feel terribly sorry for her, particularly when I found out how badly she was doing in her exams. I taught her a few computer games and we watched movies together sometimes. Then she started giving me things I didn't want, chocolates, biscuits and bits of jewellery and it was difficult to refuse them because it would've seemed so cruel. I became angry with myself for not keeping her more at arm's length. It was a bad mistake to try to befriend her, and all my other girl friends thought so too. At the same time her personal habits became even more irritating or revolting, and every time I thought about telling her to close the door or keep the toilet clean or play songs at a lower volume I just couldn't find the right way to say it.

One day I heard someone shouting outside our room and I rushed to see what was going on. Tanusri was standing in our shared kitchen with her eyes closed and her head turned away from the sink. She had dropped a glass onto the floor and broken it.

'What happened?' I asked. 'I'll get the brush.'

'It's not the glass. Look there. The hair in the sink.'

'Aww. They aren't mine.'

'I know that. It's Nabarupa's hair. That's not all. The commode water is red. She didn't flush and she's having her period. I can't take much more of this.'

We called Nabarupa to our room and she came in with Tanusri's comb in her hand. 'Tanusri Di,' she said, 'here, have your comb back.'

'What?' Tanusri said, 'you've used it?'

'Yes. I couldn't find mine, so I had to.'

'Look Nabarupa,' I said, 'you've got to learn few things and start to grow up. You shouldn't use other people's property without asking them. In this case, you shouldn't use other people's combs; it's basic personal hygiene.'

'And please,' Tanusri added, 'can't you flush before leaving the toilet. We all use it, right?'

'Okay,' she said.

'And,' I told her, 'I've often seen your soiled sanitary napkins lying on the bathroom floor. We have to call the sweeper to remove them. Isn't it your responsibility to deal with that?'

We tried our best to persuade her to change her habits, but it didn't work, and rather than tell her time and again to keep the bathroom clean, flush the toilet, or turn her music down we just gave up in the end and tried our very best to ignore her.

9. GREENISH YELLOW TIFFIN BOX

Morning 22nd December 2010

Today I have Tribology and Condition Based Maintenance – my last exam of the semester. This is the worst subject I've ever come across. I hate it. It is *so* boring. I can't really say I understand it at all, so I'm learning it all by rote and just hoping for the best, at least doing that takes my mind off things in this depressing place for a little while.

A very funny incident came back to my mind during morning attendance today, I remembered how in the first year, Bidesh didn't turn up for one of our classes and had asked Rupak to pretend he was there when the teacher called out his name. But apparently, Bibek and Suvodip were also trying to help him and the three of them shouted out, 'Yes present!' And the look on the teacher's face was one I shall never forget! To punish them, they and Bidesh were marked absent from the class that morning.

I'm awfully worried about Tanusri. She's ill. She has a high temperature and a red rash all over her face. The compounder of the prison came to see her; he just left a few minutes ago. He said she has a fever and an allergy. She looks so awful that I'm worried it might be something much more serious than an allergy and an ordinary fever; after all, he's not a doctor, but Papa is, so I'm going to get him to take a look at her as soon as he visits again.

I've packed my college bag. There was nothing much to pack, just my pencil bag which has three pencils, four blue pens, and a black one, an eraser, a ruler, a sharpener, a protractor and a compass. I am always filled with excitement at the thought of meeting Papa combined with fear that the reporters might get a photo of my face on the journey to college in the prison van. Because I'm both excited and frightened at the same time, I can't revise for my exams when I'm in the van, so I may as well just leave my books in prison.

Once the van reaches college, Kalpita, Tanusri and I are taken to a separate room where only the three of us sit for our exam. The police guards act as invigilators, but they're okay with us and let us discuss the exam with each other and I love them for that. Inside prison, we are given tea as breakfast, nothing else. I've never liked the taste of tea. So, I always skip breakfast. I used to feel very hungry, but now I'm used to it. We'll be having lunch in college and it'll be brought to us from the canteen, and that's one of the other good things about exam days, we get to eat a better lunch than we would get in prison.

I have planned many things for today – let me note them down before I forget.

- I shall ask Papa about Tanusri and her sickness. He is the only person I have ever trusted in medical matters.
- I shall talk to Mamma and tell her that I write in my diary every day. I forgot to tell her the last time I talked to her.
- I will talk to Tutul and Bubuli on the phone today. It has been a long time now since I last spoke to them.
- I will call up Aritro. I hope he still loves me.
- I will ask Papa about 306 and 309 and what they might mean.

I don't know what I'll say to Bubuli. I love her a lot. But it's always hard for me to tell her I love her and I don't know why. I'm more like a mother to Tutul than a sister, I suppose. I don't remember scolding or beating her ever. But with Bubuli, it's been different. I remember, we would fight like cats and dogs and Mamma would have to come, leaving her work, to calm us down. She would be so angry at both of us.

I remember once when I was thirteen and Bubuli was nine, we had a fight over the remote control for the television. Bubuli pulled my hair so hard that a handful of it came out. I was really hurt, not because of the pain, but because a handful of my precious hair was gone forever. I got hold of her head and wouldn't let her go and she began to shout and struggle with me. Before we knew it, her head struck the sharp edge of the marble wall and it began to bleed. I was too scared to call Mamma and so was she. I was feeling terrible about the entire episode. Suddenly, Mamma came into the room and found us like that. I don't think we got into trouble over it, but it was a bad incident.

The worst moments we had together though were on the school bus going home when both of us would try to sit by the window and we would really start fighting then. It's funny to remember this kind of thing, I suppose in jail when you haven't got anything, all your memories are important.

I haven't talked to Aritro for ages, I hope he still loves me after all the scandals attached to my name. No. I'm sure he loves me. I know him.

Midnight 22nd December 2010

Today's exam was an average one. I can't say how it went. It all depends upon the examiner. I talked to Mamma and told her about my diary. She said she'll read it when I come out and that will be very soon. I know she was only consoling me. But I felt very nice after talking to her. I talked to Bubuli as well. We were holding the phone to our ears without a word. I could understand that she felt terrible for me. She just didn't have the right words to say to me. She only managed to ask about my exam. I wanted to talk to Tutul but she was sleeping.

I tried to be brave when I was talking to Mamma and to get to the end of the conversation without crying. But my heart was almost bursting out. I wished I could hug her. I asked Papa about 306 and 309. He avoided talking about it and assured me that I'll come to know everything at the right time. I didn't force him. Papa gave me some money because when he comes to visit me in prison I have to pay the guards before they'll let me near him; we were both so shocked when we found that out. He has to pay them to see me as well. I wonder if their bosses know about how they're exploiting the prisoners. Maybe they do, perhaps bribery is thought of as part of the job.

I couldn't talk to Aritro. My thirty minutes worth of phone calls was over and I had to leave. I know this sounds terrible, but for a moment the fact that I'd run out of time and I couldn't hear his voice made me so depressed that I wanted to blame Bubuli for it, for wasting the moments she had with me, for not saying anything I mean. I wanted to take those moments back from her and have them again to use to speak to Aritro. That's what prison does to you; at one and the same moment it steals your time from you and heaps time upon you until you're drowning in it.

Tanusri is much better now. Her fever has gone down and her face isn't so blotchy. Papa said her rashes were due to the food, so the compounder was right after all. Papa told her to avoid having the sabzi. But some of the weird things Tanusri says these days are starting to upset me now. I'm going to talk to Kalpita about it and see if she's noticed anything.

Night 23rd December 2010

Actually, although I keep trying to be cheerful and practical, it's hard. I promised myself I wouldn't write gloomy things in my diary anymore, but I can't help it. The fact is, when I met Papa after my exam yesterday, I rushed through the paper, filling it with the mechanisms of wear, vibration monitoring and the things I managed to study, and then at the end I submitted the paper and ran towards him. I lay my head on his chest and I cried and could not stop. All the pain, all the hopes that were shattered, all the fear – all the unspoken emotions were expressed as Papa took me in his arms and held me. I looked up at him finally. He tried his best, but ultimately couldn't hold back his own tears – he was a helpless father holding a weeping daughter about to leave in a black van for prison. It was then and for the first time that I wanted my exams to never end if it meant I could see Papa again and be in his arms like that.

Later, as I walked towards the van with Papa, Tanusri and Kalpita, friends saw us leave and I had fond memories of class mass bunks, joining day parties, Freshers' Night celebrations. I felt as if my heart was breaking. Bibek, Suvendu, Biman, Bidesh, Sirsendu and everyone I know as true friends, stood there to bid us goodbye. I felt a hand on my shoulder. I stopped and looked around. Bibek was trying his best to smile at me. He said he'd visit me and he'd bring his greenish yellow tiffin box filled with my favourite aalu paratha. He couldn't stop his own tears and so he moved away and I carried on towards the prison van.

I felt something unusual on my wrist then. It was Papa's watch. I'd borrowed it from him for time keeping during the exam. It brought to me the grim realisation that my own watch, the one with the green dial Papa had given me, is no longer with me. I didn't want to take his watch into the prison and have the guards take it away and so I returned it to Papa although I would dearly have loved to have kept something of his close to me.

Bibek came here to see me this morning with his wonderful tiffin box. I was filled with childish joy to be able to smell it once more, even though he handed it to me in a room with a sour smell made by the pan massala the guards and prisoners spit out everywhere. His tiffin box is a long standing joke between us. He's a day scholar and the food he brings to college from home is spicy and delicious. I wasn't the only one who looked around when Bibek opened his tiffin box at recess and the air was filled with the aroma of aloo paraatha and paneer sabzi.

It was Tanusri who started the whole thing. She drew my attention to Bibek's greenish yellow tiffin box, as she called it, and described the aloo parathas she could see in it, and juicy chunks of paneer cooked with vegetables in such a way that my mouth started watering. Then she dared me to run past him and whip it out of his hands and run as fast as I could up to the terrace where she'd join me. Poor Bibek. That's exactly what I did.

When I got to the terrace and my heart beats had slowed down, Tanusri joined me with Ananya and Baishali and a couple of others and we ate his food. It became a routine joke. Sometimes we caught him and then he'd have to eat canteen food, and other times he'd hide from us, and when we got to him his tiffin box would be empty and he'd grin at us happily. This went on for months and then years. When he came this morning, the tiffin box was as full as it could be with my favourite food, and when he left, he wouldn't take the box with him, he said I should keep it and give it back to him when I got out. He thought I might find a use for it, he said.

Morning 24th December 2010

I am sitting near the huge banyan tree. This morning, Nazma Bibi approached me to write a letter for her, and I did wonder when I wrote one for Shrimati Didi if other women would ask too. Rinki is fast asleep on the cold floor. I have finished all the jailhold work set for me. Today I had to sweep the entire lawn with the heavy broom. It was backbreaking work, but definitely better than mopping and rinsing the floor of the hall with cold water, the job I had to do yesterday. My back hurts badly now and I wish I could lie on my soft and cosy bed at home rather than on the thin torn blanket on the concrete floor of this prison. Today, I noticed, the water is colder than it was yesterday and it's very difficult to bath in it, but I managed somehow. I hate having baths, not just because the water is so cold, but the baths are outside the hall, just beside the gate of the Female Ward, and I often wonder if men might be able to get in and walk through and see us.

Finally, I took out time for Nazma's letter. The letter was for Jalal and Nazma sat beside me while I wrote.

How are you my dear Jalal? I pray that you have not forgotten me completely. And that you have not forgotten your beautiful daughter Rinki. Three dates have passed in the court. Every time I have gone to court I have looked forward to seeing you there, but I never have. I think of you all the time, every minute of the day and all through the night. Do you ever think of us? Rinki asks about you all the time, she wonders where you are and she waits for you to come and see us. Please, please, please, I beg you, come and see her, come and see how beautiful she is. You will be so proud of her. She needs her abbu, Jalal, and I need you. Please come to us and save us from this place.

I found it hard to write that letter, Nazma was crying as she spoke the words and she thought hard about what she wanted to say to him. Each time I wrote a sentence she asked me to read it back and often she thought it wasn't right and would ask me to start again. Now, she's offering her prayers to the tulsi tree behind the hall.

I can hear Tanusri making shivering noises as she bathes in the cold water. Kalpita is sitting inside the hall. I have no idea what she is doing there … sitting idle, perhaps. The female guards are sitting beside me, under the banyan tree, knitting with red and green spools of wool. They've put bets on whether my toenail, which is blacker than ever now, will or won't drop off.

There is a small church outside the prison. I have heard the church bell ringing a couple of times. There is a lot of noise today, of buses and cars out there on the road. People outside must be celebrating Christmas Day with their loved ones. I just hope that they have something special for lunch. I am tired of having the same tasteless food every day; I think it's going to make my taste buds stop working all together.

10. SCAPEGOATS

When our year four class tests came up in November, most of us did really well in the first ones of the week and some of us were going out and celebrating, but I knew that there were a couple of difficult exams coming up that I hadn't studied for, so I decided I'd better get on with it.

The lobes of my ears were supercharged as I turned to page number 224, 'Supercharging of Internal Combustion Engines'. Nabarupa was playing an old Bollywood song so loudly that the walls of my room were vibrating. It was the same song she did a lewd dance to in the Freshers' Ceremony – in front of everyone and shamelessly. There was something very wrong with that girl.

I closed my book. The main door had been left open again and I knew it was Nabarupa who'd done it. She used to go to visit her Aunt Pishi at odd hours of the day or night, and each time she'd leave the door open without letting any of us know she had. I'd tried talking to her about it, but it did no good. But I used to worry about her as well because she was such a child that I'd wonder if she'd reached Pishi's place safely.

That night Tanusri, Kalpita and I decided to go to her room and reason with her yet again. 'Nabarupa,' I said, 'you have exams tomorrow don't you? Why aren't you studying? We are anyway, except we can't because of you and the dreadful noise you're making.'

She looked at me without a word.

'What *is* it you stare at all the time? Look, you're doing it now, what's the *matter* with you?' Tanusri asked.

Kalpita got impatient with her and started clicking her fingers. 'Hello Madam, you've crossed all limits now. Do you remember closing the main door tonight, after dinner?'

Nabarupa was still staring. It was as if she'd gone into some kind of a weird trance.

'How careless you are, Nabarupa,' I said, 'you leave the hostel at odd hours without informing us. Do you have any idea how dangerous that could be? We need to know when you go out.'

'How do we know where you really spend your time, though?' Tanusri asked.

'Tanusri,' I said, 'let's not go there. What's important, Nabarupa, is that you should inform us. Do we ever stop you from doing anything? Have we ever scolded you before, even when you play loud music? But everything has a limit. Tomorrow we've got a test, and it's an important one. You've got your class test tomorrow as well, so have you done any revision for it?'

'And while we've got you here,' Kalpita said, 'did you flush the toilet after you used it today? Hey look at me just for a moment will you? I asked you a question. The answer is you did not, because you never do. Does it take so much effort to engage one finger, just once, to flush? We gave you a whole lesson on bathroom use a while back, didn't we?'

'Yes Nabarupa,' I said, 'what about us? We have to use the same bathroom as you. Your habits show a lot about your character. Look, how about from tomorrow you start behaving in a decent way? Then we'll forget everything. Just imagine if I *spat* on your food. Would you have it? Of course you wouldn't, well we have the same kind of feeling each time you've used the bathroom.'

'While we're talking about weird behaviour,' Kalpita said, 'what did you have in mind when you danced in your Freshers' Ceremony?'

Nothing we said would make her look at any of us, she just gazed into the middle distance.

'What an indecorous dance performance,' Tanusri put in, 'God! How you shook your body. You're a *girl* for God's Sake. Did you forget that?'

While we tried our best to make her understand us, she simply gazed into infinity.

'Okay guys,' I said, 'it's late now. We have to study. Nabarupa, remember what we've told you. We're in our final year and will be gone in a few months. After that your juniors will come. How are they going to respect you if you carry on like you are doing? Go back to your room and all the best for tomorrow.'

She didn't move a muscle; she simply stood as if she was a dummy or a zombie.

'Look,' I said, 'we all make mistakes. But if we can rectify them, nobody remembers the faults. Its twelve now. Let's try to do some studying. Go back to your room, Nabarupa.'

She remained exactly where she was with the same stoic expression.

For the life of me, I couldn't work out what was wrong with her. Maybe not having a mother did something to her feelings, made her emotionally peculiar, but she had her aunt, I mean, how bad could things be? We'd all met her Aunt Pishi, and although she was a bit odd, she seemed okay to us. Nabarupa refused to leave our room, so we ignored her and got on with our work. By the time morning came, she was still there sitting on the end of my bed.

The morning went on and we three were still studying, but Nabarupa suddenly realised she had an exam at ten, so she got up and left us finally. By that time, the red book, 'Internal Combustion Engines' lay shut on my bed while my eyes felt so heavy that I couldn't stop them closing.

I dreamt of Nabarupa. She was sleeping and I touched her head softly and kissed her forehead. She woke up to smile back at me and I was relieved that she seemed happy. But I woke suddenly to the noise of someone shouting. I sat up and looked around me. My bed was a mess of scattered books and papers and Tanusri was standing in the doorway. She looked alarmed. 'What's the matter?' I asked.

'You won't believe it,' she said, 'it's incredible. Nabarupa has slashed her wrist.'

'*What?*'

'She got up onto the roof.'

'No!'

'It's true. There are lots of girls up there now.'

'Is she still there?' I asked.

'I think they've taken her to the Durgapur Nursing Home. There are students outside talking about us. They look really angry!'

Tanusri seemed very frightened.

'Okay calm down. Don't panic. Who found her?'

'I did. I heard her calling out for help. I went to look for her. She was lying stretched out on the roof and her left hand was bleeding. Other girls reached the roof at the same time as me.'

'Talk slowly. How bad is it?'

'I don't think it's that bad, just a cut. But when I reached her she accused you, me and Kalpita of ragging her and driving her crazy last night, she said we locked her into our room and wouldn't let her out, and we made her stand for hours in the middle of the room. Everyone was furious; I had to get off the roof fast. I'm really scared now, Dishari. All we did was talk to her; how can she say that?'

'What's the time?'

Tanusri fumbled for her watch. 'Twelve o'clock.'

'She had her exams from ten to eleven thirty right?' I said.

'Yes, she must have done it after that. She had her college bag up there with her.'

'You know she handed in a blank sheet of paper for her exam yesterday? Well she could've done the same today and that's why it came into her head to kill herself. She just got desperate and realised she was never going to make it through college at all.'

'She's saying she did it because we ragged her last night and they all believe her.' Tanusri came into our room and shut the door behind her.

'What did she cut herself with?' I asked.

'She had a blade.'

'A blade? Where did she get that from?'

'Don't know. It looked new, it was shining. What're we going to do, Dishari?'

'Have you told Kalpita?'

'No, she's still asleep. I looked in on her.'

'Wait. Be calm. We need to think now. Are you sure she said we ragged her?'

Tanusri frowned. 'Yes, I told you, that's what she said!'

'Why did she say that? When on *earth* did we rag her? But think about it, if she really wanted to kill herself, she wouldn't have called out for help, would she? Know what I really think now? This whole thing was staged. She wants to hide the fact that she knows she'll never make it through college because of the shame it'll bring on her family. So we're to be the scapegoats. Oh God! Go and get Kalpita.'

✦ ✦ ✦

The campus was filled with angry students. Kalpita kept walking up and down our room and stopping at the window to gaze out at the gathering mob. 'I don't believe this!' she said.

'Please stop saying that all the time,' Tanusri whispered.

'Yeah, well, please stop sobbing like that, then I will,' Kalpita replied.

'Stop it you two, we've got to think what to do,' I said. I felt really frightened, the mob out there was growing bigger by the minute; I didn't know if they knew which room we were in or not and if they'd find us and drag us outside. My heart felt as if it was stuck somewhere in my throat. Tanusri couldn't stop crying, half the time because she was indignant and the rest of the time because she was sorry for Nabarupa.

We tried to call some students who we thought might have gone with Nabarupa to the nursing home, but none of them answered their mobiles. Then Mrs. Sinha, Viharjee Sir's personal assistant appeared at our door. 'Are you the three?' she asked. We'd been sitting on my bed and we all stood up at once. 'Dishari Saha, Tanusri De and Kalpita Deb – the girls responsible for the tragedy?'

'We're not responsible for anything!' Kalpita roared at her. 'That kid is mentally unstable; she's implicated us in it for her own reasons.'

Mrs. Sinha gazed around the room as if searching for evidence that we three were monsters. 'Because of what you've done the class tests have been cancelled and I'm involved in a lot of the administration work for them. I just thought I'd come and see what you looked like.' She left without giving us time to protest further.

At midday we left college and set off for the nursing home ourselves, but on the way we ran into Nabarupa's Aunt Pishi and her husband, Pishoi. Before she even got within speaking distance of us, we could see by the expression on her face that Pishi was furious. Pishoi was trotting along beside her, trying to keep up. If I hadn't been so nervous, I'd have found them funny. They were both wearing red. She was dressed in a bright red sari with a matching blouse, and he, a short, fat man, had on a crimson shirt with almost bursting buttons and faded red baggy trousers to match.

We stopped in front of them.

'Pishi,' Tanusri cried, 'we haven't done anything. Please don't look at me like that. I can explain.' She turned towards Pishoi and dropped at his feet. He almost kicked her out of his way.

'Her father is coming from Kolkata,' he shouted, 'he is on his way now! See how he beats you all till you are buried into the dirt!'

'Sorry Sir,' I whispered, and I too fell to the ground so that my mouth was close to his shoes.

'You couldn't even take care of a little girl, don't tell me you're sorry now!' he said.

'But we had no idea things would turn out like this. We can explain,' I mumbled.

'Explain to the police. They're on their way. How could you treat her like that? What's the matter with you, you're older than her, you should know better!' Pishi shouted.

'All we did to Nabarupa was to ask her to be clean around the bathroom and not leave the main door open. What've you been told, Mam?' Kalpita asked. She was the only one of us still standing on her feet.

'Don't you dare question me. You're younger than me; act accordingly. You asked Nabarupa where she goes at odd hours. How can you ask the child a thing like that, what were you implying by it? She goes to my home, where else could she go? What kind of minds have you got that you can ask her questions like that? I know very well where you girls spend your nights as it happens,' Pishi said.

'It was me who said that to her and I'm sorry, I didn't mean it like it sounded,' Tanusri sobbed.

'Mam, excuse me, but you don't know anything about us,' I said, getting to my feet, and dragging Tanusri up with me.

'I know you girls well enough. You've beaten Nabarupa down slowly, a bit at a time and you've talked to her in raw slang! How could you?'

'But you're so wrong. I tried to help that girl, I tried to do everything I could to help her!' I shouted. 'I helped her with her work, sat with her, talked to her. There's something wrong with her head, there's something missing, something not right.'

I stared straight at Pishi and Pishoi and they glowered fiercely back at me. They had no idea what being ragged actually meant, and the first few months in college came to me at that moment – being made to stand for hours while I was scolded, being subjected to sexual taunts and games, being made to dance stupid dances, carrying food and water for the seniors.

By this time Tanusri was sobbing so hard that I thought it would make things worse if I said any more. I found that I was crying myself and through my tears I couldn't quite see who it was coming towards us until she came close. It turned out to be Triparna and she was grinning at us all, and her grin was very ugly. She was with Sovon Mallik, her class mate.

'I'm so glad Nabarupa is okay Aunty, she's such a lovely girl and what these three have done to her is outrageous,' Triparna said. 'They've done things to me as well, I hardly dare tell you but when we were on training they photographed me naked and made videos of me.'

'How dare you tell such a terrible lie!' Tanusri shouted at her, 'are you crazy or something?'

'What?' Pishoi said, 'they forced you to take your clothes off, is that what you're saying?'

There was a moment's silence then Triparna said, 'Not exactly. Well, they're capable of that naturally, but it was when I was changing, I mean.'

I was so hurt by what Pishi had said earlier that I blocked out what was said next – I kept hearing the words 'You've beaten her down slowly, a bit at a time and you've talked to her in raw slang.' I was really frightened now; I could sense the turmoil ahead of us. No matter how widely influential or far reaching Papa might be, he would have to come to college as soon as he was called. He might have to beg horrible Pishoi for forgiveness for his daughter's sake. He was about to lose his prestige because of me and I had no idea how I could put things right again now.

✦ ✦ ✦

We didn't visit Nabarupa in the nursing home after Triparna joined us on the street; instead we went back to the hostel. I wanted to call Mamma, but I didn't have the courage. We knew Pishi and Pishoi had reached college before us and gone straight to Viharjee Sir and that before long he would summon us to his office and then after that, he would ring our parents.

Finally it happened; the three of us were called to Viharjee Sir's room together. We climbed up the stairs slowly. 'You knock, Dishari,' Tanusri whispered.

I stared at the dark brown door and realised that my heart was beating so fast that I wasn't breathing normally. I couldn't raise my hand. 'You do it,' I said, 'I can't. I feel sick.'

It was Kalpita who knocked for us and when we were standing in front of him in a line he studied our faces carefully and his cold eyes reminded me of those of a shark.

'Do you know,' his stern voice began, 'what you've done? I shudder to think. That poor girl could've died!'

I felt tears in my eyes and I knelt down. 'We haven't done anything, Sir. It just isn't true.' Tanusri started to sob. Kalpita stood silently next to her.

'Whatever you do in life, never tell lies. Nabarupa Dash took her exam today and it has been reported that she slashed her left wrist after she returned from the exam hall at twelve o'clock. Can you explain that?' Viharjee Sir asked.

I stood up again and wiped my face on my sleeve. The fan was making an irritating sound ... Whump-whump-clunk. I tried to control my voice as I told him the story of the night before. 'Could it not be possible that her exam didn't go well? As it is, she submitted a blank answer sheet for yesterday's exam. If she'd become so depressed about the night before and our talk with her, why did she even take the exam this morning? She wouldn't have been able to. Not only that, but there are three more papers for her to sit. I know she wasn't revising. She couldn't have passed any of them.'

'How atrocious you are!' Viharjee Sir hissed.

'You are taking it the other way, Sir,' I went on, 'she screamed for help. She never intended to finish her life.'

'She screamed on the roof to raise the alarm,' Tanusri put in, 'she came down the stairs on her own and went to the nursing home on a bike which was waiting at the gate for her. She didn't need holding up by anybody. She didn't mean to kill herself at all.'

'And what do you have to say,' he asked, 'regarding what a third year student, Triparna, said about you? She said you girls had been in a training session with her where you took photographs of her while she was changing her clothes. She claims you made a video clip of her naked.'

'But Sir, that's definitely not true.'

'Of course you'd say you hadn't,' he replied. 'I didn't expect you to admit it.'

Kalpita stepped forward. 'If these photos and videos exist, ask her to produce them.'

'It isn't *her* who's got them, you ridiculous girl. It's you three. I'm amazed by your utter cheek; after all this you're still trying to argue your way out of it. I'll be seeing your parents tomorrow, and then we'll decide what's to be done with you.'

I was surrounded by numbness … photographs while she was changing clothes … nude video clips … the words just kept repeating in my ears.

I'd often seen Triparna reading the *Ramakrishna Kathamirita*. Ramakrishna said do not be like dirt-loving insects that die at once when taken to a bed of roses. It turned out that Triparna was a dirt-loving insect herself. The fan was still making the irritating sound, whump-whump-clunk, as we left Viharjee Sir's room.

Papa arrived in college the following day. Viharjee Sir handed him a notice which said: *Due to the vigorous physical, mental and sexual ragging done and the sadistic pleasure derived from the former, the following students have been rusticated from the hostel and their final results, placement opportunities and scholarships will be withheld: Kalpita Deb, Tanusri De, Dishari Saha.*

Papa and I sat in the waiting room beside Viharjee Sir's office, alone. I looked at him while he read the notice. I could hardly stand it. I touched his arm. 'It's all lies, Papa, I promise. The girl who is accusing us is mentally unstable. We didn't do anything to her.'

As we sat there, juniors drifted past the open door and looked inside. 'Hey guys, we have a shortage of beds in the Boys' Hostel,' said one.

'Don't worry about that, three beds are being emptied today in the girls' hostel. We can have those!' said another.

Finally, Bibek and Rupak put their heads around the door and called me outside.

'What on earth happened yesterday?' Rupak asked. 'Everyone in college is angry. People are saying you and the other two ought to be thrown out.'

'Everyone's heard what that weird zombie Nabarupa said, and they're all stupid enough to believe her,' Bibek said. 'So we did a bit of snooping about, and guess what?'

'What?

'Well Rupak and I went to see her and we said how dreadful it all was and we asked her to show us her – well her wound, and she did that quickly enough.'

'She would do,' I said. 'Attention is what she feeds off.'

'She hasn't cut her wrist at all where there are veins that could really bleed and put her in any danger. She's cut through the middle of her hand, through her palm. It's a hairline cut and it didn't even need a stitch,' Bibek said.

'That doesn't surprise me, it was a staged suicide,' I said, 'we worked that out yesterday.'

'I found out about the blade,' Rupak put in, 'she bought it at around nine thirty from the stationery shop outside college. That would've been before she went to take her exam.'

'Something's fishy ... the way she reacted ... I don't know; it all seemed so unnatural. Most importantly, she called out for help,' Bibek said. 'But she's fine and there was no need for her to stay overnight in the nursing home. I've worked out why she was kept in there though.

'Why?' I asked.

'Nabarupa's uncle wants the case to look serious in the hope that she gets a pass for her exam out of sympathy. At least that's what we think.'

'You see,' Rupak added, 'everyone else in Nabarupa's family would be grateful to him forever. He's such an odd little man, perhaps he's done something to disgrace the family in the past and he sees his way back into the good books through looking after Nabarupa like this – lying for her and so on. But he sure has some real interest in the matter, otherwise he wouldn't keep her in the nursing home overnight. Maybe he paid a doctor a lot of money to keep her in there, who knows?'

I suddenly felt very frightened and wanted to be near Papa again. As I turned to leave, Prateem appeared from somewhere and when he saw me standing with Bibek and Rupak he stopped dead in his tracks. 'Hey what are you guys doing with this criminal woman?' he asked.

'No one is a criminal here,' Bibek said quickly. 'Don't you speak like that.'

'We'll see when the media comes,' he answered, staring at me hard.

'Just get lost, Prateem,' Rupak said angrily.

'You used to be my good friend,' I whispered, 'what happened?'

'Not anymore. Not after what you did to Triparna.'

Now I was truly frightened and as I stared at Prateem, he clenched his jaw, turned, and walked quickly away from us.

Three days after Nabarupa had been discharged from the nursing home, the walls of the hostels and college were draped in banners which read in enormous red letters 'say no to ragging' and 'ragging is a crime.'

Viharjee Sir had summoned us again, and as we walked through college towards his office Kalpita whispered, 'Just look at the hypocrisy on the walls, will you! Funny that those banners have suddenly sprung up from nowhere.'

We entered the administrative building and saw lots of people walking around who we'd never seen in college before.

'Who are they?' Tanusri whispered, 'any idea?'

'Hard to say. Painters, workmen by the looks of them,' I replied.

'Do you get the new polish smell?' Tanusri said, sniffing the air, 'and look, those doors over there are newly painted aren't they?'

'What are those men carrying away?' Kalpita asked, 'those are all the old broken instruments from the Heat Transfer Lab, aren't they, and some of that stuff is from the SOM lab, isn't it?'

'Look at the notice on the welcome board,' Tanusri said. We all stopped. Tanusri read the words out: 'Welcome Mr. K. K. Ghosh and Mr. B. K. Moitra, All India Council of Technical Education.'

'Aha! I think I'm beginning to get the picture,' Kalpita said, and she laughed. 'I mean it's hardly likely the college has finally realised all of a sudden that those rotten machines needed mending, is it?'

'What're you talking about?' Tanusri asked.

'It's all because of us three, is what she means,' I answered. I noticed the security guard coming towards us and he was wearing a shirt and tie, which was unusual. 'Hey, what's going on today?' I called out. 'All this activity and everything.'

He frowned. 'You three ought to know! Two members of the All India Council of Technical Education are due here in the next hour to carry out an inspection; everybody's going crazy trying to get this place looking good. And it's all because of what you three girls did to that poor little kid. People like you ought to be, well I won't say it, but I hope things go really badly for you!'

We knocked on the newly polished teakwood door which now read: Mr. Anish Viharjee, Director. We walked in at his command. There were fresh flowers on his desk.

'I think you three know why I have called you again,' he said, 'two members of AICTE are coming to meet you to talk to you about the terrible ragging incident you carried out. Now remember, whatever you say should indicate that you are very sorry and feeling guilty about it. Don't try to make out you're innocent; they'll never buy it.' We looked at each other. 'And yes,' he continued, 'they'll meet Nabarupa too. I've talked to her. She'll say she was ragged and beaten.'

'Beaten?' Kalpita shouted.

'Do not interrupt. You'll get a chance to speak later. Nabarupa will speak the truth. It'll be good for you if you accept every allegation made by her. Apologise for everything. Further, they might ask you about the girls' hostel warden. Do you know her?'

'We've had no warden since Mrs. Guha retired,' I replied.

'Ages ago,' Tanusri added.

'Yes,' he said, 'but now Mrs. S. Sinha, my personal assistant is the warden. If they ask about her, say she's very efficient. She carries out regular counseling sessions against ragging and you three attend them. In reality, girls, Mrs. Sinha is very busy, and she *would* do counseling sessions if she had time, so you need to, well, just tell a little lie about it, okay? And in case you're asked why, in spite of the sessions, you *did* commit ragging, just keep quiet, or shrug. Do you understand?' I could hear Kalpita drawing in a breath beside me. 'And I want you to explain that I personally hold anti-ragging campaigns to make sure all students are aware of ragging and its evil effects.'

He looked at each of our faces. I was so shocked that I didn't know how to respond. I glanced quickly at Kalpita; her mouth had dropped open.

A waft of scented stale air brushed past my cheek. I looked upwards. Viharjee Sir had had his clunky fan fixed, and I think I hated it more now than when it made a noise, at least then there had been something honest about it. Now it had been fixed up to impress the All India Council of Technical Education and make them think the college was a well run place that cared about its students.

'How can we tell lies, Sir?' I asked finally.

'I know I can't lie about these things, Sir. No, I will definitely not lie,' Kalpita stated.

Viharjee Sir stared at her and then turned to look at Tanusri. 'And what do you have to say, Tanusri?' he asked, 'you look like a reasonable girl to me.'

'Okay Sir. I will do as you ask me,' she replied.

'See. She is so sensible,' he said, 'she realises how important it is to defend the reputation of the college. What's wrong with you two girls?'

'No sir. I won't lie. It goes against my principles,' Kalpita answered.

'And you, Dishari?' he asked me.

I looked at the floor and remained silent.

'It's all very well for you to talk about principles at your age, Kalpita, but when you grow up and understand life better, you'll find yourself in many situations where principles are a luxury you can't afford.'

'But we haven't *done* anything. That girl Nabarupa is mad. Simply mad. She used us. I know I haven't done anything,' Kalpita shouted. 'We're being used as scapegoats!'

'I see,' he said, pushing his glasses up his nose, 'but you know, if you disobey me, things won't go very well with your careers, so you need to think hard about that, don't you?'

'All right Sir. We will lie then,' I said and glanced across at Kalpita hoping that she would back down and agree, but instead, she frowned at me hard and looked very angry and flushed.

'Good. Now, I suggest you all go back to your hostel and do not stray off the college grounds, and come promptly when you are called for again.'

11. CORRUPTION-FREE INDIA

Afternoon 24th December 2010

Lunch was the usual rice, dal and sabzi. I feel terrible when I have my food, my stomach starts to ache and my throat tightens up. Today, after I finished my lunch and was washing my aluminium plate with grass and soil – God how I hate that, it's so filthy – Rekha came to me. She also wants me to write a letter for her. It was for her mother whom she hadn't spoken to since her marriage two years ago.

> *Ma,*
>
> *How are you and everybody else? I am sorry for everything, Ma. Your son-in-law is no more. I am sure that you must have received the news. Still what is it that keeps you from visiting your daughter? Why can't you feel my pain, Ma? I have nothing left. No one is there who can help me out. I am in the prison in Asansol.*
>
> *That day, when I left home to go to him, I did not understand how much the blessings of elders matter in life. Since the first day of my marriage, I have always wanted to talk to you. I did not have enough courage to do so. I felt miserable as days passed. I left home fighting with Baba. And this is killing me every moment. I thought, because you are my mother, that one day you would accept us both. But even after you heard that your son-in-law has died and I am in jail, you never came to see me! I am the same little girl who never left her Ma, no matter what. It is just that she made a mistake. Will you never forgive me?*
>
> *One of the in-mates has been here for ninety days. She can't leave because she has no lawyer. I am afraid that this might be the case for me too. Help me please. I cannot stay in this place anymore. I am in lot of pain. I want to come back to you.*
>
> *Rekha*

The bell rang three times. Rekha folded the letter carefully and looked at it for a long time. She couldn't read any of it. She was smiling, thinking about her childhood days perhaps. I saw tears coming down her cheeks. I asked her what was so wrong with her husband that her mother couldn't accept him and she told me that he was a Muslim boy and her marrying him meant that she had severed all connections with her family, but of all of them, it was her mother that mattered to her.

I have decided that I want to write a book about being in prison and how we three got here and I thought I'd call it 'Trio in the Girls' Hostel'. That's the only title I can think for now but it isn't the right one, and I hope I'll come up with something better later. Whether I'll succeed or not in writing a whole book, I cannot say … but my diary will be a great help if I write in it every day and record everything I see, all the little things like the changes in the weather, the quarrels between the inmates, the nice things they do for each other, the games Rinki invents for herself. In fact, I've been thinking a lot about writing lately. I think I'd like to be a famous writer like Arundhati Roy. I have other ideas as well, besides this. I'll write about them later. The idea of being a writer is wonderful and I have become more than just excited about writing my diary. I don't have to study anymore now because all my exams are over, so I'll be watching everything and everybody and writing in my diary whenever I can.

Afternoon 25th December 2010

I am sitting on the stairs outside the hall right now. Last night was so cold that I couldn't even lie down to sleep. The holes in my blanket always let the cold air in. Some women have blankets with no holes in them at all, and I really envy them. Others have blankets much worse than mine with big tears down them, and there's one blanket that was burnt once and so half of it has gone. The sunrays on the empty lawn in front of the hall felt very warm and I dozed off for an hour out here a while ago because I was so tired. My mind is fresh now and I'm in the mood to write.

On the day of my last exam, Papa gave me some books to read. This was, I suppose, to keep me busy since an idle mind is a devil's workplace, he kept saying, trying to make a joke with me. He said I must make sure the books are finished within one week. This is next to impossible. I've already taken four days to read *The God of Small Things*, which I loved. God really does care about little things. I'd love to read it again right away, and I would do, if it wasn't for the fact that I've got to read the two other books he's brought for me.

Nazma hasn't stopped thanking me for the letter I wrote for her yesterday morning; she is happier than I have seen her before imagining that she has finally communicated with her husband. She offered me some of her lunch as a gift today. I couldn't refuse, but I felt very uneasy about it. I feel deeply for these so called criminal women. I don't know how they stand their lives in prison, how they manage to go on; it's almost like a miracle that they do. They are real heroines.

Nazma has a scruffy photo of the husband and she keeps trying to show it to me. She is forever putting it under my nose and saying, 'Look, see him! See him! Isn't he handsome?' and things like that. I think he's ugly and oily-looking, but I tell her he's handsome just to be kind.

Afternoon 26th December 2010

Triparna is dressed in Muhammad bin Tughlaq attire. She rolls her head over her neck with a loud creak and bites her lower lip as she looks at me with hungry eyes. Then, howling, she picks me up and as her foul breathe suffocates me, she hurls me from one end of the room to the other, and I, limping, run from her as fast as I can through the open doorway. When I woke from that dream this morning I've never been gladder to find myself safely in prison, and away from her.

Now the sky is blue and the sun is shining with all its strength. Winter afternoons are so pleasant. All the prisoners are sitting outside on the lawn with me. Some are preparing to take a nap. Rinki sleeps in the arms of Nazma, her ammu, deep in her world of funny games with Abbu. She smiles in her sleep as Ammu imprints a soft kiss on her head.

Nazma has been given bail after three months. We got the news last evening. But ten thousand bucks is impossible for her to find within hours and so she cannot leave this place. Yesterday morning, she had a sudden pain. She could not do the jailhold work assigned to her. She told the female guards that she was in real agony and asked them to leave her alone for the day and said that she had to sleep. She was talking to two fat and angry guards wearing the same brown saris. They asked her for Rs. 20 and held out their hands for the money. Strange! Jailbirds should have no money, no mobile phones, no sharp or inflammable objects with them and I was surprised to see that Nazma did have that money. I watched her fumble for it in the folds of her sari and give it to one of the women. I wondered where she got it from. I wondered if it came from one of the male guards, and then I rebuked myself for thinking such bad thoughts about her. Yet if she had been given money by the male guards, who could blame her really?

The female guards told her that food in jail had to be earned by doing 'jailhold' work or paying money. I don't think this is legal – of course it isn't. The 20 bucks goes inside the pockets of the guards. Such terrible things are happening in this world, but I can't do anything about it. I feel so helpless.

Yesterday, on our television I saw school and college students, working professionals and senior citizens making resolutions for the New Year. They were calling out about having a corruption-free 2011. They put up banners saying in gigantic letters khushhal naya saal with corruption-free India. That's very optimistic. I've read articles in various magazines about corruption in our country. They describe fat-bellied policemen and constables standing happily by hardcore crimes as they go on right in front of their eyes – theft, molestation, rape, even murder. It seems that all anyone cares about in India is money. Some people cry because of their lack of it and some show their power through it. Still, reading about it and seeing it are two different things. Once you've seen it, like I have in here, you can't forget it and pretend it doesn't exist. Corruption, that is to say bribery, is like food and water here … one cannot live without it; it goes on all around us.

Shrimati Didi, for example, can never meet her father even if she wanted to because neither of them have the money; it's Rs. 20 she'd have to pay to the female guard to let him see her, and he'd have to pay Rs. 50 to the same guard to get to see her. Even if he had Rs. 50, the only way he could make sure she was given the good food he'd bring for her from the outside was to pay the guards Rs. 20 to deliver vegetables to her, Rs. 30 for fish, and Rs. 50 to give her a chicken. I am trying to remember the last time when I felt happy, and I think it was the night before the first paper of this semester, Advanced Power Generation Technology on the 7th of December.

12. THREE BLIND MICE

I did not want Papa to leave me alone there at college. If I could've gone with him back to Kolkata, I would've, without packing anything or saying goodbye to anyone. He tried to comfort me. He said he thought the whole business of us getting accused of ragging Nabarupa was what you call a storm in a teacup and it would all be over soon and she would be seen to be a needy child who was trying to cover up the fact that she was failing badly at college. I felt something darker was building up that Papa couldn't have been aware of, and I didn't know how to tell him, it was just something in the air itself.

Almost as soon as Tanusri, Kalpita and I started to make our way back to the hostel from our interview with Viharjee Sir we were picked up by a group of students and dragged to the college park.

There, an even bigger crowd of students surrounded us instantly, and if we'd tried to get away from them, we wouldn't have been able to. Everything around me seemed to be fading away ... the college park, the stage, the agitated crowd of juniors. I could hear them shouting at us, and I could see by the expressions on their faces that they hated us, but it all seemed distant. I wondered for a moment if I was going to faint. I looked for Kalpita and Tanusri. They were right beside me. Kalpita's face was mask-like and quite white. I put my hand on her arm and held onto her and took hold of Tanusri's elbow in my other hand in case they tried to separate the three of us.

Triparna pushed her way through the crowd and climbed up onto the stage. 'I feel literally ashamed to have you low life as my seniors,' she shouted, 'shame on you.' I knew that she was about to repeat the lie she'd told Viharjee Sir to make things even worse for us in front of the juniors. 'What they did to Nabarupa Dash is nothing compared to what they did to me. They took photos and made a video of me when I was trying to get dressed after training, and there I am with no clothes on and they've shown everybody.'

'Stop it. Is this the issue we've come over here to discuss?' I turned around to see who had spoken. It was Bibek, the one student who seemed to be on our side amongst three hundred. 'What you're saying is nonsense,' he told Triparna. 'So where are these photos and video clip? If you want anyone to believe you, you'd better show the evidence. How come we don't have these interesting photographs? Let me tell you one thing. Even if you took your clothes off right now, we wouldn't want to look at you. This is not the issue we came to talk about today. Don't make things complicated. I warn you, Triparna.'

'You don't know me, Bibek Bhaiya,' Triparna said, 'you don't know my contacts. I can reach the press. I've very good contacts with them. And as far as you're concerned, well I'll sort you out. I don't regard any of you as my seniors.'

She climbed down from the stage and lumbered away across the park. Eventually the students managed to contain their anger and the first year representative said, 'Are you even human beings, you three? Nabarupa could have died! You should be severely punished for what you've done. She lost at least three pints of blood.'

The second and third years shouted for our suspension and placement cancellation. We stood like objects in the midst of hundreds of students and could do nothing about it.

'Leave the Girls' Hostel in one hour. We want your rustication! This should finish your careers! You could've caused her death,' one of them cried.

We had to leave our hostel the next morning on the 17th of November. We found a house nearby on Michael Faraday Street that we were able to rent and we called it the new hostel. The street itself was beautiful and tree-lined and the house was airy and noble-looking. It was a great deal better than living in our cramped and slightly smelly room in the student hostel. It was a lot quieter as well without Nabarupa around playing her horrible music.

The house had an enormous window that let in so much sunlight during the day that it was spectacular. Yet despite its beauty and the quietness of the place, I felt vulnerable there because I was close to traumatised by what had happened to us. We all were. We weren't sure if we'd be allowed to take the semester exams. Nothing was certain, but we had to study for them anyway, and that took some discipline on our part. I don't know what I'd have done if they'd refused to let us sit the exam, go mad perhaps. One evening I couldn't bear it any longer. I couldn't concentrate. 'Kalpita, I'm going insane!' I said.

'So am I, because you keep flicking that pen around, stop it will you?'

'I can't work, I can't think, I can't sleep.'

'Where's Tanusri?'

'In her room, reading.'

'What's the matter with you?'

'I can't do it, I just can't do it. I can't revise for exams if we aren't going to be allowed to take the bloody things!'

'Talk to him then.'

'Him?'

'Yeah, you know who I mean, the Monster. It's the only way, Dishari.'

On the 7th of December in the evening, I rang up Viharjee Sir and asked him about the exams.

'Are you prepared for them?' he asked.

'Yes Sir ... almost.'

'Well, your admit cards have come. You have your Advanced Power Generation Technology exam at two o'clock tomorrow.'

'Thank you Sir. I am so grateful.'

Then the university sent our admit cards. Thank you God ... you do exist ... I thought. I called up Bibek. 'Hey ... we got our admit cards!' I said.

'Wow ... see, I knew it. Studied thoroughly?'

'Ya ... sort of.'

'Sort of?'

'Need to revise one last time.'

'Studied the AFBC, PFBC and CFBC boiler layouts?'

'Yes Sir.'

'And the gas turbine numerical?'

'All done!'

'Well Dishari, let's meet tomorrow before exams. I think you will be allotted the same room as mine, like always.'

'Don't know, let's see.'

'Had dinner?'

'Nope. I forgot about it in my excitement … food in this new hostel is a lot better, you know. And reasonable too.'

'Good for you, Dishari, see you tomorrow. Have you told Aritro about all this yet?'

'I'm just going to ring him now. He's in Raigarh.'

Aritro was working as a junior engineer in a steel and power company. I'd called him twice since we'd moved into our new place and he was very worried about me, he kept saying he'd try and get time off to come over. I was really happy about the exams and ached to hug him. I called him up.

'Hello Disha. How are things going?' he asked.

'Guess what? We're allowed to take the exams. Can you believe it? I was about to give up.'

'That's great!'

'Exactly! I am so happy Aritro. I love you.'

'You've studied thoroughly, right? You've always scored well in exams before. You need to show the world what you are. I mean that you have the will to study at such an awful time.'

'Yes Aritro. I will prove myself, don't worry, but I wish I could see you.'

'I know. Me too. But listen, don't study too late. When is the exam?'

'Two o'clock.'

'Okay, go to bed early, I'll be thinking of you. Nothing bad can happen to a sweet girl like you, it'll all get sorted out before long.'

The next day, all three of us were allotted the fourth year classroom. Bibek, Suvodip and Bidesh were amongst the others who shared our room. The fifth bench in the first row, beside the window was mine. I took my seat, looking at the dark corridor through my window. The bell rang and the exam began.

I was filled with excitement. I rushed through the three hours writing fast about the details of MHD generators and energy conservation processes. I had almost finished my paper with forty-five minutes left to go. The last numerical was almost over.

Efficiency of the gas turbine = (Work done/Heat absorbed) X100
I engaged my fingers on the calculator. I was happy to get my answer within the possible range. I looked at my watch. A sudden noise ... rushing of feet, made me look out of the window. The police were outside and I stared in utter shock because I just knew that they had come for Kalpita, Tanusri and me. For the next forty minutes I was shaking with fear as I worked. I could scarcely hold my pen as I wrote the final efficiency value. The light brown uniforms of the police, with their stars of merit studded on the shoulders, were terrifying, I couldn't help looking at them from time to time and that made me struggle through the last sentence.

Ans. Efficiency of the gas turbine is 19.38%.

Finally I put down my pen and my terror made me notice weird and pointless things like the fact that there was some pencil shavings on the floor by the desk in front of me, and there was a hairline crack running under the windowsill and that the blackboard was filthy. The cops came in when the bell rang at the end of the exam. There were three males and a woman who seemed to me to be very hard. 'Dishari Saha, Tanusri De and Kalpita Deb, come with us,' she said.

I glanced at Bibek and he looked at me in disbelief. I stood up and followed the police, Kalpita and Tanusri did the same. We walked to Viharjee Sir's room. I remembered what Aritro told me as I walked, 'Nothing bad can happen to a sweet girl like you, it'll all get sorted out before long.' The words repeated in my mind.

When we were standing in front of Viharjee Sir I said, 'Sir, if you called the police, Papa doesn't know anything about it. We never knew about any police case.'

'I'd have thought it was obvious the police would be involved if a girl tried to kill herself because she'd been tortured by other students. Do you need to be told something so obvious?'

We were dismissed from Viharjee Sir's office and escorted towards a police jeep and on the way I noticed Suvodip, Abhijit and Bibek standing at the college gate, watching us helplessly. We'd been arrested. I couldn't believe that. How had that happened? What had we done?

My heart was beating fast. There was the semester exam to come, and we wouldn't be able to do it; I felt as if my life had come to an end. I thought of Papa, Mamma, Bubuli, Tutul and Aritro. I needed to contact them but my mobile had been taken away by the woman cop.

When we reached the jeep I remembered what Viharjee Sir had said, 'Be grateful always for what college has done.' What should I have been grateful about, my weeping mamma, horrified Papa, nervous Aritro, sad sisters, Bubuli and Tutul and helpless friends?

I heard a voice behind me. 'You'll only be in the police station lockup for one night; I asked one of the police.' It was Bibek. 'You'll be in court tomorrow and you'll get bail, so don't worry.'

We sat in the jeep. Tanusri was crying loudly now. It started to rain as the jeep drove past the college park, the graphics hall, workshop, and B. tech administrative building. We were once like inseparable parts of it, but now these buildings felt distant. Above the college gate was a notice which read: Thanks for your visit, and a surge of anger came upon me at the sight of it. I must have seen it thousands of times, but I'd never taken any notice of it until now, it was as if the college was throwing us away.

We reached the police station. Guards stood with guns, saluting the police officers, as we walked in with Sankar Basu, Officer In-Charge. We were taken to his untidy room. His ugly table had files and papers all over it. A wooden board was hanging on the wall with the word 'Wanted' painted in white letters at the top of it. There were photos of criminals on it – Salim Habib, wanted for mobile theft, Nasir Sheikh, a jewellery thief, and countless others, brutal-looking men, every one of them.

'Madam ... Hellow?' I looked up at the sound of Sankar Basu's rough voice. 'Name?'

'Dishari Saha.'

'Father's name?'

'Dr. Sandipan Kumar Saha.'

'Address?'

'Fifteen, FD Block, Salt Lake City, Kolkata.'

'Age?'

'Twenty one.'

He raised his right eyebrow and looked at me. Then he turned towards Kalpita and Tanusri and asked them the same thing. Our pictures were taken, and then, a woman who looked around sixty pointed to a door just behind us. 'That's where you're spending the night,' she said, 'in the lockup. In you go, girls. Have a good sleep.'

The door had iron bars set into it and a rusty old lock, and when we walked in there we saw that rain was coming in through the open window high above us. We stood inside the cold room looking at each other and we were soon drenched and shivering. Sankar Basu brought three thin blankets and threw them inside the lockup in a heap. They stank and when we touched them we saw that they were full of sand and dust.

As we tried to lay one out, three small fat mice squeaked out of it. They were running all over the floor in their own happy world. They ran and ran and kept running all over the place.

Three blind mice ... see how they run! I thought.

I had my notebook for the next exam with me, although I was unsure if they would let us three take the exam. The copy had a few unused pages towards the end of it. I tore them off and laid them over my blanket. I stared up at the window, wanting to reach it and look outside. Every so often men came past the lockup and stared at us through the bars. We didn't know who they were, Kalpita thought they were policemen who'd come to see us out of curiosity because we were students and that was strange in the lockup because the lockup had poor women in it who couldn't read and write, not university students with mothers and fathers who knew what the world was about. When they stared at us, part of their staring was greedy and nasty and part of it was respectful and humble.

Just then, I heard a voice that sounded familiar, and when I heard the sound of his boots as well, I knew for certain it was Viharjee Sir. I watched him through the bars, standing back a bit. He shook hands with Sankar Basu and whispered something to him.

'Don't worry,' Sankar Basu said, 'I have informed them. They will all be here tomorrow morning.'

As we watched Viharjee Sir leaving the police station, Tanusri pushed past me and called out, 'Sir, we haven't done anything!'

He stopped and turned towards us, 'Whatever you do, never tell lies,' he said, and the look of disgust on his face was terrible.

'Otherwise we'll turn out to be like you!' Kalpita shouted.

I put my wet hand on Tanusri's shoulder and we turned away from the bars. We were exhausted, and in shock. We buried our faces in our filthy gritty blankets and were glad of them as we tried to get warm.

It was tremendously cold that night and I lay like a foetus, wishing I was dead.

'How did all this *happen?*' Tanusri said. Her voice was broken from the cold. Everything was silent and I could hear the chattering of her teeth.

'God knows what's ahead of us,' I replied, 'but we'll be out of here tomorrow, you heard Bibek at the jeep, didn't you, he said we'd be taken to court tomorrow, and we'll be able to show that we're innocent, surely?'

Three blind mice, three blind mice,
See how they run, see how they run,
They all ran after the farmer's wife,
Who cut off their tails with a carving knife,
Did you ever see such a thing in your life
As three blind mice?

13. CHICKEN MAGGIE CHEESE MASSALA

Morning 27th December 2010

Last night it was so cold that it was impossible for any of us to sleep. Cold air that actually felt heavy poured in through the big windows in the hall as we made our way back there at the end of the final gunti of the day and waited to hear the door locked behind us yet again so that we could settle down for the night against the yellow walls. Instead of sleeping, we told each other stories from our childhood to pass away the hours until daylight.

I told the story of how Bubuli struck her head on the wall in our big fight and how much blood there was. I didn't say it was a marble wall, and I was careful not to put in any other details that showed my family lived in a nice house. Tanusri told a story about getting lost for hours and finally being found on the edge of a city and how terrifying it was, and Kalpita told a story about a monkey who lived in a tree next to her house and how she was convinced the monkey could understand what she said. Most of the other women talked about the jobs they did as children and the money they earned and took home to their families, and they could remember every detail as if it was yesterday. Those were the stories that most interested the other prisoners; the ones that got the women talking, but that we three couldn't contribute much to.

Night 27th December 2010

I've learnt from the others that everyone has come here because they are under trial which means they haven't been sentenced to prison permanently. They are here for a maximum of three months. Hopefully, all of them will get bail and leave this place before the end of the ninety days. If, after ninety days, they're found guilty, they will be sent to a far worse prison than this one where they will be made to work all day long. I can't imagine it. It's bad enough here. We're not even proven guilty of anything and yet we're made to eat truly disgusting cockroach-infested food every day, use filthy toilets and suffer badly in this terrible and cold winter, so if we're *not* guilty why are we made to go through these things? This is the Indian judiciary system and on top of that it's riddled with corruption; to get any comfort at all, you have to bribe the guards hand over fist.

Everyone here has found a way to keep themselves busy. I write my diary whenever I can or read the Arundhati Roy book again, parts of it which I love. Kalpita sleeps most of the time these days. Tanusri hangs around and watches the television with Rekha. Nazma Bibi is busy taking care of Rinki. Shrimati Didi sits alone on the lawn, doing nothing apparently. The others, who know knitting, carry on their work with colourful wool and needles. The rest of the prisoners learn how to knit from them.

There's a prisoner here whose teeth are stained brown with the paan she's always chewing and before she even sees the yellow of the sun in the morning, she rushes from her bed to see the yellow of the stained toilet. As soon as morning attendance is over, she runs towards the open toilets at the side of the lawn. Every day she carries a bucket of water in one hand and a mug in the other and she marches off to reserve herself a stinky toilet, but she'd got no extra hand to hold soap with. She's called Nirupa Ruidas, but her nickname is 'Oh So Clean' because her white sari has a scarlet border that has faded and gone yellow-looking – some of the prisoners joke that it is urine, but I think it has gone yellow like that because she wipes her hands on it.

Oh So Clean reminds me of Nabarupa and her horrible bathroom habits. It was usually Tanusri who emptied the commode after Nabarupa had used it. The water, with the unbearable and offensive smell and suspended solid particles and pee, comes back to my memory. The most horrible days were those when Nabarupa had her period, and they still haunt me. The mosaic floor would remain stained with scarlet red drops, difficult to distinguish from the black and maroon shades of the floor, and they would stick to our slippers and be discovered much later when we'd accidentally trod them across the entire surface. The pads, drenched in blood and water, would remain in a corner of the bathroom, next to the blue buckets and inches away from her green mug. I sometimes wonder if even that disgusting habit was a weird way of trying to bring my attention to her — pretending to be completely helpless so that other people would be drawn towards her and she could make them into her friends.

Here in Asansol, Champa Mashi, with her big round red bindi and her sky blue sari with a black border, has given us new zest and enthusiasm. We call her the 'Story Telling Newcomer'. She wears her long hair neatly tied into a bun and she has a thick line of red vermilion between the parting. Six months ago she was in Burdwan Jail and then she had a breakdown and was put in the hospital there. In the midst of the endless despair we all feel in this jail, she's brought some humour in with her crazy tales.

She was talking to Nazma this evening and saying how much better Burdwan Jail was than this place. I was reading. I looked up at her. Everyone was listening. She reckoned she got a big cup of coffee in the morning. We all laughed! Nazma looked amazed as if she believed her, and Shrimati said she was straightforward lying. But that didn't stop her; she reckoned that at lunch she had two or three pieces of chicken or mutton. She was beginning to make me feel really hungry. Then after that, ha-ha, they apparently got as many rasgullas as they wanted. Some story! I asked her if she was feeling terrible now that she was here, and she rolled her eyes and said, 'Of course I do.' She's told us a lot of outrageous stories about Burdwan and although we don't believe a word of them, they make us laugh. Even Tanusri smiles at her stories and it helps pass the dreary time away.

Her sky-blue sari with its black border brings me tender memories of my grandmother with her serene smile. I can see her beautiful face in my mind in perfect detail. When he visited yesterday, Papa told me that Dida is in hospital with breathing problems. The entire universe crazily revolved around me … everything became zig-zagged and irregular as he spoke. I asked him if she would be all right soon. At first, he refused to answer. Then, he assured me that things would be okay. I didn't ask anymore about it. I could understand from his reaction, though, that Dida is very ill. How much I long to be with her now. I believe in numerology because it's always worked for me. Papa said that Dida's bed number is 268, and so I did a quick mental calculation. 2+6+8=16. 1+6=7. Oh I was so happy. 7 is my lucky number. She will get well very soon.

I have no mental work now other than writing my diary. I don't enjoy watching the serials that the others watch on the television, I've tried to sit with them and pretend to be enjoying the stuff they watch, but it doesn't work, I just want to see the news channels so I know what's going on in the world. I don't fight with them over the remote control like I used to with Bubuli though, I wouldn't dare. So all I can do is keep myself busy by writing. These are the most terrible days of my life and I am feeling sad and angry about them, and I want to write about the way I am feeling because I think it will make me feel better.

I am sitting on my blanket in the hall. I try to close my eyes to meet Mamma in my mind − Mamma in her red and white Assam silk that Papa brought once from an official tour. I tremble in fear wondering if I can remember her face. I am desperate to tell her that I love her.

When I first had to go to school, I hated it, I didn't see why I should have to leave my own world of people I knew, especially Mamma. At that time, I was four and Bubuli was yet to be born. Papa, who was an intern doctor at a hospital, wasn't at home then, I think he was away on some official work. I remember that our street would be quite empty in the morning with very few vehicles on the road, but there'd be school children, some of them laughing and some of them sad waiting with their parents for school buses or cars.

I hated having to go to school so much that I shouted and screamed and it took our car driver to force me into the car. I remember looking into Mamma's eyes expecting her to stop this terrible thing happening to me and she just looked back helplessly. One day I was so deeply hurt by this that I decided to stop talking to her all together; she was my mother, the most important person in the world, if she wanted to stop this horrible thing happening to me, she could. When the car collected me from school that day and pulled up in front of our house, Mamma was standing at the gate waiting for me. The driver came around to my door and opened it for me and I got out, walked past him, walked past Mamma without looking at her and went straight to my room and closed the door behind me. Later, she came to talk to me and bring me some food, and that was the first time I had ever seen tears in her eyes and it was I who had caused them. Even though I was very tiny, I made a vow that I would never do anything that would make my mother cry again. Now I am in prison. Now my mother is crying because of me. I feel terrible to have broken my vow. Sorry, Mamma, I would do anything to change it.

Mamma's beautiful face fades away into darkness and through the darkness I can see a pink background and I know we are all together, me, Mamma, Papa, Bubuli, Tutul. There is a cake with candles on it and pizzas and a crusher. I can see drinks. People are laughing and clapping. It is someone's birthday. We are in Pizza Hut. I feel myself smiling and as I do, the vision moves away from me, slowly at first and then rapidly until I am alone.

The thought of pizza and cake has made me hungry, I wish I could reach into my own mind and pull them out and eat them. But what I'd really like now is some Maggie noodles. I haven't tasted them for a long time and I miss them. We used to cook them in college in our little kitchen when we were in the middle of heavy revision and didn't want to have to leave the hostel. They only took five minutes to cook and they tasted like heaven. I once boiled them and then fried them and I put in massala, egg and chicken pieces, then finally I added cheese and coriander leaves. Tanusri and Kalpita said it was great and we called it Chicken Maggie Cheese Massala.

I'll have to remind Kalpita and Tanusri about Maggie noodles tomorrow, but it isn't only food that I think about a lot in here, I've become crazy about everything to do with nature lately, that is when I'm not angry or sad. I remember the days when a deep blue sky, the chirping of the birds, moonlight and blossoming flowers didn't move me … even though I tried to be as poetic as Wordsworth. That's changed since I've been here. I've realised that I often stare at the banyan tree's leaves as they move in the slight winds. I spent time, too, watching the midnight sky become the beautiful morning sky. I hadn't known before I was imprisoned that nature was so fantastic. It is this place that has brought me close to its richness and now I am longing for everything. I am thinking of Aritro and my friends and I miss them all so badly. I hope that I'll dream of Aritro tonight.

14. HAZY, HALF-LIT WORLD

'How do we know there aren't rats in this lockup as well as mice?' Tanusri whispered.

'We don't. We don't know anything,' Kalpita answered. 'Just say nothing to anyone, Tanusri, and please don't cry, otherwise they've won.'

It was morning. I was beginning to feel really sick about the lockup. I don't know how the three of us managed to sleep at all the night before in the stinking sand-filled blankets, maybe we'd been exhausted. We found some food someone had left behind, wrapped in newspaper and lying in a corner. We were burning with hunger by then. People kept coming to stare through the bars at us as if we were apes and their curiosity about us disgusted me. I tried to concentrate on revising for the exam; I kept my eyes on my notebook, and didn't look up when I heard the sound of their footsteps.

The walls of the lockup room were wet and sweet smelling. Weird, we thought. I was pretty sure it was mould; there was white furry stuff high up on the walls. Papa would know that kind of thing. The face of the officer in charge was covered with a large number of irregular marks on a rough, undulating dark skin and he had a tilted smile that made a distinct angle. I looked at my copy. He laughed, and the sound of it made me cringe. 'My, my!' he said, 'these sluts are studying but their career has been totally spoilt. My! My!'

I kept staring at my copy and watched as the letters changed from distinct to blurred shapes as tears began to fill my eyes. All I could think about was Mamma and how I wanted to be in her arms, but she was miles away and I had to wipe my tears on my own as best I could. I thought about my two sisters and what was to become of them, Dida's failing health, and Mamma and Papa's anxieties. I closed my eyes hoping to create a different scenario out of what seemed to be a very bad dream.

A minute later, someone began to shout: 'Take them out! How long do you plan to keep them in? Bring out the convicts!' and the female cop came into the lockup to tell us that we were to be taken to court and on the way we would be stopping for an interview with a doctor. My heart started to beat and I heard Kalpita groan.

There were scores of reporters waiting outside the police station to take pictures of us – the convicts responsible for stripping a girl naked and making a video of her. We used the dupattas of our salwar suits to hide our faces as best we could from the crowd and the reporters, as they were all we had.

We had to struggle all the way to the police van, we couldn't keep the media people away from us, they were like savage dogs with their questions and comments. Each one wanted to get a better view of us and so they pushed each other about trying to get close to us. I could see them all faintly through my dupatta with their notebooks and cameras and their slick faces.

'Why are you hiding your faces?' they shouted at us. 'Show us your malicious faces!'

Finally, we reached the van and were pushed in roughly by the guards. My heart was beating loudly, the press banged on the windows, but we sat with our heads down. The questions almost buried me with terror. The van stopped at the Durgapur Hospital. The press followed us there in cars. The dupatta was still supporting me as I went inside trying as hard as I could to ignore the reporters.

The typical smell of hospitals filled my nose. I removed my dupatta from my face and saw that we had been taken into a shabby room. The doctor was sitting at the huge table that had on it a laptop, a pen stand, and a prescription pad. He looked through his frameless glasses at us and started plucking his moustache with his left hand.

The three of us stood in front of him in a row, the same as we had done in Viharjee Sir's room.

'Were you tortured inside the lockup at all?' he asked us. 'Just a routine question,' he added.

We nodded our heads to mean no. He looked at the police guards and slightly raised his right eyebrow and then made a little tilting movement of his neck. The gesture suggested that we could be taken back to the van.

'Please help us, Doctor,' I said as the guards came forward.

'Help you, what on earth for?'

'We are innocent of what they claim we've done, you can use your authority. My own father is a doctor; he is Dr. Sandipan Kumar Saha from Salt Lake City in Kolkata.'

'It's a lawyer you need, not a doctor, you silly girl. Guards, show them the way outside,' he said.

At that point, Tanusri started to sob, and the guards, who were standing behind us, moved forward and dragged her by her arms to take her out. 'Leave me,' she shouted. 'Doctor, we are innocent. We did no ragging. The girl pretended to commit suicide.'

'What should I do about it?' the doctor asked, standing up.

'You asked about torture. Yes, we were tortured … mentally. The reporters, the police guards, our college director, our juniors, everyone has tortured us. People all over the country will be reading newspapers and watching television and being told a total lie!'

Kalpita stood with her arms folded watching everything as if it was a play, but, like us, she was scared.

I saw that the doctor was becoming angry; I sensed that he thought us despicable criminal women who were beneath his contempt. 'Stop this! You're embarrassing me. Get out!' he shouted and his voice was arrogant and piercing. A couple of patients were peeping in at us and others were standing coolly, disinterested in Tanusri's shouting and the doctor's fury.

'The reporters are asking questions. What should we do? They are following us everywhere. We can't show our faces,' Tanusri sobbed.

'Security! Guards!' the doctor shouted, 'get on with it, will you, get these women out of my hospital.'

The guards dragged Tanusri outside the doctor's office and we followed behind. As she struggled with them, Tanusri shouted out bravely, 'Yes, Doctor. Sit and enjoy the news. What else can you do?'

I was surprised at her, she'd suddenly found some strength and anger in her that I hadn't seen before, and I was glad. Outside the doctor's door we covered our faces again and were taken back to the van. I could, very faintly, see people gathering to form a crowd around us. They were looking at us in a way that was supposed to make me know I belonged to the dirt beneath their feet. Kalpita and Tanusri stood behind me; I could feel them. We got into the van quickly, desperate to get away from the reporters. I remember thinking when I was a first year student that my seniors were like treacherous jackals – always looking out for their prey, and here I was again in the exact same position. The van began to move slowly forward.

'Hey, girlies, let's see your pretty little faces then, angels' faces, eh?' one of them said. 'Feeling shy now after what you've done?'

'Is it your habit to torture little girls?' a woman shouted out.

We reached the court. It was a huge building. It seemed that the reporters had been waiting for us there also. I could hear one of them very clearly: 'These are the three culprits who are being taken to the court now. You can see the huge crowd waiting to know what the court decides for the brutal ragging of a first year student.

The ragging was so violent that the girl tried to commit suicide. This event took place on 15th of November late at night. The question is why it has taken so long to arrest them, a whole twenty-three days later. Did they try to flee? Well, we are yet to find out. The college Director, Mr. A. Viharjee, told LTV News this morning that he had thought about having the girls arrested earlier. But he thought it better to wait for the semester exams when he knew for certain that they'd be in college. It would have been foolish, he said if they'd been alerted to my intentions by someone else and then made a run for it. Yesterday, on 8th of December, the girls had their semester exams, at the end of which, the Durgapur Police arrested them. This is reporter Abhishek Mondal with cameraman Ashish Ranjan, L TV News.'

I had no strength left; I may as well have been a paper bag in the wind. But then I heard the voice of Papa somewhere, and some of my terror and shame vanished because he'd come to save me. I was going to be free soon, I could do the exam tomorrow with no problem, Papa was somewhere outside the court and I was dying to be in his arms.

We entered the court building and walked down a long corridor and into a hall in which there were many guards, lawyers and policemen. I was glad to see that reporters were not allowed to go in there. Within the hall there were two small rooms with iron bars at their windows. These were the court lockups. One held around ten male convicts. The other was empty and was meant for the three of us.

The shabby blue walls of the lockup had turned scarlet red with the stains of the paan spit. The room was huge and I felt that it was filled with loneliness and fear. I imagined the tears of all the people who'd passed through there and it made me shiver. The room stank of urine, and I could see that the smell came from a toilet in one corner that had no walls around it, and I shuddered with revulsion. I felt sick and dirtied, and hoped I wouldn't have to use that toilet; I couldn't bear the thought of it. All three of us were starving as we sat on the cold concrete floor with our backs against the stained walls.

It was time for lunch at court. One of the guards gave me three newspaper-wrapped packets. I spread the greasy paper out on my lap and Kalpita read out to us what it said, although parts of it were unreadable because of the food stains.

'You're not going to believe this but it says here that the accused students are not even going to be offered jobs in the IT sector,' Kalpita said. 'The detailed report is hidden in this gobi ki sabzi, four kachoris and a juicy, sweet, white rasgulla!'

'Don't make a joke of it, Kalpita,' Tanusri whispered.

'What else can I do?' she replied.

I dipped the kachori into the juice. It melted in my mouth like some long forgotten pleasure. I really had been hungry. I felt my eyes close in delight. I was, for a moment, completely lost in a hazy, half-lit world in which there was only the wonderful taste of the food. Tanusri was not eating. She sat in silence facing the dirty wall.

'Did you hear what that reporter was saying, Kalpita?' I asked.

'Yes. I heard.'

'Viharjee Sir had it in his mind to have us arrested for some time!' I said.

'Yes, and because we knew nothing about it we have no lawyer now.'

'He didn't want us to have the chance of getting a lawyer and therefore avoiding arrest,' I said, and as I spoke the words, I knew them to be true.

'Why?' Tanusri asked, turning to face us.

'Well, by making examples of us, and getting us arrested, he can make out that he's a supporter of the anti-ragging campaign, and that would make the college look like a good place for parents to send their kids, wouldn't it?'

'God! How is it possible for a man like that to be running a college at all?' Kalpita said loudly.

'Today is the 9th of December, right? It is twelve-thirty. Nabarupa must be doing her exam right now,' I said.

'And, I'll bet you,' Kalpita added, 'that even if she does badly, she'll be given a pass mark out of sympathy.'

'Do you think that's why she faked that suicide in the first place, so she'd be given a pass knowing she'd fail otherwise?' Tanusri asked.

Kalpita sighed. 'Yes, I do. You remember how she stared at us after we'd told her off that night, and how she wouldn't go away and study when we told her to?'

'Was it my fault though?' Tanusri asked.

'What do you mean *your* fault?' I asked.

'Don't you remember, I said we didn't know where she spent her time when she went out at night?'

'That's hardly ragging, though is it?' Kalpita said.

Tanusri looked away. 'I still shouldn't have said it.'

'Well, you did, so forget about it. This is not your fault. I think she was actually planning that pretend suicide while she was staring at us in a spooky way that night.'

'But she wouldn't have known Viharjee Sir would do what he's done, would she?' Tanusri whispered.

I looked at Kalpita. I was glad she was here with us; she was so direct and practical. 'No, of course not,' she answered. 'Anyhow, I'll say it one more time, Tanusri, what's happened to us isn't your fault, so you've got to stop crying and be strong about it all.'

'Okay, okay!' Tanusri replied and wiped her face on her arm. 'What I've been trying to work out is how come she had to stay in hospital overnight when she just had a stupid cut on her hand.'

'It is all about money, Tanusri. The uncle bribed the hospital doctors. That's got to be what happened, there is no other way.'

'I think so too,' I said. 'He reminds me of Mr. Haley from *Uncle Tom's Cabin*, and he's completely corrupt, I'm sure of that.'

'I don't care about that man, he's in the past now. I'm really scared of the reporters,' Tanusri said. 'I felt so helpless out there with them; it was as if they wanted to tear our heads off!'

'What I'm thinking is that we don't have a lawyer,' I said quickly in case Tanusri started to weep again. 'I saw Papa in the crowd; I'll bet both your fathers were there as well. I'm sure they'll try their best to free us.'

'I really hope so. It is terrible here. So stinking!' Kalpita said.

'I am thinking about our exams tomorrow. I'm not even sure I'm going to be able to do it,' I said.

'Oh yes,' Tanusri said, 'tomorrow … we've got another exam! What are we going to do about that?'

'Yesterday's exam was good for me at first. But the end was terrible!' I answered. 'You know, I was sitting beside the window. I was just writing my last sentence when I looked outside and saw those cops. I was so scared. My heart was beating against the edge of my desk so that my body was jerking about.'

'I was so afraid when I saw the cops that I thought that I might have a heart attack,' Tanusri whispered. I don't want to think about tomorrow's exam. Our careers are spoilt anyway, aren't they? I can't live this way … without a career, a job, or respect.'

She began to weep again and I saw a flash of irritation pass over Kalpita's face. 'We can only deal with one thing at a time,' she said, 'we don't even know if we'll be allowed to take the exam, yet.'

As we sat wondering what was going to happen to us, a huge female guard with big glasses and a pierced nose came into the room and glared at us. 'Time to go, girls,' she said, putting her hands on her hips and pushing her face forward as if to see us better. We put our dupattas over our faces, and I could sense her impatience. 'Hurry up, stop fiddling about, you stupid girls; everyone's going to know your wicked faces soon enough! Come along now!'

I learnt later that her name was Kalpana.

The male convicts were taken out of the adjacent room and their hands were tied behind their backs with rope. Two expressionless guards waited, one in the front and the other behind the queue. They had huge polished, light brown loaded guns on their shoulders. We three were pushed into place at the end of the queue by Kalpana

Di, but we weren't tied up. I could hardly see anything through my thick, dark green veil. 'Please, I can't see anything; can you guide me in case I fall?' I asked her.

'You are your own ress-pon-see-bee-lee-tee,' she replied, 'I never forced you to tie that thing on your face. Un-der-stand?'

As we struggled to climb the stairs to the courtroom, I could dimly see scores of flashing lights as cameramen took photos of us. There was so much noise and commotion that I started to sweat with fear – and I knew it was us three who were the cause of it, not the other prisoners in front of us.

When we got into the courtroom, I took off my dupatta so that I could breathe properly and see everything once again. There was a long green table at the front of the room, and the men sitting along it, engrossed in conversation, I supposed were lawyers. I looked around the room, there seemed to be hundreds of people in there and I gradually distinguished the faces of people I knew. Rupak, Suvendu, Kaustav ... they were all there, Suvodip, Abhijit, Ananya and Baishali ... I was highly comforted ... Sangkha, Pallab, Biman and most importantly, Papa. At first I couldn't look at him – my throat started to ache and my heart began to beat loudly. I kept my eyes lowered, but he was looking straight at me, I knew it, and finally I looked up, and it was as if we were alone in that vast place. Tears came to my eyes, hot ones, and I watched Papa crying too on the other side of the room where I couldn't get to him.

The magistrate made his ceremonious entrance. His brown eyes were large, slightly protruding, and seemed filled with a kind of wonder as he looked us, as if he were on the verge of some new and exciting discovery. We stood up to greet him as he sat down behind a large desk, and then we took our seats again. The hearings began. The cases were being put up before him in the order of the crime date and time.

The convicts stood up as and when their names were called. Everyone was nervous ... the lawyers, the convicts, the guards ... everyone. Kalpana Di was sitting beside me. She whispered to another guard and pointing at us, said, 'These girls, ragging case!'

'Oh! I've heard the lawyers talking about this. I think they'll get bail.'

'No-no-no … not that easy! Let's wait and see.'

None of the prisoners before us got bail. They were all given another date to appear in court. We had no lawyer, yet, but I had unfailing trust in Papa, he was my father and so of course he would save me.

When our case was put up, we rose to our feet and then I could see the court room clearly. The magistrate ordered us to wait in the court lockup till decisions were made. I could feel that everyone was looking at us. I was never more nervous than at that moment. We left the room with Kalpana Di and walked down the stairs with our faces covered once more. Tanusri began to stumble.

'Please tell us what happened,' a reporter asked. 'Why did you make a video of that girl?'

'Who did you supply the videos to?' someone else asked.

'And did you get money for it?' put in a third voice.

Again we found ourselves in the stinking lockup. I was convinced we'd all be released soon and I was planning a grand celebration with Papa. I had my second exam on the following day. I wanted to return to my books and copies and sit for the exam after all the turmoil. I didn't remember anything I'd studied earlier in Protection and Instrumentation and I had a lot more work to do on it.

The first exam came to my mind again. And then, after knowing I'd done well, I had the vivid memory of having the cops arrest us, and ending up in the prison lockup and not being able to sleep the entire night on the gritty blankets. Every second came back to me – every insult, the horrible pock-faced guard, the reporters who followed us everywhere bombarding us with intolerable questions, but soon the nightmare would be over, and knowing that was what kept me going.

The male convicts were being brought back to their lockup room. I saw a woman in a torn, once yellow sari, running across the hall. Her hair was in a terrible mess, streaming down her back and tangled. The guards stopped her.

'Please let me see my husband, just for a little while, please!' she begged.

'You need money for that. Rs. 50. Do you have the money?' one of the guards asked.

'You can't take money off me, you're not allowed, I could tell someone and then you'd be in trouble! I know because my uncle told me.'

The guards laughed at her. 'Go ahead, then,' they cried, 'try your luck!' I saw the woman leave the hall wiping her tears away. The guards were laughing amongst themselves and one of them said, 'She says it's illegal, huh! If everything follows legally what'll happen to our bonus money?' and they laughed even louder.

Through the bars of the lockup we could look into the hall. It was four-thirty by the clock high up on the wall and we were still waiting for the decision. I chalked out a quick plan in my mind. I had to finish the syllabus for the exam, latest by next day noon because the exam started at two o'clock and I had a lot left to study. But I was confident, and I felt optimistic about everything, yet as the minutes went by waiting for the court result became more and more difficult. I tried to concentrate on all the different sounds I could hear, the noises out on the street – the sound of cars and their horns, people talking inside the courtroom building.

Finally Kalpana Di opened the door and looked in on us, grinning. 'You've been given bail. You'll be free to go in a minute!' Although I'd been expecting it, it was still somehow unbelievable; I was free. Mamma must have been weeping until now, I thought, and she would be so happy to get the news.

'So you three are in the middle of doing exams, are you?' Kalpana Di asked. All we could do was nod and smile; we were so glad to be out of captivity that we couldn't even speak properly. 'Okay. Study well and all the best to you.'

While I waited for Papa to come and get me I was trying to decide which things I'd tell him about what we'd been through and which parts I'd pretend hadn't happened. I wasn't going to tell him about how the officer in charge of the prison lockup called us sluts, or about the terrible things the reporters and cameramen called out to us to make us respond to them, or the way the arrogant doctor treated us. I'd tell him about the white stuff in the lockup and how we couldn't sleep, and about those little mice, and how someone had left some food in the lockup.

116

I'd been so thankful to see all my friends in the courtroom, if ever I'd taken any of them for granted before, if ever I'd been impatient with them or had unkind thoughts about them, I knew I never would again – I had the best and most loyal friends in the world and I couldn't wait for things to get back to normal so I could be with them all again.

15. LITTLE, RING, MIDDLE, INDEX, THUMB

Our friends and families were all waiting outside the courtroom, expecting us to be released at any minute. Tanusri, Kalpita and I were waiting in the lockup with the door open. We were impatient for it all to be over and done with, and then suddenly Kalpana Di appeared in the doorway and stared at the three of us. I watched as she pulled an odd face at us, and then turned back to talk to the main guard who was sitting at a table in the room outside with the other guards. Already my heart had started to beat uncontrollably. The guards stopped talking and turned to look at us with the same hostility we'd been greeted with when we first came to court – yet minutes ago, they'd been giving us friendly looks and silly winks.

I rose to my feet. 'Uncle,' I called out, 'Guard Uncle, what's the matter?'

'The public prosecutor,' he replied roughly, 'has turned against you and the case is being reconsidered. I hope God will save you.'

'How can that be?'

'That is exactly how it is. I've just told you.'

'But we *have* got bail, right?'

'Apparently, you did get bail at first. But things have changed now. Do you have a lawyer?'

'I don't think so. Papa couldn't get one. He couldn't arrange for one in time because he hadn't been told about our arrests.'

'Now God will be the only one who can save you, I guess.'

'What do you mean?'

'You girls are going to Asansol Special Correctional Home.'

'What? When?'

'In few minutes.'

'But we have an exam tomorrow.'

'No exams … this is the decision by the court.'

'But no exams mean that we will have a one year lag ... that means we're failing at college!'

'You're *still* thinking about exams! Think about how you're going to get out of jail without a lawyer instead, girl.'

Kalpita and Tanusri were standing beside me, listening silently. I lost all hope then. We had no lawyer to defend us, and Papa, how could I talk to him? I didn't have my mobile phone with me.

Viharjee Sir made a complaint to the police about us three days after Nabarupa was discharged from hospital, but it was a whole sixteen days before the police actually arrested us, and if we'd known about the complaint, if Viharjee Sir had had the kindness to tell us what he'd done, Papa could've got an anticipatory bail condition for us and we wouldn't have been arrested like we were – that's what we found out later, anyway.

I could hear, but very faintly, the media reporters talking outside the room, on the long balcony perhaps. 'I congratulate the authorities for taking appropriate action. MMS scandals are against Indian culture. The culprits should be punished!' one of them said.

Our lives and careers were at stake. That would be the end of all my dreams ... life, love, career, job. My heart was beating faster than ever and I felt as if I was going to faint.

Just then, Bibek and Rupak came into the room with Papa. I rushed to him and hugged him tightly. 'I am so sorry Papa,' I whispered, 'I promise you we didn't do anything to that girl, I even tried to help her with her work. She would never leave me alone, she tried to force me into being her friend, like a little kid would; she shouldn't have been in college in the first place, someone should've been looking after her.'

I could feel him patting my back. 'Dishari ... I have good news for you, so don't worry. We have a lawyer now. Meet Mr. Sood, Suvodip's father's friend.'

'What's the point Papa? My life is ruined. I can never live my dreams of becoming an engineer now.'

'C'mon Disha, calm down. Just talk to him.'

I looked at Mr. Sood. He was wearing a formal black coat and trousers and was very tall.

'Don't worry,' he said, 'I'll try my best to get you out.'

'We're not really going to jail, are we? That means college life is finished for us, doesn't it?' Kalpita asked.

'You'll be able to study for your exams in jail, and travel to college to take them; I've arranged it that way. Do you have your books with you?'

'I haven't got any books,' Tanusri whispered.

'Sir, we have the girls' books here,' Rupak said.

'And they can study our notes for tomorrow's exam,' Bibek offered.

Your next hearing will be in nine days time. Let's hope that on that day you will be free again. So stay calm and just work. Keep focused on your exams and try to think about nothing else,' Mr. Sood advised us.

'Thank you Uncle. For everything,' I answered.

'But I've got to tell you that it'll be a really difficult case to fight, girls, you should realise that.'

'But why?' Tanusri asked, nearly in tears now, 'we haven't *done* anything, we keep saying it and saying it and nobody believes us!'

'Shush, Tanusri,' I whispered, 'don't go to bits now, we've got to concentrate.'

'Go on, Mr. Sood,' Kalpita said, 'what do you mean difficult?'

'Well, your head of college – what's he called?'

'Viharjee,' I said, thinking of other names for him.

'Yes. Well, he's gone all out to make things bad for you, I'm afraid.'

'He's crazy!' Kalpita shouted. 'He's a mad man!'

'Shush,' I said, 'can you explain it to us, Mr. Sood?'

Mr. Sood loosened his tie. He seemed nervous and wouldn't look us in the eye. 'Just concentrate on your exams,' he said, 'and forget about the rest of it for now.'

I hugged Papa tightly. He stroked my head and rocked me from side to side. As I felt his tears fall on my shoulder, I panicked suddenly and was filled with the idea that this might be the last time I'd hug him again and the thought of it made me very frightened.

'Life has not ended,' Papa whispered, 'it has just begun – you have to show the world that you can tolerate what's happened to you and still do well in the exams, darling.'

'I'll try my best, Papa, all I care about is that you believe in me and know that I'm innocent.'

By the time Papa and I got outside, all the reporters had gone. 'Can I talk to Mamma?' I asked him.

Kalpana Di was already getting irritated by the delay, but Papa turned to her, 'Can she?' he asked.

'Yes-s. But ma-ak-e it fa-a-st,' she replied rudely.

Papa dialled Mamma's number from his phone.

'Hello. Hello Mamma?'

'Disha! It's you at last, where are you?'

'Mamma, are you crying, please don't. Everything is okay. Papa is here, we've got a lawyer, we'll be out in no time. Please Mamma; I can't bear it if you cry.'

Before I could finish, Kalpana Di snatched the phone from my hand and disconnected the line. 'Enuf-f-f,' she said, and handed the phone to Papa, 'start moving now.'

I climbed into the jail van. It was dark inside. Tanusri and Kalpita came in behind me. The van windows were covered in fine wire mesh and I stared out with the palms of my hands flat against it. Papa was right there, trying to touch my fingers through the mesh. The van started. It moved off slowly. The familiar faces were fading away. Papa had to gradually leave all my fingers … little, ring, middle, index, thumb.

Kalpita was staring through the van window with her hand clutching her throat, and Tanusri was moaning softly with her hands covering her face. It had stopped raining and the sky was clear and the moon full. I could feel my eyes flood with tears as the image of Papa with his fingers on the mesh window of the van came back to me, and so I tried to think of life in school where I had been happy. I remembered my English teacher, Mrs. Jonathan. We used to call her Johnny Baby, and it was she who told us that charity was unconditional in Hinduism. She said, 'Rajadharma ordains that even a King cannot have a good night's sleep if one of his subjects is sleeping on an empty stomach.' She knew all about the bible as well. I used to love the song 'We Three Kings of Orient Are'. I started to sing the words under my breath as the van stopped at a traffic light.

'*Stars with royal beauty bright,*
West-ward leading still proceeding,
Guide us to Thy perfect light.
We three Kings of Orient are …'

'Shut up!' Kalpita shouted, 'I can't bear it. Just be quiet will you?'
'Who?' I asked. 'Tanusri or me?'
'Both of you; just shut up!'

I closed my eyes. Suddenly I could see everything very clearly – the song is on page number thirty in the red hymn book. Mrs. Bula Raju is sitting at the one hundred and fifty year old piano, belting out the tune as we sing loudly, and Johnny Baby sings with us. When the song is over, the choir girls sit down on the long, black, wooden benches. The green wooden doors let in the fresh air as Jonny Baby begins her speech. She tells us that the Calcutta Girls' High School motto 'Deus Et Humanitas' or 'God and Humanity' is a century and a half old, and that since 1856, when the institution was established under the patronage of the first Viceroy of India, Lord Canning, the idea of all men being equal was our central creed. Then she announces the thought for the day – Charity Lies Above All._

Viharjee Sir's cold unflinching face floats into my mind at that point and I shudder. He'd been taking some of our classes in the last few months if he had nothing better to do. But, some clever students had been finding out in advance that he was coming, and they'd go missing, while the rest of us would have to sit through two forty minute sessions with him, or if he didn't appear, sit through eighty minutes of idleness. We'd hear the noise of his boots coming down the stairs, and if we'd been talking, we'd shut up and sit quietly. He'd come into the classroom and his little frameless specs would be half-way down his nose, and every minute or so, he'd push them up again. He never had anything with him but a pen that he put on the teacher's desk very carefully.

'Where are the rest?' he asked us on one occasion, staring around the room.

'Sir, they didn't know about today's class. So …' Bibek said.

'What do you mean by that? If I can come, leaving all my important work for a bunch of brainless students who have no future ahead of them, can't I, at least, expect full attendance from this class?'

There was pin-drop silence in the room. I looked down at my desk and hoped I'd become invisible. I didn't dare look up again, in case he was staring directly at me.

He took the pen from the desk and stared at it for a minute. 'A hopeless, worthless batch!' he continued, 'I'll make sure that such irresponsible students don't get placed in the top companies. One of you will give me the names of the absent students. They won't be appearing for the next company who comes here.'

'That's not fair, Sir,' Suvodip said, and all of us turned to look at him, startled that he dared to challenge him.

'Is that so?' Viharjee Sir replied.

'Yes, Sir. How long do you expect us to hang around waiting for your classes when we never know if you're going to turn up or not? It's eighty minutes each time, we could be doing other things in that time, we could be in the library working. We wait for weeks for your classes and we get tired of it, it's no wonder some of us wander off. Of course there are some students missing today, what do you expect? But just a phone call will bring them back here in five minutes. It's unfair to call us irresponsible and worthless because of this.'

'So now I have to listen to you?'

'I'm sorry Sir, but I think it's about time you did. You've got our futures in your hands. You do the same thing every year. You fail students on purpose if you don't happen to like them so that they can't get the good jobs or get near the good companies. Every year some of us are left unplaced or placed in some run down company that pays badly or that has a lousy profile. Everybody here knows what I'm saying is true.'

'Yes, Sir,' Bibek raised his voice now, 'take Suvrojit Mondal for example. Three years back, you failed him in the sixth semester and failed him again in the review of the paper. He couldn't sit for good companies till he cleared the paper again the following year. For two years now, he's been working in the worst profile companies and looking for an average profile job. It's the same story every year for someone or other. I'm sure today will be the beginning of the same old story for our class too.'

'If the same thing happens again,' Viharjee Sir shouted, 'it's only because you stupid people deserve it! You shouldn't be absent from class.

'Absent from a class that never takes place. How does that make us stupid?' Suvodip asked.

I looked at Sir. His face was red with anger now.

'I'll screw your future! You don't know me.'

'We all know why you do this to your students,' Bibek replied.

'Yeah, that's right, we know,' someone shouted from the corner of the room.

'We won't let this happen to us!'

'We shall stand up against your whims and fancies!'

'It is high time now!'

They shouted from every corner. People started using their mobiles and in a few minutes the missing students came into the room.

'Sir, I don't personally feel that way.' We looked around to find out who had spoken and it turned out to be Prateem.

'What do you mean by that?' Suvodip asked.

'I just don't feel the way you do. Is it mandatory that we should all think alike? I think Viharjee Sir teaches very well, and you lot are talking rubbish.'

'Hey Prateem … sit down or go outside,' the students shouted together. He left the room after, of course, first getting permission from Viharjee Sir.

'Sir,' Bibek said, 'we know that your son couldn't get admitted to a good college and so is still jobless. That's why you want us and our futures to be doomed! You want to take your bitterness out on us.'

'We'll see who comes out of this best. My subject is one of the hardest in the curriculum, and the companies are going to keep coming here, and they're not going to be impressed by students who haven't passed it. So, you'll be the losers, not me.' Viharjee Sir drew in a deep breath and left the classroom, leaving the door wide open and banging.

Everybody fell silent and we all looked at Suvodip who was sitting on his desk and staring down at the floor, smiling slightly. Since he'd handed me the rose three years ago in our welcome ceremony, we hadn't talked to each other. I felt like congratulating him and patting his shoulders for his courage. He too, got up and left, and so I thanked him in my mind because without his intervention, perhaps Viharjee Sir might have been able to collect the names of the absentees.

Thinking about bullies like Viharjee Sir, reminded me of when I was in third year in our Electronics class. The teacher at the blackboard was only two years older than us. We called him Nilanchal Sir. He received his B. Tech degree from an average engineering college. Now that should never happen. A B.Tech holder teaching in a B. Tech degree college! He should have some degree higher than that. We called him Nutty.

He was teaching bipolar junction transistors. I was sitting with Baishali and Ananya on either side and Bibek and Bidesh were behind us. We were copying the circuit diagram from the blackboard.

'What is that thing?' Bibek whispered in my ear.

'Which thing? There are things all over the board.'

'That thing labelled drain.' he said.

'I think I missed it,' I replied.

'You are idiots!' Bidesh said, 'drains are things which drain bathroom water to safety tanks!'

'What?' we all, including Baishali and Ananya, burst out into laughter.

'Outside go. Go now. Out of room all of students go!' Nilanchal Sir shouted. Slowly, we all moved out of the classroom and walked towards the college gate.

'Why does the college take teachers like him?' I asked.

'Yes, why do they? They can't even speak in proper English,' Baishali said. 'Outside go, go now!'

'I think it's probably that Viharjee Sir hires them for a very low salary,' Bidesh replied.

'Yes, he's a mean old man,' Bibek said, 'he'd never spend money to get good teachers in here, look at the state of the place anyway. When do you think it was last painted?

'Did you notice Prateem in the classroom?' Ananya asked.

'No. Why, what was he up to?' I asked.

'He was doing his usual cunning smile,' she replied, 'when we were told to leave. He is so …'

'Disgusting!' Bibek added.

'Hey!' Bidesh said, 'have you guys thought anything about Rahul?'

'Rahul Bose of our class?' Baishali asked, 'what about him?'

'See,' Bidesh began to explain, 'His family hasn't got enough money to pay for his college fees. For the past two years he's been paying his fees by selling property for some company or other, and now he told me he's reached the point where he really can't do it anymore, can't afford to study and he's going to pack it in and leave. He's desperate. He gets such good grades too.'

'Why didn't he apply for a scholarship?' I asked.

'Even for scholarships you need to show a minimum family income. His condition is worse,' Bidesh replied.

'Third year now. The fourth year is yet to come. How will he manage?' I asked.

'We must do something,' Ananya said. 'Let's collect money from everyone in college. All juniors and seniors. I'm sure everyone will help.'

We decided to talk about this to all the batches, and when we did, everyone agreed to help Rahul, except, of course, a few. The fourth year guys were the batch mates of Aritro. That batch didn't create a problem since Aritro handled everything. The first year guys were the fresher batch, fresh and helpless. Hence, they paid up willingly and without a fight. We were the third years and none of us created any problems except for Prateem. He rose up angrily to his seat and said, 'Why should I suffer for an irresponsible student? Is he my headache?' He banged the door loudly behind him and walked out of the classroom.

The only batch left to be convinced about the idea was the second year guys, Triparna's batch. We entered their classroom. She was alone sitting on a bench meant for two.

'Guys we have come to collect some money for Rahul Bose of our class,' Bibek began, 'he can't afford the college fees anymore and we really don't want to lose him. Any small contribution will do. But try and feel his condition by placing yourselves in his position. What do you say?'

There was a silence for some time. They looked at each other and after discussing it for a while, said, 'We agree. Okay. We can't let this happen to him.'

I was very happy. It was a job well done.

'No, wait a minute. Money doesn't grow on trees,' Triparna said suddenly, 'I'm sorry, but I can't support this campaign!'

'Ok Triparna, just think if you were …' I tried to say, but she stopped me by raising her hand.

'These boys should know what they can afford and what they cannot. Who told him to get admitted to this expensive college?' None of us could ever imagine talking like that in such a rude tone and to seniors. We were dried off words. 'But still if you insist. Here. Take these five hundred bucks and go. I am doing this because I have moral values!' she said, and threw the five hundred rupee note at us.

There was pin-drop silence in the class. I couldn't believe what I just saw.

At one and the same time I admired and loathed Triparna for her dismissal of one of our best students just because he was struggling with money, yet her generosity in giving so much of her own money to our campaign was puzzling, but again, throwing the money at us as if we were dogs or beggars was terrible. We decided not to take it and left it lying on the floor and walked out of the classroom without a word.

I remember how humble and timid I would be when a senior talked to me. When I was in the first year, a fourth year senior boy disturbed me every day. I would be called out of my hostel by him and made to stand every evening in the college park until dinner time while he asked questions about my past crushes. I found it unbearably irritating and yet I always answered him politely.

One evening, when he was getting drunk on the volley ball field, and I was walking towards the canteen to get some coffee, he called me over. I couldn't pretend I hadn't heard him because I'd jumped at the sound of his voice and stopped on the path, and so I walked to where he was, feeling scared, and I stood in front of him. He was drunk. He caught hold of my hand and made me sit beside him and watch him drinking more liquor. I was helpless in the situation and was forced to talk stupid talk with him. I kept trying to inch away from him, and he kept grabbing me and pulling me back closer to him and saying, 'Hey, baby, where do you think you're going?'

'I don't know what you mean,' I said.

'You're trying to wriggle away from me like a little fishy, aren't you?'

'No, I'm just a bit uncomfortable, and cold.'

'Cold? Well come closer and I'll warm you up, Baby. Come on; don't be so timid, do you think I'm going to bite you or something?' He reached over and got me by the wrists and pulled me violently towards him.

Just then, someone from behind got hold of my shoulders to help me get up and we ran, holding hands, across the field to a safer place. He was my second year senior and none other than Aritro. We were not in a relationship then but I was slowly beginning to like him.

I was thrilled that he'd saved me. I was shocked as well that he could show such courage in front of a fourth year guy who was his senior as well. It must have been highly embarrassing for that guy as we run away from him. We could hear him shouting behind us, but we didn't pay any attention to it and he was too drunk by that time to follow us.

The next day, before class, Bibek caught up with me. 'Dishari, you know Aritro, don't you?'

'Yes, of course I do. I saw him the other evening.'

'Look, can I talk to you about something. Just come by the canteen for a second.'

Bibek looked slightly strange and so I followed him, but I had the feeling it was going to make both of us late for class. 'We better be quick,' I said.

'You said you saw Aritro last night, Dishari. Someone told me they'd seen you with him as well.'

'Yeah? So what's this all about?'

'Some fourth years and him. I'm trying to work out what happened.'

'Well, if this is about fourth years, you know that vile fourth year guy, the one who drinks? He got me to sit with him on the volley ball field while he was drinking and I couldn't get away, and Aritro rescued me from him.'

'That'll be it then. Some fourth years beat Aritro up late last night and he's not coming into college today.'

'How badly was he beaten?'

'He's covered in bruises and his face is swollen up and his lip's cut badly.'

I didn't care about being late for class anymore, I didn't go to it; I went over to the library and sat at a corner table with my head in my hands and thought about Aritro for the whole morning.

✦ ✦ ✦

Back in the black prison van that night, the sky was alive with stars. I'd been staring at the full moon. Kalpita was shaking me. 'Where did you disappear to, Dishari? We're at the prison, wake up.'

The van had stopped and we could hear the prison guards tramping towards us as the doors were opened. We were ordered to follow the guards who took us to a small locked gate. One of the guards unlocked the gate and as we walked through it, two female guards were waiting for us inside.

'Even the women guards are imprisoned behind this gate,' I whispered to the others.

'Don't talk now,' Kalpita replied, 'you don't know what they'll do to us.'

The gate opened onto a big empty lawn with a huge banyan tree at the centre of it. We were marched across the lawn towards a building, and the same guard who'd opened the first gate opened the building, and we were taken into a vast and dilapidated hall by the female guards. It seemed to me that they themselves didn't have access to any keys and so they were as much prisoners as we were.

'My name is Kanta Singh,' the man with the keys announced. 'You will see me every day, in fact several times a day. I check that all prisoners are present and that none of you have escaped, although of course escape is completely impossible. Nevertheless, that is part of my job.'

He stared at each one of us in turn and I didn't know what we were supposed to do. Introduce ourselves or smile at him?

I gripped my bag tightly because he was staring at it and it contained books and notes for the next day's exam. I was very tired after our two days of exam, arrest, lockup, media and court and my eyes were beginning to hurt me. I walked into the hall with Tanusri and Kalpita. I noticed that it had dull yellow walls, the kind of colour that could drive you crazy if you had to sit looking at it all day long – a colour that made me think of despair and boredom and sadness. The floor felt very cold and thirteen prisoners and a small girl were fast asleep on that floor, and all they had around them were dirty blankets like the ones we'd been given in the lockup.

We walked towards the end of the hall. A tall woman in a sari covered with a green shawl, came up to us. 'Take these,' she said, and gave us three very worn-looking blankets. 'I am Shakila. You can call me Shakila Aunty. I am the in-charge of this place. I will treat you the way you treat me, if you behave in a decent way, things will go well, if you behave badly, it's going to be tough for you here. Go to sleep now. Let's talk tomorrow.'

16. CHAUVINISM!

Morning 28th December 2010

I am sitting under the banyan tree now. I don't feel hungry any more after skipping the nasty tasting tea we have for breakfast. I regard this place as a dangerous adventure but interesting at the same time. I am learning a lot about the lives of different people who I wouldn't have met normally and I'm grateful for that.

Every time I write something in my diary, I feel better in myself, but at the same time, little things upset me as well that wouldn't do if I wasn't here. Stupid things become important, like when Nazma moved my blanket from where I'd left it and I thought it'd been stolen, because all of a sudden around here, things are going missing, and I shouted at her, and then I felt sorrow about it but it was ages before she'd accept my apology. But even so, I feel that each day I'm developing inwardly. I feel I'm becoming mature and I love this change.

Rekha Di told me yesterday that when she was brought here, the guards didn't ask her age. They simply told her she was fifty-five and wrote something down in a book, and when she said she was only twenty or maybe thirty, but definitely not fifty, they told her to be quiet and said what would she know about anything anyway? She said she's been curious about it ever since and one day she asked Heera Aunty what she thought because she knew that she was more than fifty-five herself because she'd heard her saying so. Heera Aunty told Rekha Di that she should thank her stars that her age was almost doubled by those men. There's a jail some place in West Bengal (Rekha Di couldn't remember the name exactly but said it sounded like Aalua or Halua) where Heera Aunty was posted two years back as the female guard. She said the male prisoners there used to bribe the guards so that at night they could freely molest and torture the women prisoners in any way they fancied.

When I heard that, I was almost shivering with fear and disgust. I thanked *my* stars that I hadn't been flung into a place like that. I was feeling very angry indeed with Viharjee Sir yesterday. We three have been abandoned by the college, a place that is supposed to be nurturing and protecting us as young people on the verge of starting our adult lives, and instead it's put us into a situation where we could get raped by men, how bad can that be! And what kind of advertisement is it for adult life that he can do such a thing?

A thought: Women don't matter one bit in society, they never have. Men stomp about with their great inflated egos, shouting and kicking up dust like buffalos and making wars, and doing just whatever they want – nature created them like that all full of spit and fight – and the societies we live in make sure that women are there just for the purpose of serving men, and punishes them or even kills them off if they dare to do otherwise. I wish I could do something about it ... at least tell Mamma. I am feeling so horrified. I want to lie down and think about it all. But Papa isn't like that at all, so maybe some men are really fine and gentle and other men, most of them maybe, are plain brutal.

When I finished my jailhold work this morning, I noticed that my hands were hurting me a lot, much more than they were yesterday; the joints in all my fingers were in pain, they still are, and I think they are beginning to swell up. I should take a bath now, rather than writing this, because I'm filthy with all the dust and muck, but I know the water's extra cold today and so I'm reluctant to do it.

Oh, I meant to make a note about the water supply here, so I didn't forget it. Water's available in the morning at eight-thirty and cut off again at ten-thirty. Within these two hours we're expected to finish any of our work which needs water. So we store some water in a big tank and use it from there throughout the day and we have to be very judicious with it because it's so precious, and we take a bucket of water into the hall in case we need some in the evening when we're locked in.

An argument took place a couple of days ago in the hall between Rekha and Nirupa Ruidas, our Oh So Clean.

Rekha: Where is my toothpaste? I always keep it over here. Who's taken it?

Oh So Clean: Here. You mean this?

Rekha: Why have you used it without my permission?

Oh So Clean: I haven't used it, I just picked it up.

Rekha: Oh dear toothpaste, do you have wings? Nirupa, does it have wings?

Oh So Clean: I don't know what you're talking about. I've never used tooth paste in my life! Why should I take it? In the morning I just gargle with water. If I needed to, I would use the soil from the lawn.

Rekha: You dirty thing. You could get ill that way; don't you know there are diseases in the soil? So why have you got my toothpaste in that case?

Oh So Clean: I don't know what you mean *got it*.

Rekha: I mean it's in your hand, stupid. Why is it in your hand?

Oh So Clean: I picked it up to show you, Rekha, what's so wrong with that? You asked where it was, I was trying to help.

Rekha: I don't believe you. You stole it, and I don't think that's the first thing you've stolen around here, so you better watch out because I'm going to be keeping my eyes on you from now on.

Oh So Clean: You can't go calling people thief whenever you feel like it, you can't prove it.

Rekha: So what's that white rim round your mouth, then, a new kind of lipstick?

End of the duel. Rekha left the hall. She was talking to herself. Oh So Clean sat down slowly on the floor and stared straight ahead. I really could not help laughing. Tanusri laughed too, and I was glad of that. Kalpita was biting her lips and *trying* not to laugh. I better go and take my bath before the water goes altogether. My toenail is not going to drop off, the black is fading away now, I'm so glad.

Afternoon December 28th 2010

I have just finished my dinner. It is only half past four now. This is how things are here in this dreary place, one has to have dinner at this odd hour, and it doesn't matter if you are hungry or not. We had our lunch at one o'clock, only three hours ago. I long for some decent food, or even some fresh fruit, anything but the terrible stuff they serve us up. I've swopped two pencils with one of the knitters for a small ball of wool, and I'm going to try to darn the biggest hole in my blanket using my compass to make little holes all around it to thread the wool through. I hope it works.

Tanusri wanted me to see some abandoned rooms that she found today. There are five of them and they're behind the hall. I've never noticed them before. All of them are bright red inside. They're very tiny and completely empty. I didn't like them. I can't imagine what they were used for, but they don't look like storage rooms and they aren't old toilets. Tanusri sat down in the middle one and I didn't want her to stay there. I asked her to get up and come back with me, and she said it was the most peaceful place in the whole prison and she wanted to sit there for a while. So I left her, but I felt really depressed, and before we went there I'd been feeling good; I had my blanket project to do and I was thinking about other things I could swap for wool so I could mend more holes, but by the time I walked back into the hall I wanted to cry and I had no idea why except that a great cloud of sadness seemed to have settled on me like dust.

Evening 28th December 2010

It worked, it looks really lumpy, but the big hole is covered now and I've still got some more wool left. I'm really pleased about it. Later on, I turned over some of the pages of my diary to read what I'd put in about Nabarupa. I remained sitting for a long time with the diary open in front of me and thinking about how it came to be that I was so brimful of rage that I wrote about her in such complete detail. Someday, I'd love to be able to ask her why she thought she was unloved, and how she imagined trying to harm herself would help.

It is around six. Rinki sleeps quietly in her ammu's arms and so does everyone else in their thin blankets. They are shivering in their sleep, with clothes piled up under their heads to act as pillows in the little space allotted to them. I can't sleep, and finally I can write about Aritro without being disturbed. I saw him this afternoon. My eyes had tears flooding the corners when they met his eyes. He had come with his helpless hands to hold the fine mesh between us, all the way from his work place in Raigarh ... to touch my fingers through the fine mesh … to see me cry through the fine mesh … to watch me smile through the fine mesh. He looked tired. His eyes were swollen; he must have cried a lot in the past few days. I couldn't speak, all I could do was gaze at him, and live each second I was with him. Neither of us knew when we'd see each other again. Those ten minutes that we were together come back to me time and again when the love between us was so powerful that words became meaningless and so were not spoken.

17. TERRIBLE DREAMS

Night 28th December 2010

I'm so glad I have my precious diary with me so I can write things down; I've just had the weirdest dream and it was so vivid it was almost as if I could've reached out and touched her – it was Nabarupa. I saw her in front of me, clothed in rags, her face thin, her eyes worn-out looking and tired. She gazed at me sadly and I could read in her eyes: 'Oh you said we were friends. How, then, could you scold me? Why, then, didn't you stop your friends when they were scolding me? Oh how horrid of you to treat me the way you did! So what if I left the toilet dirty or kept the main door open? So what if I played loud music? So what? I took you as a friend. And you scolded me!'

I saw her expressions changing. She looked at me with big and angry eyes now. Her eyes told me: 'Now I've got all I wished for. And now you are burdened with a terrible fate. I have been chosen to live, and you to die. Now suffer in your misery, Dishari Saha!'

I woke up from the dream and I was sweating profusely. It was only nine o'clock; I heard the bell chime. I clenched my teeth together to make myself feel courageous. I couldn't stop thinking about it – and here, it has come back to my mind again. I keep seeing Nabarupa's big cow-like eyes staring at me and I can't free myself from them.

It is strange that I should often see such vivid images in my dreams here. First, I saw Triparna, dressed like Muhammad bin Tughlaq, hurling me from one end of the room to another, and now I dream of Nabarupa who seems to be like the symbol of my sufferings. Terrible dreams these are!

Whenever the new shift of guards come in from outside the prison with the wind in their clothes and the cold on their faces, I bury my head in my blanket to stop myself thinking about when I will be allowed to leave. This morning Manju had her hearing and she returned from court happy and full of high spirits. She got bail, and the minute she told us, we started thinking about her in a different way, it was almost as if she'd accomplished something impossible. I noticed that some of the other women seemed to treat her with new respect. I don't know about anybody else, but I had mixed feelings about it, I was glad for her of course on one level, but I couldn't feel properly happy for her because I was so jealous. Even this evening she was still talking to everyone about how it feels to get bail and what she'll do once she's permitted to leave tomorrow. I think Kalpita and Tanusri were irritated with all this talk and chose to go to sleep rather than hear it. Apparently, Manju – the rice eater as we call her, was brought here on charges of theft. But it's her husband who's the thief and both of them were granted bail today. We call her the rice eater because she eats a lot and always asks for a share from everybody else's meals and rice is her favourite food. She once told me she loves rice so much that she could eat it with just salt and chilly. I can't imagine what that would taste like, neither can I imagine how happy she must be feeling right now.

The bell rang nine times just now – nine o'clock. I've realised that all goes well with me on the whole, except I have no appetite anymore. The other prisoners keep telling me I don't look well at all. I think they're doing their best, making sure I have my food. So now whenever I have to eat something which simply won't go down, I put my plate in front of me, pretend it's something delicious, look at it as little as I can, and before I know it, I've managed to eat. Whenever I wake up in the morning, which is the most unpleasant thing in winter, I move out of my bed quickly, promising myself that I will be back here again shortly after I've been to morning attendance and done my jailhold work.

My nerves keep getting the better of me though. The atmosphere sometimes becomes so oppressive. I feel as heavy as lead and so *tired* these days. Sometimes I can't hear even a single bird singing and a deadly stifling silence hangs everywhere. I feel as if this silence is pulling me down into a terrible underground place. At such times, I wander from one end of the hall to another, and then out onto the lawn, or I go downstairs and up again several times and then back again to walk the hall. I think sleeping is the best option to force time to pass more quickly, and to make the silence and stillness go away for a while, even though there is no way of getting rid of them completely.

It annoys me that I am so dependent on the atmosphere here. And I'm sure that it's not just me … I think we all feel the same way. I was reading my diary a while back. It struck me that I'd been having frequent mood swings lately. Sometimes I am furious with everyone and at other times I think I'm going to choke on my own boredom – my throat literally closes up. The other day, I really tried to fight with my boredom, I sat and stared at my fingers and I was trying to remember the games Papa used to show me with his hands when I was little. He could make birds, little people, houses, churches, but I couldn't remember how to do any of them.

We had a bit of excitement this morning around eleven o'clock. The entire place began to stink very badly. I thought I had been smelling something horrible for some days, but not strongly enough to say anything about. This morning, though, none of us could deny the stench; it was the worst thing I've ever smelt. It was like fermented human waste, rubbed on the armpits of a sweaty, hairy bear. We looked all around the place to find out where it came from. Some women thought that it was our Oh So Clean though it is impossible for a living human to generate such a nasty smell.

It was Heera Aunty who spotted the dead cat beside the waste bins behind the hall. She called us all over to look at it. It had decaying flesh all over its body and we hung back from it. Maggots were wriggling in and out of holes in it everywhere, busily, as if they were in a little city. I turned away quickly and just as some of us turned to walk off, she ordered us to stop because she wanted one of us to pick the thing up and take it away from the Female Ward and throw it into the rubbish pit next to the Male Ward. Of course, no one volunteered, we all had our backs turned to the stinky thing. She told us to turn and face her and we had to do it.

Then she called out Rekha's name and made her step forward, and Rekha's face was a real sight. I was much closer than I wanted to be to the cat and I was trying hard to hold my breath and not breathe in the stench, but I was beginning to feel light-headed and wobbly. The smell seems to be sticking to my nostrils even now as I write. I just can't come out of it. I wonder how the male prisoners are feeling about the stench. I hope they don't pick the thing up and bring it back over here. I'm sure when this cat was a kitten it used to be really cute. But now that it's dead, it's nothing but a stinking burden for the rest of the world. I need to stop thinking about it right now, it's depressing me.

I miss so much being in here, so very much. I long for my freedom and some fresh air and some decent food and some proper conversations and kind words. I have so much to tell Mamma, Aritro and friends. Everything in here is so different from ordinary times and ordinary people's lives. When I lie down and think about the many sins attributed to me, I get so confused by it all. Just this evening, I learnt what the world thinks about me, and I can't decide if I should laugh or cry with the cruelty and horror of it all. I just wonder what Nabarupa and Triparna are doing now, those two crazy women who, between them, were the cause of all this, I don't suppose they've even given it a second thought.

18. TEN LITTLE FINGERS

On the day of my last exam, the 22nd of December, after I'd finished writing my paper, Rupak came to visit me. 'You know,' he whispered, 'your mother called Viharjee Sir yesterday.'

'What? Mamma called? Who told you?'

'Your mother calls me and Bibek often to ask about you and the exams and stuff.'

'So what did she call him for?'

'To ask him to withdraw the case against you all. She pleaded with him. She told me all about it. I hardly dare tell you, but he laughed at her.'

'He laughed?'

'Yes. He said that since she was the mother of one of the convicts, he'd expected her to call and that he was waiting for the other two mothers to call as well, but there was no point in pleading with him and crying down the phone, he wasn't going to drop the case and that was the end of the matter.'

'Something is seriously wrong with Viharjee Sir. He's a sick man!'

'I could never imagine that he can be so greedy! He only cares about *his* own reputation and nothing else. It's so cheap on his part to push his students into these conditions. I've never seen or heard anything like this before.'

'He's our *teacher*?' Bibek said putting his hand on Rupak's shoulder, 'Someone who should be *protecting* his students than putting them into trouble?'

'Shame on him! Really!' Rupak said.

'Not only him, Rupak. Shame on *all* those in our country like him who can go to *any* extent for personal reasons.'

'I can't imagine that Mamma cried before him and all he did was to laugh it off!' I said.

'It's making me burn with anger whenever I'm thinking about it,' Rupak said.

'How can he be so much obsessed with his selfish desires before a mother who is crying for the sake of her child?' I said.

'That makes it clear, Dishari,' Bibek said, 'that it isn't for Nabarupa's sake that he's doing all these. It's not that he feels that Nabarupa is a poor girl who was tortured. He's a selfish bastard! He sees his own benefits in this.'

'I'm feeling sorry for Mamma, Rupak. He's just like the villains we watch in movies, isn't he? She's a weeping mother on her knees in front of him and he's standing laughing at her.'

I felt terrible and furious and sad all at the same time and I wished Mamma had stayed out of it and never called him and humiliated herself on my behalf like that.

Everything upset me again later that evening and I was burning with anger. The news about how the outside world thought about our case had not really penetrated through to us until then, and I'd always thought it was best to remain as cheerful as possible and just get on with things in jail. I mean what else could we do? Even though I felt twisted inside that we should be here when we were innocent, I was prepared to try to bear it with dignity. It never occurred to me that there was another sickening layer of punishment waiting for us.

I switched on the television and for a change from the regular idiotic Bengali serials I was watching a news channel and none of the other prisoners who were watching complained. The weather conditions were depressing outside, not that that mattered to us. The first cricket match between IndRed and IndBlue was to be held in the Vidarbha Cricket Association Stadium at nine o'clock the next morning. Good, glad to hear it. I was about to change the channel when a middle-aged woman reporter appeared, hosting a show called 'Crime Files'.

The reporter began:

'Now here's a story of how it's just not the boys who enjoy ragging. Three students of the Royal College of Engineering, Durgapur, who have been accused of ragging and filming an MMS clip of a first year student getting undressed, have spent six days in police custody. The arrested students were produced in the Durgapur Sub-divisional Court today. This is the first case in West Bengal where three girl students have been arrested for ragging another girl student. Nabarupa Dash has alleged that she attempted suicide after being tortured both mentally and physically on the night of the 15th of November. All the three accused are final year students of a B. Tech. College. Sources say that the accused girls were asked to vacate the hostel. The primary investigations have revealed that the three students were involved in ragging.'

They showed our college and few agitated students. But what did they mean by primary investigations? My eyes were fixed to the television screen. I couldn't move. My hands turned cold. I could feel the other prisoners staring at the three of us. I turned quickly to look at Kalpita and Tanusri.

The reporter continued:

'This is one of the rare instances where the college authorities took strong action against a complaint of ragging. There have been numerous instances when campus officials sat on complaints, even when the victim had died, committed suicide or was critically injured.'

They'd interviewed people all over India and this is what they thought:

Shiva (Kolkata): A very good job by the college administration of convicting the girls and sending them to jail. It is a big lesson to colleges all over India and this case will be an eye-opener to the future.

Navin (Chennai): They should be put into some jail where there are mostly hard core criminals and rapists. Only then they will repent and understand the meaning of fear.

A.K. Mitra (Gujarat): I congratulate the authority for taking appropriate action. We have seen that in spite of having laws, institutes do not proceed to take action for fear of losing reputation. Now let the law take its own course. An exemplary action should be taken against the accused if they are proved guilty in court.

Souvik Mallik (Durgapur): The difference between the West and India is that mostly Indian girls are from very traditional backgrounds. Any type of MMS, real or fake, means destruction of their lives. It will become impossible for their parents to find a good match for them in future.

I want to cry out aloud before all of them that there *was* no MMS clip. Of all the wrong that had been done to us, of all the lies told, and the way Viharjee Sir had treated us, what Triparna had added to the mix was somehow the nastiest part. She'd seen an opportunity to damage Tanusri and me and she'd taken it. I found that I was digging my nails so hard into the palms of my hands that I was almost drawing blood.

The reporter continued:

'Sreeparna Banerjee, a third year student said today to our reporters: We are very happy for the actions which I believe are true and appropriate. They have ragged us and now ragged our junior. They deserve this for making a dirty MMS clip. They have done this with us also.'

'Who is Sreeparna?' Tanusri asked.

'Be quiet a minute, will you?' Kalpita said. 'I want to hear all this rubbish.'

'The President strongly condemned ragging in educational institutions and made a strong pitch for an end to this "criminal and disgraceful practice".

'Sankar Basu, Officer In-charge of Durgapur Police Station, said that the police had taken up the case after the college authorities lodged the police case. The girls have been charged under sections 306, 511, 143 and 34 of the Indian Penal Code, and bail is not possible for these charges. They were produced in the court on the 9th of December and sent to jail custody.

'Ujjwal Kumar, another first year student of Birbhum's Mallabhum Institute of Technology, jumped off the second floor roof of his hostel on the same night. He was allegedly ragged and thrashed by a senior.

'Ujjwal, who is in hospital, is in coma. He jumped off the hostel roof after dinner and was found lying in a pool of blood. No complaint has been lodged, in this case, yet.'

At this point the programme moved to another crime report in Jharkhand. 'But who is Sreeparna?' Tanusri asked again.

'Write these numbers down, Tanusri,' Kalpita said, 'quick before I forget, 306, 511, 143 and the other one was 34.'

Tanusri wrote them on her arm with her biro. 'Yeah, but Sreeparna? Who the hell *is* that?' she asked.

Kalpita shrugged. 'They made it up, someone gave them the name and they believed it. I think it's meant to be Triparna. Maybe she supplied them with that name. Complete fiction and the public are even more sheep-like than the press itself and so they're going to believe Sreeparna Banerjee exists.'

'How about that student from Birbhum's Mallabhum Institute of Technology who's in hospital in a coma, and no complaints have been lodged against whoever ragged him,' Tanusri said. 'He really did try to commit suicide. Not like Nabarupa.'

'Viharjee Sir must be happy now,' Kalpita said.

'How do you mean?' I asked.

'Everyone is praising the college authorities. He is now the ideal for all Indian colleges. He might even get a double promotion for all this hype.'

'Can you believe Nabarupa did this to us? She was always so fond of me,' I replied. 'Everything has gone haywire.'

'Oh I think you're wrong about her, Dishari,' Kalpita said, 'I don't think she's as innocent as we thought she was.'

'If I'd known she was so disturbed,' Tanusri said, 'I would never have talked to her or said anything about her vile habits that night. I've been thinking hard about what we said to her, and sure, if I'd been her, I'd have been embarrassed, but that's all. Anybody else having to live around her would've said the same thing. Don't you think?'

'Yes, Tanusri, none of this is your fault,' I told her. 'But I'm so angry, I can't tell you. How can those people say such cruel things about us? And what is the MMS thing? And those codes – we've got to find out what they mean.

We fell silent for a while and then Shrimati Didi and Champa Mashi came closer to us. 'What do you mean by M ... M ... ?' Shrimati Didi asked.

'And who is the man you're talking about, what did he do to you?' Champa Mashi added.

I looked at Kalpita. She stood up and walked away towards the other end of the hall. I turned towards Tanusri, but she'd settled down to sleep with her blanket and put it over her face.

'MMS means Multimedia Messaging Services,' I replied, 'a way of sending messages to and from mobile phones.' The two women stared at me blankly and I suddenly felt silly. 'Video clips then, do you know what those are?'

'We don't understand all these equipments, mobiles and so on. I'll bet they're a lot of money to buy,' Nazma Bibi said, coming up behind Shrimati Didi.

I didn't feel like having a conversation with them. I was feeling angry and depressed.

'I'll bet Shakila Aunty could sort out this man for you,' Champa Mashi announced, and that made everybody laugh, including me.

'Yes,' Nazma said, drawing her finger across her throat, 'She could fix him good. So what is it that you girls did, you've never really told us. You're famous, aren't you? So it must have been a really bad, bad thing you did.'

'Nothing. It's all made up stories. All rubbish!' I replied, and I lay down beside Tanusri. Then, I heard a loud noise coming from the hall gate, and with the others, I went to see what was going on. Kalpita was having an urgent conversation with a man I hadn't seen before. 'Please, let me have it just for tonight, I'll return it tomorrow,' she was saying, 'I promise.'

'It's the Deputy Superintendent,' Nazma whispered, 'I wonder what he's doing here today.'

'Deputy Superintendent of here?' I asked.

'Yes, of course of here, silly. He usually comes once a month to look in on us.'

I watched the man smile at Kalpita and thought him unlike any other man I'd seen in this place; he was dignified and quiet. He handed her a book between the bars of the gate and went away.'

'What − what − what?' I asked her, 'what is it?'

'Guess.'

'I can't, come on, tell me.'

'It's only the Indian Penal Code manual. We can find out what we're charged under now.'

We went back to the corner of the hall were Tanusri was sleeping and woke her up, the other women had drifted off and so the three of us were alone. 'Give me a number, Tanusri,' Kalpita said.

'What? Oh! 306,' she said, looking sleepily at her arm. 'Why?' I handed her the juice bottle that I kept with me and she took a long drink from it.

'306, abetment of suicide,' Kalpita read out. 'If any person commits suicide, whoever abets the commission of such suicide, shall be punished with imprisonment of either description for a term which may extend to ten years, and shall also be liable to a fine.'

'Did you say ten years?' I asked. '*Ten years!*'

'That's what it says. 511. Punishment for attempting to commit suicide with imprisonment for life or other imprisonment.'

'What the hell does that mean?'

'No idea. 143. Whoever is a member of an unlawful assembly, shall be punished with imprisonment of either description for a term which may extend to six months, or with a fine, or with both.'

'*What?* What unlawful assembly, being a student, what?' Tanusri asked.

'Listen to this one. 34. Acts done by several persons in furtherance of the common intension of all, each of such persons is liable for that act in the same manner as if it were done by him alone.'

'So these are the different cases against us,' I said, 'and Rupak told me that our lawyer wanted to change one of them, he mentioned 309 when I saw him last, find that one, Kalpita.

She turned the page and read out: '309 is attempt to commit suicide. Whoever attempts to commit suicide and does any act towards the commission of such offence shall be punished with simple imprisonment for a term which may extend to one year, or with a fine, or both.'

'Ok', I said, 'so 309 means that Nabarupa should get punished for committing suicide, or trying to. Suicide is a crime … yes?'

'Now I understand what these numbers actually mean,' Kalpita said, 'I'm even angrier. What on earth does unlawful assembly and common intention mean? It's all complete rubbish!'

'I think it's Viharjee Sir by himself doing this. He lodged the complaint, right? So he's the one who must have decided which laws to get us under,' Tanusri said.

We fell silent for a moment trying to understand the insanity of it all. 'I've always been afraid of Viharjee Sir, his eyes give me the creeps, but I couldn't imagine him treating anybody like this,' I said.

'I think I forgot to tell you this small thing,' Kalpita said, 'my father heard that Viharjee Sir told the reporters it was he who'd taken Nabarupa to the hospital!'

'One of her classmate's took her on the back of his bike,' Tanusri said.

'Remember Nabarupa's uncle?' Kalpita asked suddenly.

'Pishoi? Yes. How could I forget that *Mr. Haley* from *Uncle Tom's Cabin*?'

'That's another conniving bastard. There's no one who comes out decently in this saga is there, whatever their age or status? Nabarupa wanted to be noticed by the world and she managed that all right. Triparna wanted revenge, and she got that with her horrible lie. Viharjee Sir wanted to be seen as the head of an excellent and modern college and that little fat man, Pishoi, was probably looking for more status with his family.'

'God! It's so depressing!' I said.

'I don't want to hear anymore of this,' Tanusri whispered. 'I've had enough. More than enough.'

'That's not the end of it though,' Kalpita said, as if she hadn't heard her, 'it's like a disease in this country, corruption, I mean. Even the hospital has made something for itself out of the situation. I think it made a false medical report for some extra money.'

'What the whole hospital?'

'No, I mean someone there who was looking after Nabarupa, idiot.'

I suddenly realised that Tanusri had crept away and left me and Kalpita alone. I looked around for her. 'Tanusri's in a bad way,' I said. 'She can't deal with all this stuff anymore.'

'What's she doing now?'

'Gone to sleep, I think. She was crying a lot earlier. She shivers all the time as well; she's really frightened by all this. I'm worried she might catch something if she carries on this way.'

'Yeah, I'm worried about her too,' Kalpita said, 'but what can we do?'

'We've just got to try to be optimistic, and maybe watch what we say in front of her a bit.'

'Yeah, of course, but it's hard, I'm feeling really depressed and I've got to talk about it sometimes. Give me the juice Bibek left you, would you?'

I handed it to her. 'He left it with the guards. I didn't even see him, and that's what's depressed me today. I wanted to see if he had any news from the outside. I crave for it.'

'When are visiting hours?' she asked, handing me back the bottle.

'I think it's from nine to four,' I said. 'Our friends are really trying to fight for us out there, there's a petition going round apparently.'

'I know. They're great, and they've got to think about exams as well as all this stupid idiot stuff!'

✦ ✦ ✦

That night, I couldn't sleep at all, my brain felt bruised. I'd been missing Mamma, and thinking of her a lot. I hadn't seen her for ages and I knew she'd be in a complete panic about me and not eating properly. God knows how Papa was feeling, I was sure he wasn't sleeping either.

I felt sick with shame that I'd brought all this on my family, but the instant I felt shame, anger came roaring into me because I was *innocent*, we were all innocent. Sometimes the mixture of shame and anger was so strong that it hurt my stomach and my throat and gave me a headache as well.

All this had done something weird to my brain. I was thinking twice as fast as I used to and I could barely control the thoughts I had. It was like being haunted, I kept thinking about the accusations against us, about begging Pishoi there on the road – being on my knees in front of him – and in Viharjee Sir's office, on the floor again. Triparna's big flat face and her twisted smile kept drifting into my mind and Nabarupa was always there in my thoughts with her funny staring eyes. Even the bathroom and the way she left it came back to me and I went over and over what we said to her that night until I thought I'd scream with it, and there was nothing, absolutely nothing we did that you could possibly call ragging. I wished so hard that night that I could be a child again. I remembered when I was small, Mamma would sing a bedtime song every night and I would soon fall asleep …

Ten little fingers,
Ten little toes,
Two little ears,
And one little nose,
Two little eyes,
That shine so bright,
And one little mouth to kiss …
Mother goodnight,
Goodnight, goodnight.

19. GOOSE BUMPS

I was still worried about Tanusri. I don't know what the day was, a Monday perhaps, and she'd been sleeping for a long time in the corner of the hall. She'd bent her body as much as she could to reduce the effect of the cold. 'We're innocents, Sir,' she murmured in her sleep, 'let us go.' There was the usual expression of fear and helplessness on her face and a deep frown on her forehead. I was sitting next to her trying to write my diary, and it was just before four o'clock. 'Wake up Tanusri.' I shook her. 'It's dinner time.'

She sat up slowly and rubbed her eyes. 'What?' she said. 'I want to sleep.'

'Dinner. Get up; you know the guards are going to start screaming at us in a minute to come out with our plates and so on.'

'I hate all that clashing and banging. Why can't they just do things quietly?'

'I don't know. Boredom maybe?'

'But they're so angry all the time and it's not as if any of us give them cause.'

'Are you two coming?' Kalpita asked, walking over to us from across the hall, 'a wonderful dinner has just been made for us all, aren't we lucky? We had a glorious lunch, just a couple of hours back and now they want to feed us some more to make sure we're not still hungry. I think I'm going to go insane in this dump soon, I want to scream all the time, or break something.'

I tried to smile at her and she pulled a face back. We took our plates and formed a line with everybody else. Shakila Aunty was serving the food. We had only found out recently that she was a prisoner like us and had been in prison for two and a half years. That's quite a long time, and she'd been given the role of dealing with the problems and quarrels of other prisoners. She had to do all kinds of things like close the windows every day, make sure prisoners did their jailhold work properly and serve out the food. She couldn't have been paid for this, and so someone whose job it was to do all this had passed it on to her. Anyway, she did the job well enough, but I kept wondering what her crime was. So I asked Shrimati Didi, and it turned out that she'd committed three gruesome murders with blunt instruments. Wow! Knowing that, made me stare at her to see if it was possible to recognise such a destiny in the lines and plains of the face itself.

After Shrimati Didi told me, I tried to work out how a serial killer could be as polite and responsible as her. It was like trying to do a tricky jigsaw puzzle, and I couldn't put the bits together. Most of the prisoners had false charges against them or they'd been put into situations where they had no other option *but* to commit crime. So I wasn't willing to believe that Shakila Aunty really was a murderer at first; I slept in the same room as her at night, she was really quite close to me, maybe only five women away. 'She isn't really,' I said to Kalpita, 'I mean she hasn't actually killed anyone, surely?'

'What on earth makes you say that? You're hurting my arm, Dishari, stop clutching me, will you?' We were walking around the lawn together.

'Well because all sorts of women get thrown in here who haven't done a thing. What about us for example?' I asked her.

'I talked to her about it. She really, really is one. It's no use staring at me like that. She *is*. She killed three men. Ask her yourself if you don't believe me.'

'I wouldn't dare! How could you just go up to her and ask her … ?'

Kalpita laughed and took my hand off her arm. 'Because otherwise how would I know?'

'So she really is?'

'Really, truly.'

'Well, did she say why she killed them?'

'She said she killed them because they were men, what other reason did she need she asked me, and then she did her laugh, you know?'

I couldn't tell if Kalpita was joking with me or not because she had her expressionless face on.

Now, as Shakila Aunty slopped the food onto our plates, I looked at her again, but she just looked like any woman of her age. Then she looked straight into my eyes. She knew exactly what I was thinking, and she smiled at me and winked and it made me blush very hard.

'Just look at the wonderful food,' Kalpita whispered as we three sat down on the hall floor to eat, 'this roti has already become so hard that I can't tear it off. Impossible.'

'But it's free of cost! Criminals always have bad food … don't you watch movies?' I asked.

'Hey, Dishari. We're not criminals, ok?' Kalpita said. 'Just keep remembering that, and you especially remember that, Tanusri.'

'The entire world can't be wrong, right?'

'Be quiet and show gratefulness for our food,' she whispered back, looking around to see who was listening to us.

I fell asleep for a short while in the afternoon and woke up from another terrible dream. Thousands of rats were running after me. I was running for my life … and very fast, faster than I'd ever run before. I was running through streets, and alleyways, across stinking puddles and around corners, and through marketplaces full of people who shrank away as I came towards them. The rats were fast too, coming in a great swarm behind me. So, I had to run faster still. I looked back and to my horror, the rats had changed into a pack of vicious wild dogs and then into wolves and next they became a great colony of scabby bald-headed vultures. I realised that they represented the press men and women who had been hounding us three.

I woke up and found that I was screaming, and that scared Rinki and she cried out loudly, and her mother was angry with me for a while – she said she was feeling sick and was having awful pains in her stomach and needed all the sleep she could get. My face was wet with sweat and I couldn't stop shaking, or get back to sleep for a long time after that.

While I was writing my diary this morning I engaged myself in some deep thinking about the order of events before our arrest. It was on the 14th of November that I was so happy after a great class test. I felt that everything was good about the world and my place in it. The next day, Nabarupa slashed her hand, followed by the heated episode with Nabarupa's uncle and aunt, and the tense meeting with Viharjee Sir in his office, and then facing the crowd of agitated students and Triparna's attempt to make matters worse. It was on the 7th of December in the evening that we three were so excited about being able to take the exams and then when we'd finished them, we were immediately arrested. After the night in the awful lockup, we found out what it means to be harassed by the media, made truly frightened by them. And following all the tension and waiting and uncertainty we had about bail, we were finally brought here to this prison.

What if we don't get bail this time? I can't imagine what it would be like to spend another fourteen days in this disgusting place. I have no expectations, though, after I saw the news on the television and Kalpita quoted the exact meanings of the charges against us. Our friends are trying as hard as they can to help us with their signature campaign, I do know that much, but will it help us? I just hope Mr. Sood is able to please the public prosecutor with those signatures.

I hope, pray and write most of the time these days, I've grown tired of talking to the women in here; I've got so little in common with any of them that it's a struggle to know what to say. They talk about money a lot and the different ways they know of making money, little tricks they have, things they've seen other women do on the streets. I don't think they really like the idea that we're engineering students; they think only men should do things like that, yet they half admire us for it anyway. Champa Mashi said that if we kept thinking in that way all the time about maths and sums we'd probably end up not being able to have babies and we'd regret it in the end. She's just like Heera Aunty in a way.

I'm having a weird feeling that I'm living through a very strange winter indeed, for while it's cold, I'm experiencing it as if it was really hot – as hot as a bubbling bed with the heat of confusion and all the terrible tension and agitation. Maybe that's an exaggeration, there have been funny moments here in prison and tender one's too, so 800 degrees Celsius – bubbling bed hot, as it's called it in engineering – is a bit extreme I suppose, but one thing's for sure, I'm tired of suffering here.

This evening, before Kanta Singh locked the gates, I was just flipping through the pages of my diary. Kalpita came over to me. 'My father came to visit me this afternoon,' she said.

'Oh, I'm dying to see my papa again. I can't wait.'

'No, listen, Dishari. You won't believe what he told me,' she said.

'Why, what is it? It can't be that bad.'

'It was; it was terrible.'

'Don't frighten me, Kalpita, tell me what it is! I can't take any more surprises.'

'It's about college placement fees.'

'What do you mean? There are no such things as placement fees, Kalpita.'

'That's where you're wrong. When we leave college, we have to pay fifteen thousand rupees each as a placement fee to Viharjee Sir,' she said.

'Fifteen thousand! That's outrageous; I'm sure no other college asks for money like that.'

'It's more outrageous than you think, because our college used to take five thousand rupees from each student who got a placement, and this year it's been trebled.'

'Papa never told me a thing about placement fees. What if you or your parents *can't* pay?'

'Then you don't get clearance, and that just means you don't get your B. Tech certificate, so you don't get a job, do you?' she said.

'I wish you'd never told me that. But anyway, we don't even know what's going to happen to us. I can't bear to think about it right now, let's not talk about it until we get out of here, or I think I'll go mad. By the way, have you seen Tanusri this evening?'

'Yes, you know those dilapidated single cells behind the hall, those tiny ones with red walls? She's sitting in one of them. She went there after lunch and she's been there since.'

'What on earth is she doing over there alone?'

'Someone told her the cells were where they put the prisoners who were sentenced to death and were going to be hung,' Kalpita said.

'That's giving me goose bumps!'

'Yeah, same happened to me when Tanusri told me about it. I asked her to come back into the hall and she wouldn't. It's really morbid.'

'Let's go and bring her back then,' I suggested. I remembered the feeling of sadness that came over me when Tanusri first took me to the little rooms.

'No, let's wait until Kanta Singh comes to lock us in, then go and get her,' Kalpita said.

After the evening attendance, when the Female Ward was locked up, I saw Tanusri, sitting quietly, facing the wall; she'd come away from the cells by herself. She was murmuring something. I went and sat by her side and placed my hands on her shoulders.

She turned slightly to face me. 'Yes, what do you want now, Dishari?'

'Kalpita and I are worried about you; she said you spent half the day in one of those nasty little cells with red walls, the ones you showed me a while back.'

She shuffled around to face me fully then. 'Oh Dishari, don't worry about me, that's the one place in this prison I can tolerate, it's so quiet. You know I hate the noise and banging, and shouting.'

'But why do you go there alone? You could have called us to go with you.'

'I don't want to be with you two all the time, you talk a lot and complain about things, there's no point in complaining, what's going to happen to us is going to happen. There's nothing of interest for you there in the cells anyway.'

'So what's interesting for you about those creepy little rooms.'

She looked at me for few seconds. 'I like to imagine the women who were sentenced to death. I think I can see them actually. I think they come to me if I wait long enough.'

'Eh? How do you mean, Tanusri?'

'I like to think about them. I imagine them locked up. There's one little cell in particular, the one on the end, you see. You can feel the women who have been in there, almost touch them. You just have to close your eyes and reach your hands out slowly.'

'I think you should stop doing that right now, it's weird and horrible, and it's not good to be on your own in this place.'

She turned her face away from me and I dropped my hands from her shoulders. 'They're company,' she said.

A sudden shiver went through me. 'Imaginary women are company?' I asked her as gently as I could. 'What about Kalpita and me; aren't we company enough for you?'

'I see them moving around in that cell and we talk about our lives, and they give me lots of hope and courage. They say that if something ends badly, then it hasn't really ended at all because all endings are happy endings and you just have to have patience and wait.' At that moment she lifted her face slowly and looked straight into my eyes, and she seemed truly happy. 'See,' she continued, 'now I don't cry at all like I used to do, and I know my crying annoyed you both, so you should be glad for me.'

'No, don't say that, Tanusri. Of course we were worried about you, but this is even more worrying. These women aren't *real*. Kalpita and I are real.' I put my hand up to brush her hair away from her face and she flinched almost as if she didn't know who I was any longer, as if the ghosts of the condemned women had claimed her for their own. Neither Kalpita nor I had realised how bad things had become for Tanusri, I thought we had been looking after her, but it seemed she preferred the company of women who didn't exist to ours.

So many problems were hovering around me. The biggest was our hearing. We'd heard that people all over India were praising Viharjee Sir as if he was some prophet or wise man and that was making me very angry indeed. I'd have done anything to have been able to expose him for the liar he really was. Yet, I knew I had to try to control my feelings. It was hard though; I was helpless and yet brimful of rage and the combination of those feelings was hideous and all I wanted to do was run away and get lost somewhere.

Of course, out of everything bad taking place, the sudden and surprising visit of Aritro gave me fresh hope. His visit meant he was still there by my side and loved me as he did before; the world couldn't turn him against me. So I was trying to stay happy, thinking about as many good things as I could because I resolved to try to do positive thinking as I had written about it in my diary. It would've been terrible to have started to behave like Tanusri who was becoming more and more unapproachable, and shouldn't have been in the prison at all but in a hospital where she could've been properly taken care of. But perhaps you have to be a little mad to think happy thoughts in an institution like Asansol Special Correctional Home. I even hated the name of the place. When I tried to look back on myself from before we were arrested, it was like looking at a child with no problems in the whole world. Twenty or so days in prison had turned me from a girl into a sad older woman. So what it would've been like to have been in prison for ninety days like so many of the others was unimaginable to me. But Shakila Aunty had been in prison for a lot longer than that.

I was very nervous about the 31st, I imagined my friends seeing me looking haggard and dirty as I stood in the courtroom in front of everybody. There weren't any mirrors in the prison, so none of us knew what we really looked like – what the prison had done to our faces. I imagined that my face was distorted and my lips weirdly bent downwards; that I looked like a really old woman. We probably smelled of this prison as well, because it did have a kind of dreadful smell all of its own.

20. A RESOLUTION

Evening 29th December 2010

Early this evening, just before Kanta Singh visited the Female Ward to lock us in the hall, a woman called Anima was brought in as our new inmate. Her clothes were dirty and she looked very untidy with her dust laden skin and unkempt hair hanging down her back in great matted clumps. Her eyes were red and swollen and we could see that she'd been crying a lot. She is lying in one corner of the hall now without a proper blanket to cover her. She's using Nazma's old sari to comfort her for the night. But I don't think that it is close to being comfortable.

I can hear her crying from time to time, but the noise is feeble and pitiful, like the mewing of a kitten. We've all tried to make her feel better by giving her some of our food we've stored up for night and by talking to her, and taking her mugs of water from the bucket. But it doesn't do much good, she rolls over and says she's all right, but she's not.

Shakila Aunty repeated her famous line about the jail being a game and asked her what she'd done that she'd been put in here with us. She said she's very poor. Her husband, who was a water seller, died recently in a road accident and since then she's had no source of income at all. Sometimes she begs for money. Often she cleans roads and gets a bit more money, just enough to live on. She has an eight years old daughter to look after.

A couple of days ago, she had nothing to cook food with, but she had a bit of rice and a few onions, and her daughter was starving, hadn't eaten anything for two days. So Anima went to steal lumps of coal from the stockyard of some industry not far away from the place they lived in. She said that it was a common practice among people she knew, her neighbours, but she'd never done it herself because up until then, she hadn't had to. She thought that a little coal for her daughter would not harm the big industrialists so very badly. Apparently, she was caught. While the others who were with her managed to escape, probably because they were good at it, she, being inexperienced, couldn't flee fast enough. And after a day or so inside the lockup where she was thrashed by the guards, she was brought here to us. She could hardly finish telling her story when she thought of her daughter, and started crying again. She was terrified that some man, or some gang of men, might steal the little girl, she said she was very pretty, she could easily get kidnapped. She'd often seen men gazing at the child with that particular look they have.

I felt terrible thinking about her daughter, because she would be about the same age as Tutul and the idea of someone stealing her is unimaginable. Or what if Tutul solely depended upon me, and I suddenly disappeared from her life? I thought about my sister – her huge eyes with their intense expression came to my mind and the way she always calls me Di-Di. I am thankful to God that Mamma, Papa and Bubuli are around to take care of her.

Night 29th December 2010

I've just woken up because there's a wild cat in the hall somewhere, I can't see where it went. It ran straight over my body and across my face – trod on my face. I thought it was a giant rat at first because it was a brownish colour and its tail was thin, and it looked like it had bad mange. It scared me, those filthy animals can bite, but I didn't want to wake anyone up and make a fuss about it because people were bad tempered today, so I started writing again to keep myself calm. Tanusri was telling me the other day that she's seen horrible mangy cats entering the hall at night before. They're getting in through the two broken windows. They might have rabies, and if they do bite or scratch any of us, then we're in serious trouble. There was that dead and stinking cat that Rekha had to take over to the rubbish pit by the Male Ward. They never did bring it back over here, I'm glad to say. Perhaps the cat died over there in the first place and one of the men had been sent over to put it by our bins to get it away from theirs. We hardly ever see the male prisoners; we just occasionally get a glimpse of them. We're as curious about them as they are about us I expect. The ones I've seen look very ordinary, like men you might see on the street selling things, and if the same thing is happening to men as it is to women in this city, then they aren't dangerous criminals at all, anymore than we are.

It's dark outside, pitch black in fact. I have to go to pee in the toilet attached to the hall. But I don't think I dare go alone, and everybody else is sound asleep, even the new prisoner. Tanusri's imaginary women have come back to my mind. She nearly had me believing in them because she talked so convincingly about them, and this is exactly the kind of place that would have ghosts if they existed. The funny thing is that what Tanusri claimed her ghost women were telling her about endings only being happy events was something I once read in a spiritual column of a magazine and I really liked the sound of it. If the end is not beautiful, it is clearly not the end because all endings are happy. That is true positive thinking, and while we have to be in this place, I have to start practising positive thinking.

I want to make some serious resolutions. First, I shall always think positively and let this positivity in me overcome all the negative thoughts and emotions around me. I will try to be happy about the conditions I've been put in here and find out the good things about this place. I know I've said this before and written about it, but I've really got to try this time, and it's not so hard to do, I've already found out a lot of positive things. The other prisoners are kind, they look after us as if we were their sisters, and yet us three have a much greater chance in life than they have. We've got proper families who will support us and I hope we've still got a chance to have the careers we want and the independence that should be ours in modern India. And my experience of these prisoners is the exact opposite from what I've read in books and seen in movies where prisoners are savage and fight amongst themselves and rob each other.

The food we get here is really bad, there is no doubt about that, and I'm thankful Papa has managed to bring me fruit from time to time even though he has to bribe the guards to give it to me. But if at all possible, I'm going to try to find something positive about the food as well. Maybe there are vitamins in cockroaches, who knows?

Heera Aunty is very irritating most of the time. But I am thinking positively now, so I will put it this way that she doesn't beat me up with a stick or something hard when she easily could do if she felt like it, and she's got that pain in her knee and I should be more forgiving towards her.

We can't go outside the Female Ward but we can enjoy the open sky, the sun, the shade of the banyan tree and the fresh smell of the grass from six in the morning to five in the evening, after which we are locked in the hall. But then you could say kind Kanta Singh locks us in for our own safety because he wants to protect us from the cruel outside world. If I wanted to, I could get one of the knitting women to teach me how to knit, so I would leave prison having learnt a skill I didn't know before. Also, I have my closest friend, my diary, here with me, and I am able to write in it undisturbed for the most part, because the women are getting used to seeing me writing and are bothering me less about it now, and I get a great deal of comfort from it.

When I really look at some of the women prisoners in here I do wonder how they would survive out there on the streets, where they would sleep, how they would make money. Would they, in the end, have to become prostitutes? Just looking at little Rinki and her mother really does make me wonder. It's so obvious that Jalal has no intentions of saving them from this prison and that he's gone off and left them and probably got himself another woman. They don't have a home to go to when they get out of here. What will happen to them? As hateful as this place is, maybe for some women it is a bit like a sanctuary. There's regular food and men can't molest them easily and there's the company of other women and a television to watch and that's something they wouldn't be able to see out there on the streets. Maybe someday they could learn to read and write in a place like this, if some charity thought it would be a good idea, and I'll bet that could never happen if they were outside having to struggle and fend for themselves every single day.

Wow! I am so good when I am optimistic! I am great at positive thinking, it really works; I am feeling much better. I should tell Tanusri and Kalpita about it. Especially, Tanusri … she badly needs something to keep her strong. Both of them are fast asleep now of course. I think I should tell everyone about this great thing I've discovered. I will definitely tell them tomorrow.

Morning 30th December 2010

I am feeling very good this morning. I am very, very nervous, of course, because the hearing is tomorrow. The weather is lovely. I am sitting in my favourite spot under the banyan tree, writing. I am looking up at the blue sky and at the banyan leaves. On the branches, little dewdrops are shining like silver. The leaves are green ... the shade of this green is so lively. I love the word 'lively'.

Earlier on this morning we were discussing what each one of us will do once we are released. The other women had come over to us to wish us luck for tomorrow and we began to talk about our hopes for release and our dreams for what comes afterwards. Nazma said she'll look for her husband, Jalal, and that she is almost dying to see him. She seemed worried about him and what food he's having every day. It amazes me that she doesn't realise that he's gone and left her; he never came to court once when she was there. She looked a funny yellow colour to me; even the whites of her eyes looked yellow. I was about to say she should think about feeding herself properly first when she got out of prison, but I decided not to in case she thought I was being rude. Rekha said she'll go back to her mother but she looked sad and was unsure if she'll be accepted into her family again. I know that when I get out I'll go home and hug Mamma and eat some good food at last, and hug Papa, and see Bubuli and Tutul again and pay attention to them properly, I mean spend time with them. Then I'll call Aritro ... I have so many things to tell him. I have to talk to my friends too ... oh, I have a lot of things to do. Kalpita said that she'll sleep. I thought that was strange but that's what she has planned. She said she'll simply doze off for a week, and then wake up and start her life again, as if this weird thing never happened to us at all.

Tanusri isn't sure what she's going to do; she didn't want to talk about it. She said she'll decide later, and then she wandered away from us across the lawn towards the little cells. I hope she wasn't going to ask her ghosts for advice. Shrimati Didi wants to hug her son and cry her feelings out. I saw two huge tears race down her cheeks. When we turned towards Shakila Aunty, she covered her head with her sari and left us too. I hoped we hadn't hurt her feelings by talking about being released. I suppose we had though, and it's a very bad thing to do in this place as we're already in enough sorrow as it is. We were very thoughtless; Shakila Aunty isn't getting out of prison anytime soon.

I am breathing in the air, it is so fresh today. I think I have finally and fully become optimistic. I think the best remedy for those of us who are afraid, lonely or unhappy, is to go outside; somewhere we can be alone with ourselves, nature, God and heaven. Because only then does one feel happy and realise that God wants us to be cheerful and discover the beauty of nature. Nature is the best healer. No matter what the problem is, it is nature that provides solace in every trouble.

I used to condemn the bad weather. I hated bathing in the cold water. I found nothing amazing in the air, birds, leaves, water or anything when I was first here. I think I forgot about God and the presence of God in everything. I've decided that He has made me suffer and cry so I can feel Him ... call Him day in day out, intensively. Yes, I think He wants to see our intensity and I believe that this is the understanding He wished me to have. Now that I have it, He, probably, doesn't want me to suffer any longer. I have a firm belief now that we will get bail tomorrow.

21. AMMU-LESS WORLD

The day before our hearing Papa visited me unexpectedly and I, being so on edge, panicked. I knew he'd come up from Kolkata already, but I wasn't expecting to see him until we'd arrived in court. I looked at him through the iron mesh and could see that something was disturbing him. Usually, the very first thing he did was to put the palm of his hand against the mesh and I would lay my hand against his and feel his warmth. That morning, he hung back and was looking from left to right and frowning a little. I was instantly convinced that it was to do with the court hearing – that the date had been changed, and that we would have to wait for weeks more and he didn't know how to break the news to me. I felt dizzy for a moment and then suddenly quite sick and in a panic. I began to sweat and tremble. I felt like screaming.

'Papa!' I said. 'What's wrong? I know there's something, I can tell. Please don't keep it from me.' I banged my hand flat against the mesh several times. 'Something's gone wrong with the court date, hasn't it, just tell me! It's off tomorrow isn't it? That's what they've told you!'

'No, no!' he said. 'Stay calm, Dishari. 'It's nothing to do with the hearing. It's just that I don't know if I should tell you the news right now, right at this moment before the hearing.'

'Well, what is it then? You *have* to tell me. Is it something from home? Is it Mamma?'

'Your Dida was not doing well over the last few days, she was not eating and she was very weak.'

'You told me as much when you were here last. But she's okay now isn't she?'

'Yes, I did tell you, I remember.' Papa looked down. 'Look, last night, she died, darling. There, now you know. That's what it was; I didn't want to have to upset you before the hearing because you need to be strong for it.'

Papa looked up again and put the palm of his hand on the mesh between us and I stared at it and didn't raise my own hand; I was too much in shock for a moment. Dida, my grandmother was dead and I would never be able to tell her how much she meant to me and how I loved her. I didn't cry.

'In hospital?' I asked.

'Yes, during the night. We found out about it in the morning when we went to visit her.'

'Was there anyone with her when she died?'

'We don't know, Dishari.'

'I'll bet there wasn't, I bet she died alone.'

'We can't know. Maybe a nurse was with her.'

Papa gave me some money and some fruit and I went back to the hall thinking about Dida and for the whole day memories of her came back to me of when I was a child and used to visit her. Kalpita asked me what was wrong and reminded me about my positive thinking idea but when I told her about Dida's death she gave me a hug and said how sorry she was that a family death should happen while I was stuck in prison.

Later on as the sun was going down, Rinki came to sit with me. I think she sensed that I was feeling sad because for a long time she didn't say anything to me. We sat side by side and watched the golden and faded blue of daylight merge into the coming darkness.

'Count the leafs,' Rinki asked eventually, pointing to the banyan tree. 'How many of them?'

'What, *all* the leaves on the banyan tree? There are far too many to count, Rinki. Thousands of them. You'll be able to do counting yourself one day though,' I told her, putting my hand on her delicate little shoulder. 'Maybe you'll go to school as well. Would you like that?'

'Yes. Ammu will take me when she gets better. Ammu is sick now.'

'Yes of course she'll take you. When her stomach doesn't hurt anymore and she's well again. Then she'll hold your tiny hands and these tiny fingers of yours and take you to school.'

'Will Abbu take me too?'

I looked at her for some time and she looked back at me with such hope and innocence that it was hard to know what to say to her next. 'Oh yes, your abbu. Well, he's away working at the moment and he'll be back as soon as he's finished and then of course he'll go to school with you too.'

'Why doesn't Abbu come here now?'

'He's very busy with his job, but he will come.'

'When?'

'I don't know, Rinki.'

'I want to see him.'

'Yes, love, I'm sure you do.'

'So does Ammu want to as well. She told me.'

'Yes, she talks about him, doesn't she?'

'Ammu says he is coming here to get us out and take us away to live in a house.'

'Then I'm sure he will come, Rinki.'

'I love my abbu and my ammu.'

'Yes, Rinki, of course you do.' I smiled at her and she put her head on one side and looked at me, and at that moment the bell rang six o'clock. It was properly dark by then and the sky was studded with stars and they did seem to twinkle and shine very beautifully. It might have been the first time Rinki had really looked at the stars properly, and each time another one appeared above the banyan tree, she pointed at it and laughed. 'Count those things,' she said.

'One, two, three,' I began. 'They're stars, Rinki. Stars way up there in the sky.'

'What are they for?'

'What are they for? Well, I don't know, for us to look at maybe, to make wishes on. They … bring us hope for better things.'

'I've got another ammu. Choti Ammu.'

'Have you, Rinki? Your ammu didn't tell me about her.'

'But she shouted all the time, she shouted and shouted and shouted, and she hit me sometimes like Heera Aunty.'

'Oh, I'm sorry. Were you frightened of her?'

'Yes. I don't want her to come here, only Abbu.'

I watched her rub her sleepy eyes and I was glad she'd fallen asleep before the storm broke out and before she heard her ammu scream out in pain. Nazma's hair-raising cry startled everyone. She called out for help. She couldn't sit up, neither could she lie down. She began to hold her stomach and we could see she was in terrible distress.

'Get the guards,' Kalpita shouted, 'quick, something's really wrong with her.'

'What's the matter with you, Nazma, where is the pain?' I asked. She was too much in agony to give me any kind of answer. 'Shakila Aunty!' I shouted, 'please call the guards quickly!'

Kalpita, Shakila Aunty, and Tanusri ran to one of the broken windows and screamed out for the guards as loudly as they could. The rest of us sat beside Nazma and tried to comfort her. I touched her forehead. It was burning hot. 'Get this soaked in water from the bucket. Fast!' I gave my handkerchief to Rekha.

After about five minutes, Heera Aunty came to the window. 'What's all the fuss?' she asked, 'and at this time of night? What's the matter with you women?'

'Nazma isn't well. She has a terrible pain,' Tanusri explained.

'And a terrible fever too,' I shouted across.

'Have you tried giving her a cold compression?' Heera Aunty asked.

'Dishari is doing that now, but things look really bad,' Kalpita said.

'Things always look worse at night. Let's wait until morning, see how she is then. She's had stomach aches before, especially when she doesn't feel like doing her jailhold work, then she gets very, very bad ones.'

'Are you crazy? We need a doctor now,' I shouted. 'Please come into the hall and have a look for yourself, Aunty, you can't see anything from outside that window.'

'Call the doctor, and do it now, otherwise you'll be in trouble!' Kalpita told her.

'Don't you dare talk to me like that, girl!' Heera Aunty said. 'I can't do a thing about it. The gates are locked. I haven't got the keys so how am I going to go out to find a doctor? I can't even get into the hall to look at her, you stupid girl. You've got no choice; you lot will just have to look after her the best you can. It's not my fault so don't you go accusing me, little college girl. The minute Kanta Singh comes here tomorrow we'll be able to get a doctor to see her. So just get on with it, and keep the noise down will you. What are you, jackals or women?'

'You must be kidding me!' Kalpita answered. 'You're supposed to be the guard, and you can't do a thing to help us.'

'That is exactly correct. How clever you are to have worked that out, go to the top of the class.'

Nazma was shouting now and trying as hard as she could to sit up. I didn't know if I should help her to sit or try to restrain her and make her lie down flat. I wished so hard that Papa could be right there beside me to help. He'd know exactly what had to be done. I wondered if she'd burst her appendix; she was clutching her stomach so hard and her face had turned the colour of clay. I thought at any moment that the noise she was making would wake Rinki who was sleeping not far away from us.

'There is no point in talking to that stupid woman,' Kalpita concluded, coming over with the others when Heera Aunty had gone.

Nazma was silent now, but the pain was showing on her face and her fever was very high. Tanusri held her hand while Rekha went back to the bucket to dampen my handkerchief again. 'Bring me some water in a mug,' I called out after her.

'She looks such a terrible colour,' Tanusri whispered. 'I don't think she's conscious anymore, is she?'

'Try and lift her head, Tanusri,' I answered. 'Gently though. She is conscious. Her eyelids are moving.'

Tanusri, Shakila Aunty and Champa Mashi tried to lift her head while Kalpita and I massaged the base of her feet. The others were putting cold water on her stomach.

'I think it's getting worse with every passing minute,' Kalpita said.

'Shut up, will you,' Tanusri said, 'you don't have to state the obvious.'

'How are you feeling now?' I asked Nazma. 'Is the pain less than it was, do you think you could sleep? Rinki is all right. She's asleep over there. We'll look after her, you don't have to worry.'

She turned her head and tried to see where her daughter was lying, and a wonderful expression of love passed across her face, but it was followed immediately by a look of terrible fear that really frightened me. Tanusri saw it too and tried to catch my eye. I knew what she was thinking; the same as me. I shook my head as if to say I don't know what's going to happen.

'With your father being a doctor, had you ever thought of becoming one, Dishari?' Kalpita asked.

'Yes, when I was younger, for a while.'

'You would know better than us what to do for Nazma,' Rekha said, 'because of your father.'

'That's not true,' I told her.

'Doctoring would be in your blood. You should think harder about what to do for her. She's burning up, look and the handkerchief; it's bone dry again. Think, Dishari, think what to do.'

'All right. We're going to put the fan on and move her underneath it,' Kalpita said, 'there's nothing else we can do until morning. And Rekha, just because Dishari's father is a doctor, does not mean she knows anymore than you do about this situation, so don't put the problem onto her.'

Moving Nazma under the fan made no difference to her fever, she became weaker as the night went on. She drifted in and out of consciousness, but when she was conscious, she couldn't speak to us. We took it in turns to hold her hand. At some point during the night, a noisy wind began blowing through the broken windows and shortly after that, a storm rose up.

Around midnight there was a particularly loud clap of thunder, and her grip on my fingers tightened. She raised her eyebrows, widened her eyes and raised her body slightly in her struggle to breathe. Her eyes were still open as she died and abandoned her grip on my fingers. The end of her deep green sari moved slightly in the wind. Her inanimate form made a blurry vision through the tears at the corners of my eyes, but when I could look at her properly I saw that she was beautiful in her death.

I looked quickly over to Rinki and she was deep in sleep and smiling. Perhaps she was dreaming of going to school, escorted by her ammu and her abbu. There would be no one Rinki could get support from when she woke the next morning ... no one to hold the back of her head and massage oil into her face ... no one to run behind her with food when she refused to eat. She could now run around the prison whenever she wanted to, there would be no one to stop her and make her calm down.

We laid Nazma out as best we could with her arms by her sides. We combed her hair and straightened her sari, we washed her face and her feet with water from the bucket, we closed her eyes, and we prayed over her. None of us could sleep that night, we couldn't even think of it. We sat in silence around Nazma's body and then at about two o'clock Rinki woke up, although she'd slept through the worst of the storm. We watched her walking towards us with her tiny irregular steps and we made room for her. No one spoke. Rinki stared at each of us in turn and most of us were crying, then she stared down at her ammu. She frowned and blinked and seemed to look harder at Nazma, but strangely, she didn't call out to her, didn't ask her to wake up. It was as if she knew, as if she had accepted that her ammu was dead and that she was now in an ammu-less world. She sat down quietly by her mother's head and bent her face even closer to gaze at her. Then, after some time, she lay down beside her, and hugged her, holding Nazma's deep green sari tightly in her tiny fingers. She closed her eyes, and although she made no sound at all, I saw a tear form in the corner of her eyelid and twinkle like the stars had done earlier that same night.

22. HOME

My head throbs; I still don't know where to begin. On 31st December, in the morning, Nazma's dead body was removed by three men and Kanta Singh. We kept watch over her body until dawn came, and we watched over Rinki who slept beside her. Rinki was still sleeping on the dirty floor when her ammu was taken away from her.

Just as we were leaving, I heard Rinki cry out. She had woken up and was searching for Nazma. I wished I'd been able to see her before I left, to try to comfort her, but the van was waiting and the guards were shouting at us to hurry up.

Tanusri suddenly refused to go on. She stopped on the path and crossed her arms. 'That child is wailing for her mother, is nobody going to comfort her, hold her?' she shouted.

'That does not concern you!' one of the guards called back to her. 'Your only business is to get into this van; we can't wait here for you all day.'

'Damn you, but it does, we watched the child's mother die. Sat with her through the night. Don't you go telling me what concerns me, Madam! Don't you dare!'

Kalpita and I smiled at each other and stopped alongside her; it was great to see Tanusri rearing up again like she had when we'd been paraded in front of the arrogant doctor at the beginning of this farcical episode in our lives. Four of the female guards came marching towards us, got hold of our arms, and pulling us towards the van, pushed us inside.

We didn't talk to each other in the van, I think we were all dwelling on how Nazma suffered in prison and how she'd died, and I couldn't forget the sound of Rinki's crying.

We reached the court building and were taken to the stinking room where Kalpana Di was waiting for us. The reporters were not there and so we did not have to use our dupattas to try to hide our faces, and we were at least glad of that. Kalpana Di hadn't changed; she was the same arrogant bullying woman as she'd been when we first came across her, it was horrible having to look at her face again. She was not friendly with us at all, but I didn't care now; people's rudeness didn't count for much after our days in prison and the thought of Rinki being alone without Nazma. I had the feeling I was surrounded by terrible misfortune; death seemed to be all around me, first Dida and then Nazma, and so I felt pessimistic about what would happen in court; I had forgotten entirely what I'd written in my diary about trying to see everything in a positive light.

We walked up the stairs to the crowded courtroom. On the way I saw Papa and my classmates, but I couldn't look at them because I knew I would cry if I did, and I wanted to try to be dignified. A man in a red uniform with a long stick in his hand stood next to the magistrate who took his seat as we walked in. The lawyers did likewise and sat at their places around the huge green table, then after that, everyone else sat down. The last time I'd been in the courtroom I was very scared ... my face was almost covered, and so I hadn't been able to see everything that went on.

The man in the red uniform announced, 'Ragging case – convicts Kalpita Deb, Tanusri De and Dishari Saha.' He gave a letter to the magistrate and we three stood up.

'Sir,' our lawyer began, 'the petition before you carries the signatures of students who support the three accused.'

'Objection Your Honour,' the public prosecutor said, 'the students who have supported these girls are extremely young and shouldn't be allowed to govern the course of this case.'

'Objection sustained,' the magistrate replied. My heart began to beat very fast.

'Sir,' Mr. Sood said, 'the West Bengal government passed the Prohibition of Ragging in Educational Institutions Bill in the year 2000. With the new resolution, ragging will be liable to a fine of Rs 5000 or two years of rigorous imprisonment or both. Offenders may also be expelled from their institutions without any scope for re-admittance. A charge will be non-bailable only if the offence is punishable with three or more years of imprisonment.' The magistrate nodded his head. The room was deadly quiet. 'This ragging case will be punishable for two years. Hence, bailable. So,' he continued, 'considering the life ahead of these girls and that they are unmarried, I appeal for their bail, Sir.'

There was a long silence. The magistrate was writing something. I started to feel faint. I looked at Kalpita. She was staring at the magistrate and frowning hard. Tanusri had her eyes closed and her fingers twisted together. She was murmuring something to herself. I felt sick quiet suddenly and really did think I was going to faint, I looked down at the floor and tried to breathe deeply and slowly. I thought of lovely times with Dida when I was little.

'Given that they maintain peace in college premises and outside' – the magistrate read out what he had written – 'I grant them bail of Rs. 1000.'

I thought I must have misheard him but when I turned again to look at Kalpita, her face was crumpled up and her chin was trembling slightly. I felt like crying too, because at long last we were to be released.

Papa went to collect my clothes from prison the following day, but before he went, I asked him to see if he could find out what they'd done with Rinki. 'The little girl I told you about, Papa, remember?'

'Of course I do, it's tragic for a child to be in a prison.'

'Her being there in her beautiful innocence helped us all. She wanted me to count all the leaves on the tree and the stars in the sky once. Then, later, and we don't know of what, her mother died. That child has no one now. They'll have put her in an orphanage somewhere.'

Papa hugged me tightly. 'You've seen far too much of the dark side of life for a girl of your age, Disha. You've been very brave through this awful time.'

When he came back with my few things that somehow smelt of the jail, he took hold of my hand. 'Apparently, she's in an orphanage in central Kolkata, it's called 'God Cares.' He frowned and looked away. 'Let's hope he really does.'

✦ ✦ ✦

I am lying on my bed in my own room watching the fan go around silently. It doesn't squeak like the one in prison, the correctional home as it was called. Am I corrected? After those twenty-four days of hell, have I come out a different person? I think so. It's made me realise how much I am loved by Mamma and Papa and Bubuli and Tutul. All I have to do is walk downstairs and there they will be.

I am thinking a lot about the times when the media had attacked us and how we had finally survived through those situations. It terrifies me, especially now that I know about the interests of Viharjee Sir behind everything. I was surprised to find out yesterday from Papa the answer of a question that I had been thinking about lately. I was reading the newspaper when Papa wished me a good morning and then I put up the topic.

'Papa, what do you think the reason was behind the U-turn of the magistrate from giving us bail to sending us to the correctional home on 9th December?' I asked.

'Disha, that's how the world *is*. People want fame, popularity and recognition. And this, being the first case where girl students are arrested for ragging another girl, the magistrate and the prosecutor, both, wanted to create history by sending raggers to jail for the first time. Do you understand what I mean to say?'

'But would they not think about our future, even for once?'

'I'm afraid they won't. Their reputation is more important I believe. I'm certain that this is not the first case of injustice on innocents and will not be the last either. The system is all corrupted and we can do nothing about it. We can only be its prey.'

I thought about Dida suddenly today. She told me once that if you can find a path with no obstacles, it probably doesn't lead anywhere, and I think that's one of the coolest things I know. Now that I am at home, I can actually feel her absence in everything I do. I dialled her number three times when I first got home and couldn't understand for a while why she wasn't answering. I pictured her on her way down the long staircase in her huge house and tried to give her time to get to the phone, until, like a sudden slap across the face, I remembered that she was dead.

While I was in that rough and dreary prison, that place of ghosts and stray cats and weeping women, and bad tempered guards, I missed Kolkata terribly, even the pollution and the traffic and all that noise, and even the water flooding the roads in June. Sitting in that stinking yellow hall, I used to think about the Victoria Memorial, the Academy of Fine Arts, and the films of Satyajit Ray, Mrinal Sen and Rituporno Ghosh. And food was always, in fact forever, on my mind, I daydreamed about different dishes of fish curry and sweet yoghurt and I was always grateful when Papa was able to bribe the guards to let me have the fruit he brought me when he visited.

I've been hearing a lot about my college lately, reading about it in newspapers, and coming across internet articles about it. Apparently it has become a bit famous for banning ragging. And it's become a very popular place – of course Tanusri, Kalpita and I have faded away into the background now. I still see Viharjee Sir's face sometimes in my mind with his eyes as cold as the eyes of a shark. But we three did have a kind of revenge for what he did to us. We came out of university as eight pointers. When Papa heard about that he laughed out loud and Bubuli wanted to know what eight pointer meant. Papa explained that the highest point was ten and so we were really good students. Kalpita and I had no trouble getting jobs. We got placed in big companies, and I'm posted to Pune on the 31st of August to work for Thermozite Ltd. I was frightened I wouldn't get the job because the people in the company would've read about me in the papers, and so when I got my confirmation letter, I was thrilled. But it was harder for Tanusri to find work when she got out of prison. Eventually she managed to get a job in Madhya Pradesh, but when we were released she had a throat infection and had to consult a doctor and see a psychologist for a while. I found out that Nabarupa managed to pass her exams with a backlog. She failed in one subject and just passed in the rest. I still dream about her sometimes, and about the monster, Triparna, but I'm sure those dreams will fade away in time.

As I struggled throughout those twenty four days of captivity, I realised the importance of Aritro in my life. I love him much more now because he still loves me, even after knowing me as a jailbird, and I just wonder how many men would've stood by me under those circumstances. He has promised to come to Kolkata and celebrate our four years of love soon. I can't wait to see him; I'm going crazy with the waiting. Mamma is very fond of him and Tutul and Aritro make great friends. I know Papa likes him too, he just doesn't show it.

Last week, after seven months of trial, Nabarupa's family signed a compromise petition stating that the case had ended as a result of mutual understanding. This has proved us innocents. I strongly feel, whenever I think about it, that there are hard core criminals roaming freely in our society. Then why did *we* suffer so much though we did nothing? I believe everything that goes around comes around. I've read it in some magazine, or book, I can't remember where. Though I know that all these were unnecessary and that we shouldn't have been to prison, yet the very next moment I feel that my twenty four days stay in the correctional home definitely has some underlying purpose.

✦ ✦ ✦

I went to visit Rinki yesterday and took some little toys with me and some clothes I thought might fit her, and I brought her a book of paper that looked a little like my prison diary, and some pencils. The street the orphanage was on was hard to find, it was in one of the old, narrow, twisting streets in central Kolkata, the kind of street you'd never go to unless you really had to. I could still bring back to my mind her haunting cry as she awoke to find Nazma gone when Kanta Singh came for her. I know that that this dirty game of inhumanity, corruption and ill treatment goes on in prisons and perhaps hundreds of Nazma die every day, though not literally, but living under such conditions is definitely like struggling to breathe every moment.

I went by taxi to the orphanage, but the driver couldn't take me all the way there as the streets in that area are so narrow and full of people that vehicles cannot enter. As I walked through the last of the streets towards Princep Street, I thought of turning back several times, thinking that perhaps my going to see her would only bring back memories of Nazma that would cause her pain, or that my visit would mean nothing to her – that she'd have forgotten me. But having gone that far, I went on.

There were stinking piles of rubbish lining the edges of the streets and flies in great swarms were everywhere. Princep Street was noisy, full of litter and bordered by an untidy and irregular fence. I came to an old dilapidated building that I suspected could be the place because there were several small children, too young for school, yet old enough to grub about by themselves in the cracked playground in front of the building. Their eyes shone happily in their grimy faces as they laughed, screamed and fought with each other. The games they were playing overflowed onto the footpath and I walked around a group of kids doing 'ring-a-ring-a-roses'. I soon located the nameplate on the building's wooden door written in faded red and gold letters: 'God Cares'. When I knocked, a small, dark-haired boy in blue jeans and a discoloured once-yellow t-shirt opened the door immediately. 'Hi,' he said. 'Who are you?'

'I've come to visit a little girl called Rinki, do you know her? She must have been here for about six months now. Is there a grown up person I can talk to?'

'Rinki! Yes, I know that girl. She's upstairs playing with the other girls. Are you her ammu?'

'No, but I did know her mother a while ago.'

'Rinki says her abbu is coming to fetch her today. But she says that every single day, so no one believes her anymore.' He stared at the bag I'd brought with me. 'Have you got presents?' I nodded. 'Have you got one for me?'

I looked into the bag I'd brought with me and found a sparkling rubber ball. 'Would you like this ball?'

The boy smiled. 'Can I have it really just for myself without sharing with anyone?'

'Yes. It's yours if you want it.'

'Thank you Rinki's ammu! Thank you, thank you!'

'I'm not Rinki's ammu. Just someone who knows her. My name's Dishari. Is there an adult I can talk to?'

'Mrs. Gupta that will be. I'll take you there, but she'll be asleep because she always is until dinner time, and if you wake her up too suddenly she'll be cross and shout at you.'

The boy took me down a narrow pink-painted corridor that smelt of onions and urine, and onwards to a shabby broken glass door at the end. He pointed to it and ran off quickly. I knocked softly and waited a while, but hearing nothing I opened the door and looked in. Mrs. Gupta was asleep with her head on a desk. The window behind her was open and the flimsy curtains drifted in and out slowly in a garbage-smelling breeze. I stepped inside. 'Hello, Mrs. Gupta,' I said. 'Hello.' The room was tiny and apart from several boxes stacked on top of each other, the desk, a chair, and Mrs. Gupta herself, it contained nothing else.

'Who are you?' She had awoken suddenly and was blinking at me and rubbing the side of her face that had lain on the desk and was now raw-looking. 'We're not due for an inspection for two weeks at least, who let you in? You can't just come in like that.'

'I've come to see Rinki, a child let me in. I'm not an official.'

She straightened up and looked slightly friendlier. She attempted to smile at me, but it was a poor effort. 'A relative, you're a relative, a sister, an aunt maybe? She stood up and held out her hand. 'I'm sorry; I'd offer you a chair, only …. The child thinks her abbu is coming. She talks about him every day, I never imagined anyone *actually* coming here to enquire after her.'

'I'm not a relative, but I did know her mother.'

'Ran off and left the child, did she? They all do that, abandon their children. Have them, then dump them. Same story every time. Did you know that there are now twenty-five million orphaned children in India?'

'No,' I said, 'I didn't know that, but not all mothers have them and dump them as you put it. Rinki's mother loved her dearly. She died quite suddenly. My father is a doctor and from my description of her symptoms, he thinks it could have been cancer of the liver.'

'Well, that poor little thing,' Mrs. Gupta said, 'and such a nice dear little girl too. She's no bother to anyone. It's just so sad that she keeps thinking her abbu is coming to take her away. Come on, I'll take you to meet her. You're not a relative then?'

'I'm afraid not, Mrs. Gupta.'

'Ah well, never mind. Come along, then, come along. The children are all together in the playroom.'

The stairway was narrow and smelt of years of collected dirt and dust from the street. We reached the second floor and walked along another pink-painted corridor until I heard noise coming from one of the rooms. Mrs. Gupta led me there and opened the door. There were around ten girls of Rinki's age playing on the floor, but Rinki was not with them. I looked across the vast untidy room as I could hear the sound of weeping.

'There she is over there. She doesn't usually cry like that. Perhaps another child hit her. Did any of you hit Rinki? You'll be in trouble if you did.'

I walked towards Rinki very slowly so as not to startle her. I wondered how Mrs. Gupta could know what any of the children did if she spent all day sleeping until dinnertime. She would have no idea what happened to any of them. They could easily run away if they wanted to, or go anywhere unescorted throughout the city.

Rinki was sitting with her hands over her face, and so she didn't see me. 'Rinki, I don't like to see you crying.' I touched her head and she looked up at me and in an instant was hugging me, and I found that I too was crying. I hadn't expected to feel so deeply. Finally I stood her away from me and looked at her properly. She seemed a little stronger and taller. 'You've turned into a big girl since I last saw you Rinki.'

'I can count now too, Dishari Didi.'

'Can you *really*? That's very clever. Do you remember the great big banyan tree with all those leaves on it that you wanted me to count for you?'

She nodded and for a moment looked sad. 'Tree and stars, I remember. When Ammu was there.'

'Have you made some friends here?'

'Yes, lots of girls and some boys too, but not the ones who try to push me about.'

'Those girls over there are your friends?'

'Yes.'

'So why aren't you playing with them?'

'Wasn't feeling like it. I was thinking about my abbu. He's coming to fetch me today to take me to his house. Ammu is dead you know, so she can't look after me anymore, so Abbu must come and fetch me.'

I felt my throat close up, and for a moment I found it impossible to look at her face. 'Rinki, look what I've brought for you,' I said, 'lots of toys and a little book and some pencils, all of your own.'

'This will be for school,' she said, holding up the book, 'when Abbu takes me there. I've got my own bed in this house, Dishari Didi, can I show it to you?'

'Of course, Rinki, I would love to see it.'

She took the bag tightly in one hand and got hold of my thumb in her other hand and led me out of the room. Mrs Gupta followed behind us, beaming, but not speaking. Rinki led me back down the pink corridor and around some narrow corners past great rifts of dust that rolled away from our feet as we moved until we came to a room so full of little beds that there was no space between them.

'Dormitory,' Mrs. Gupta said. 'The girls must clean it themselves. No cleaner, we can't afford it, anyway, it's good for girls to learn housework for when they get married, so they can please husband.'

I felt a faint wave of nausea pass through me; I'd heard similar words before not so long ago. Rinki showed me her bed and her blanket and looked up into my face to see if I was impressed. In fact I was in a way. Life in the God Cares Orphanage was better than life in prison in many respects; Rinki had children of her own age to talk to and the food was better by the looks of her. Except that if it had been a choice between staying in prison and keeping her mother, or being in an orphanage without her that would've been a different matter to think about.

Mrs. Gupta drifted off to her office and I went back to the playroom with Rinki and sat with her for some time, encouraging her to share the presents I'd brought for her with the other girls. Before long, as she laughed at something one of them said, I glimpsed her as an older girl, and I had for a second, a strong sense that she would grow up to be a woman whose life would turn out to be a little better than that of Nazma's.

23. I WAIT FOR THEE

Aritro was working for Jindal Steel and Power in Raigarh and although we talked a lot on the phone, I hadn't seen him in person since I was in prison, six months ago. It was July, and he'd promised he would come on the 15th of August so we could celebrate our four years of being together. I can only pay tribute to all the lovers who manage long distant relationships for years; I don't know how they do it. I felt as if I was going mad waiting to see him. He wouldn't be in Kolkata for another one thousand, one hundred and four hours. If only he wasn't so far away – four hundred and eight miles.

I used to spend a lot of my time thinking ridiculous thoughts like how long it would take to walk to Raigarh from Kolkata. I imagined us meeting somehow, someplace, maybe by accident, and being so overwhelmed to see each other again that it physically hurts us. Mamma and Papa were very careful with me, and I suspect they thought my restless dreaminess was a result of my experience in prison. Of course they'd never allow me to meet Aritro alone, so I had no choice but to wait until he came to Kolkata. I couldn't just get on a train and go to Raigarh, although I knew Mamma did like him.

I could not find peace in anything I did, when I was inside the house, I wanted to be outside in the fresh air, when I was outside, I couldn't stand the noise, and wanted to be back in my room thinking about Aritro. I wanted to run to where he was. When I moved to Pune at the end of August, it was going to be even harder or maybe impossible to see him for months at a time. So we'd only have one meeting here in Kolkata on the 15th. I found I couldn't stand that idea. A few hours together, and then pulled apart again by circumstance.

I couldn't imagine running away from my home, at midnight, through the window. That was foolish. I needed a perfect plan to be able to meet him. First, I had to move out of Kolkata. The only place my parents would allow me to go alone out of Kolkata was Durgapur where my college was, but I'd still have to have a good enough reason to go there. And I needed a reason to be able to go there for a couple of days at least.

The idea I came up with in the end was that the Librarian's computer had crashed and he'd lost all the records of students who were issued with a clearance letter before leaving college that year, and so he was calling them to return to college in person and show him their letters, so that he could re-create his records. I could buy train tickets for Raigarh for Monday morning and get home again on Wednesday morning. It was a crazy plan, but worth it. I was going to lie to Mamma and Papa, but I just couldn't help it.

Telling the lie was awful because I did it with such cold skill. They believed me instantly and I felt thrilled and horribly guilty and very excited. Aritro, I thought, I am coming to you. I had to tell all my friends about my plan just in case my parents should call them, which was unlikely, but not impossible.

I was standing on Howrah station just next to a tea stall. The place was almost overflowing with people, and so noisy that I could hardly hear the train announcements. I could hear different dialects and languages amongst the din. People were pushing each other, quarrelling about seats, rushing around with crates and boxes and baskets. There were coolies in red uniforms, food stalls, weighing machines and sacks piled up on top of each other all along the platform.

I felt nervous and very alert; my train was supposed to come in very soon. I thought: What if something happens to me? What if someone kidnaps me? What if the train meets with an accident? Mamma and Papa would get the shock of their lives. I tried to drive these thoughts out of my mind, and the minute I thought of Aritro again, I felt strong.

I'd been thinking about his parents since I'd come out of prison. I was frightened that they wouldn't accept me because of it. I knew Aritro would stand by me even if it meant severing all connections with his family. But that was something I couldn't bear to think about. I wanted to be able to take care of the people who had cared for Aritro for all these years. I desperately wanted them to accept me.

I finally found the courage to be able to discuss the issue with Aritro on the phone. He told me it had been his mother who said that if he loved me he should go to the prison to see me. His parents had known what had happened to the three of us all along and had not judged us.

An eventful incident came back to my mind as I waited for my train. I was in the third year and Aritro in his fourth. Aritro and his batch were at a party held by some heavy drinkers who'd been suspended from their hostel many times before and had poor attendance records and did badly in exams. They were celebrating having got jobs against all the odds and against Viharjee Sir's deliberate attempts to see that they failed.

By twelve o'clock most of the boys had left the room puking, but Aritro was still there cleaning up the bottles and was more or less sober. Earlier in the evening there'd been a fight between a student called Bowery-Bum and one called Pinhead Potter. There was a knock at the door.

'That Pinhead bastard has returned,' Bowery-Bum said, staggering to his feet and lurching towards the door. Aritro told me that he grabbed whoever was at the door by the collar and pulled him inside and it turned out to be Viharjee Sir who had heard about the drunken party and come to investigate. The parents of all the party-goers were summoned to the college.

Things didn't go too badly for Aritro over this incident. He learnt that his father had been suspended for a month for breaking glasses after getting drunk when he was in engineering college himself. However Aritro's father hadn't known that his son had a girlfriend until Viharjee Sir told him about me. Aritro called me on my mobile. 'Disha, everything's okay, but you've got to come and meet my parents. We'll be in the park in ten minutes. Please don't be late, and wear something good.'

'I can't do that, not in ten minutes.'

'Please.'

'No.'

'Look. They know about you. Viharjee Sir told them and they're a bit upset that I hadn't said anything about you to them, and they had to find out from him.

'Oh God! That's not good.'

'Yes, so you see, you've got to come and meet them, Disha.'

It didn't matter how I looked. I put on whatever I found in front of me in my room and rushed to the park. There they were, waiting for me. All the three pair of eyes turned when I walked towards them. I looked at his mother. She looked like a damn serious woman, and she was staring at me as if I was a dreadful creature, a monster, a witch, who had snatched her baby boy out of her arms. I tried to keep my cool. It wasn't easy.

'Hello Aunty,' I said, standing in front of her. I managed to smile at them both. 'Hi Uncle.' I looked at Aritro, and he looked back at me helplessly.

'Dishari ... are you Dishari?' Aunty asked. Uncle was looking up at the trees. He did not seem interested, but I think he was.

'Yes ... but you can call me Disha,' I said and I looked again at Aritro. He'd started frowning at me and the message I got was that I shouldn't be informal with his mother.

'You know, don't you,' she said with her arms crossed in front of her, 'that Aritro got caught while he was drinking?'

'Yes Aunty.'

'If I had been you I would never have let him drink in the first place.'

This statement really struck me; she was challenging my ways. I could no longer be formal with her. 'Aunty,' I said, 'some new research done in England has come up with the idea that drinking could be good for you, well, drinking a bit that is, because it could help blood vessels work properly. Apparently they need nitric oxide to function well, and nitric oxide is in champagne. Something like that anyway.' Aunty was staring at me with her mouth open. 'Two glasses,' I went on, 'a day might be good for a person's heart and circulation – apparently.'

'That sounds quite ridiculous to me,' Aunty said. 'Sounds like an excuse for heavy drinking.'

'It's to do with the chemicals in the grapes,' I told her, wondering if I should go on and deciding to risk it. 'They say that if you drink a couple of glasses a day you reduce the risks of getting heart disease and stroke, and it can stop blood clots forming as well.'

'Everyone knows the English are total drunkards,' Aunty announced. 'I'm surprised you were taken in by that rubbish.'

'How do you know all this?' Uncle asked me. 'It's extraordinary.'

'My papa is a doctor. He regularly reads the Journal of the Indian Medical Association. I read it in there.'

'I see. Why didn't you become a doctor like your father then?' he asked. 'It would seem you have a flair for it and a big interest in it as well. And a very retentive mind which I am sure doctors need.'

'I hated biology. I left it after class ten.'

'Okay,' Aritro put in, 'Mamma, Dishari has an exam tomorrow. Can I please ask her to go now?'

I liked Uncle and I wanted to talk more to him. I frowned at Aritro. 'No Uncle. I don't have an exam tomorrow. Aritro's nervous that I might do or say something wrong here and so he made that up about the exam, I don't have one.'

'You talk a lot, don't you?' Aunty said. I didn't know if she was irritated by me or not.

'Yes, I suppose I do,' I said. 'But again, you see, talking is good for health too. Research says – well would you like to know what research says?'

'No. Thank you.' She scared me a bit with her strict tone. She turned to look at Aritro. He was still standing helplessly, not knowing what to say. 'You talk a lot more than what is required and that shows that ...' she was interrupted.

'Mamma, leave her be. She is really stupid!' he said, giving me one of his angry looks.

'Don't call me stupid, Aritro,' I said. 'I won't put up with that.'

'Will you let me finish please, you two?'

'No Mamma ... let her go, please!'

'Aritro! Just shut your mouth for a moment,' she said and turned to face me, 'as I was saying ...'

'Mamma please! Stop all this.'

She widened her eyes and looked at him once more. Aritro gazed down at the ground and waited for the important verdict to be announced. I was beginning to sweat now.

185

'Dishari ... or Disha, if I can call you that. My son is very naughty.
He has been like that since childhood. I want you to take care of this
fellow properly.'

I was spellbound ... highly surprised. It felt very nice. I was
accepted, and very well accepted. I returned to my room after that,
feeling extremely lucky.

✦ ✦ ✦

I concentrated hard, trying to hear the train announcements. My train
would be at the platform in another seven minutes. Just then my eyes
fell on a man in a blue T-shirt who'd just got off an incoming train.
I had the oddest feeling about him; I was so excited at the prospect
of being with Aritro soon that I was inventing him in front of me. I
asked the man at the tea stall where the train had come in from and
when he said Raigarh I was shocked. But it was only minutes later
that my imagined Aritro became the real Aritro. It was him all right;
there was no doubt about it!

'Aritro!' I called out. 'Over here, over here!'

He stopped and looked about for the caller, turning this way and
that. I picked up my bag and began to make my way towards him
through the crowds, calling to him still. Then he spotted me finally
and waved at me wildly and crazily. I saw him smile and then frown
and smile again as he tried to make his way to me, weaving in and
out of the crowd that had become larger now as tired passengers
from a train disembarked between us and moved slowly along the
platform with awkward luggage.

For a few minutes I couldn't see him at all. I stopped where I was
and waited for him to come to me. The crowd didn't like that, they
bumped into me and pulled faces, but I was so happy that I didn't care
what they did. At last Aritro reached me and we were like an island in
the moving people. We clung to each other for ages in silence.

'You,' he said finally, drawing back from me and kissing my nose,
'right here in the station.'

'You too,' I replied. 'What a fantastic surprise. My train is due in
a few minutes. I could've been on it and gone from here, and never
even seen you, Aritro.'

'Ah! I was going to call you and say, rather than just risk it. Now it's too late. I was stupid. But where you're concerned, I am stupid, I always have been. Where are you going? I see you've got an overnight bag with you.'

I beamed at him. 'Let's get away from this crowd before they crush us to death. Come over by the wall where we can talk.'

'I wish you could stay in Kolkata,' he said when we'd found a bench to sit on away from the noise and people. 'I was going crazy wanting to see you Disha, just to be with you for a few hours today. I jumped on a train this morning without thinking too much about it; I couldn't bear the thought of not seeing you again before you went to Pune. I've been so restless without you lately. So irritated with everybody at work. I haven't been able to sleep, or think, or settle to anything. I hate being apart from you.'

'Mamma and Papa think I'm going to Durgapur to show my library clearance letter at college,' I told him, speaking very slowly, and trying not to smile too broadly. 'Because the Librarian has lost all his records.'

Aritro shook his head and sighed. 'Your train's due now, then?' he asked, looking at his watch. 'We haven't even got a hug's worth of time together. Life is so cruel to lovers.'

'Look at me, Aritro.'

'I should get back to Raigarh. Long journey. What a shame. I won't be able to see you now before you go to Pune, Disha.' He took my hands and kissed each of my fingers.

'You don't listen to me, do you?' I said. 'You never did. I wish you would. I was right in the middle of telling you something. Something important.'

'Sorry. Go on. Tell me. Your mother and father you were saying ...'

'... I said they think I'm going to Durgapur, but, Aritro, guess where I was really, really going? Because it certainly wasn't there.'

He turned his head slowly and studied my face for a moment, and then he knew the answer. 'How is it possible that we had the same idea at exactly the same time, Disha!?' he asked. He was so excited that he stood up and scooped me up with him and hugged me tightly. Our laughing made people stare at us and we tried to restrain ourselves and behave like the rest of the world, but it was hard.

It wasn't until we'd left the station and were standing outside on the road that I remembered that I wasn't due home until Wednesday morning. Just being with him had put everything else out of my mind. I'd touched him again after such a long time, heard his voice, felt his warmth, and remembered the way he talked, the things he said, his laugh that I loved. Everything around me seemed slightly unreal as I stood beside him watching people and traffic moving past us as if in slow motion. I could've just stayed there with him and done nothing else; I was so contented at that moment.

'What do you want to do, Disha?' he asked, putting his arm around my shoulder and pulling me close to him. 'We've got the whole wonderful day together, hours and hours and blissful hours.'

'Well, we did have *much* more time than that. I'm expected back home on Wednesday. I've got to think up a reason to be home later on today, Aritro, one that my parents will believe.'

'Oh, don't tell me that! I wish you'd never said it. It's like showing me a pot of gold and then taking it away. So you mean if I hadn't had the same idea at the same time, you'd have come to me and stayed until Wednesday?'

'Yes, that's right.'

'Damn!'

'Well, it's too bad now. We've got to think up a reason for me to be home again today.'

'Okay, that's not so very hard. You can easily travel from Durgapur to here in a day; couldn't you say the process only took fifteen minutes?'

'I suppose I could. That'll have to do. I don't want to have to worry about it anymore; I want our day to be perfect. I'll call Mamma later on this afternoon and tell her I'm coming back tonight. She'll be pleased about that.'

'Okay, let's go some place and have something to eat, I'm really hungry. I'm always hungry when I'm around you; I think that's what love does.'

'Same here. I'm starving.'

'But just a minute, where, dear girl, did you think you were going to stay on Monday and Tuesday night? I hope you thought about that. I mean you could hardly just turn up at a strange hotel on your own, could you?'

'Yes, I did think about it. Your parents visited you in October, you told me, and they stayed in your company's guest house didn't they?'

'Ah, you remembered that?'

'Of course, and that's what I was planning. I am able to think things through, you know, unassisted by a male brain.'

We walked along the road slowly, hand in hand. The sky was the most beautiful blue I had yet seen. We were together, if only for a brief time. I was completely happy. I heard the noise of the train I might have been on leaving the platform.

'So, tell me, Disha, because I do need to know this. Those twenty four days in prison, have they harmed you – any part of you? I used to be in torment seeing you through that mesh and not being able to touch you.'

'I don't think so. I see myself as stronger. I've witnessed things and experienced things that I wouldn't have done in a life like mine is supposed to be. Although I did know there was more than one India.'

'Yes, of course, everybody knows that. You're always reading about it in magazine articles and so on.'

I stopped and put my hand on his arm and looked up into his face because I wanted him to listen properly to what I said next. 'Before I was imprisoned, if anybody had told me that one of the other Indias – a far cruder India – might also be more beautiful at times than the one I was born into and know, I'd have thought that ridiculous and insulting. Now I wouldn't.'

'Is that really true, Disha?'

'Yes, that is really true, Aritro. Prison was terrible, and I wasn't corrected as they call it, in the slightest. But being there, especially with little Rinki when we were under the tree looking at the stars made me think about nature, about God, and about time itself – and most importantly, about how precious life is, all life I mean, not just mine, but life itself.'

Lightning Source UK Ltd.
Milton Keynes UK
UKOW040948300413

209977UK00001B/9/P